FAMILIES FIRST
A POST-APOCALYPTIC
NEXT-WORLD SERIES

VOLUME 3 ~ SECOND WIND

LANCE K EWING

COPYRIGHT

DEDICATION

To my wife, Hannah, our three awesome crazy boys, Hudson, Jax and Hendrix, and to my mom, Shareen, for her tireless editing.

To the readers who took a chance on a new author without knowing if there would be a second volume.

Thank you to all readers who left honest reviews on Amazon, Goodreads and Audible, making this continued series possible.

What Readers are Saying

flows quickly without having to stop and try to decipher what the author is trying to say. I'm very much looking forward to book 3 in this series.

* * * *

Clean enjoyable fun

A nice change in the apocalyptic genre. Characters based on real people obviously are likable or hated, with some in between. A very interesting story that draws me in and down the road with all the characters. Highly recommended!

* * * *

Families First is a fresh approach.

Lance, this is an amazing first effort. Congratulations. *Families First* takes a rather unique approach to the EMP genre. It is the emphasis on keeping your own humanity despite the breakdown of society, working to keep family first.

* * * *

5.0 out of 5 stars

OK, I'm hooked. Let's get book 3...4...5 out for us to read... Can hardly wait. Thank you for the ride.

* * * *

Better than five stars.

Awesome book. It is well thought out...and the characters in the book. I can't wait for the next book. Keep up the awesome job!

* * * * * * *

DEAR READER

D ear Reader,

If this is your first look at my *Families First* series, please consider reading Volumes One and Two first. This is a complete series of 7 volumes, depending of course on you, the reader.

Thank you for purchasing and, most of all, for reading the first two books in the series. In this day of Internet publishing, I realize you have many other choices in this genre, and I am honored you would spend your money and time with me. As writers, we now, more than ever, are judged by our reviews online. If you enjoyed this book, please leave an honest review on Amazon and Goodreads.

For those of you interested in this series, please consider keeping in touch by visiting my website at *LanceKEwingAuthor.com* or Lancekewingauthor@gmail.com for upcoming books and projects, as well as weekly updates on what I am up to. I will not distribute your e-mail anywhere and will only contact you in reply to a question you may have or to let you know of an upcoming volume or series I am about to release.

In return for your e-mail, I will forward you my Quick Guide e-book (free of charge and not available for sale) with more information on the characters of *Families First*, including their backstories, much of which you will not find in any of the volumes.

Lance K. Ewing

RECAP OF VOLUMES 1 AND 2

I n Volumes One and Two of *Families First ~ Post-Apocalyptic Next-World Series,* we were introduced to a cast of characters spanning multiple locations across the United States, all with diverse points of view and hardships to overcome.

We learn that North Korea dropped an EMP in the center of the United States, knocking out power to all states, except Hawaii, and parts of Canada and Mexico. With no electricity, food or running water, and few working vehicles, the country is instantly reduced to the hardships of days long gone. It's every family for themselves in this new and hostile world.

Lance and Joy, along with their children, like-minded friends and neighbors, embark on their journey, headed to Saddle Ranch in the Colorado Rocky Mountains by way of Raton Pass, New Mexico.

The first leg of the trek to Raton Pass would prove more difficult than they could ever imagine, plagued with injuries and losses along the way. Relying on faith, and loyal to the group, they soldier on and finally arrive at their destination.

Vlad is transferred to a FEMA camp, and eventually to Trinidad, for surgery following a life-threatening injury.

The sons of Lance and Joy each face hardships and potentially catastrophic situations.

Former McKinney police officer, Mike, proves to be a hindrance to the group as well as an invaluable help when safety is on the line.

Lonnie and Jake keep everything running as smoothly as possible.

Joy, Nancy and Tina earn MVPs of the first leg of the trip.

Mac, on Saddle Ranch, falls in love with a beautiful medical doctor, but the relationship is complicated from the very start.

Crossover has begun between the communities of Saddle Ranch, led by John, and The West, led by Samuel.

David and the Jenkins family in Raton, New Mexico, suffer a devastating loss after an accident involving mistaken identity.

James and Janice, in Weston, Colorado, start their new family, taking in a young orphaned boy named Billy. With both James and Jason in new town government posts, they try to remain neutral as the Sheriff and Judge passively battle for control of the town.

It is clear to all that Ronna is working with the US Military in some capacity.

* * * *

CONTENTS

Chapter One ~ Raton Pass, New Mexico

Beatrice helped to serve a communal breakfast this morning, outside at the guests' camp.

After cleanup, she pulled Mel aside and asked him for a favor. Telling him about the DVD her late husband had made for his son and grandson, Mel agreed to bring the TV to her house later in the morning.

"Please have them here at 10 a.m." she asked, as Mel headed back outside.

The morning was bustling, with inventory being taken by Joy and Lucy, and the sounds of children playing in safety for the first time since leaving their homes in McKinney, Texas.

Getting with Lonnie, Steve and Jake, we looked over the map of Colorado and alternate routes for the larger cities of Trinidad, Colorado Springs, and Denver.

Having taken this route many times over the years, I had a good idea of the possible choke points on the map.

Jim, tasked with attempting to get a radio connection with Saddle Ranch, went right to work, asking for no interruptions.

He had kept a close ear on the crazy guy in Topeka, Kansas, who now was heading west with his ever-growing group of loyal followers.

* * * *

David entered his mother's house, with Mark close behind. Mel had only told them that Beatrice had a surprise for them.

Handing the DVD to David, she began.

"Your father made this video only a couple of short months ago for you and Mark. I helped him create it, so I will leave you two alone to view it."

David held the disc out to his son, asking Mark if he was ready. "Not really, Dad, but if something happens to this TV, we may never have another chance to see it."

"I agree, son," replied David, as Mark loaded the disc.

Pressing "Play," Dean's image came into focus.

"Is this on, Beatrice?" asked Dean at the beginning.

"David, Mark... I'm making this video for you, and if you're watching this I must surely be gone to the other side.

"I'm sorry you will find out like this, but I have been diagnosed with stage four pancreatic cancer and have decided to skip the chemo part.

"After a second, and even third, opinion, I have come to accept my fate. They all tell me that I have a few months to live, at best.

"I've sworn your mother to secrecy, David, as I didn't want you to see me differently in my final days.

"Don't shed any tears for me, as I have lived a great life and have been truly blessed with you both and my beautiful wife of 43 years.

"I want you both to take care of her in my absence, as she has cared for you all these years. Rest assured that I will be waiting patiently for you all on the other side.

"Pray often, and live your lives to the fullest.

"I love you, boys."

The short video ended, with a smile from Dean.

David replayed the video several times, until he committed the short speech to memory.

Mark smiled at his dad, saying, "I miss Grandpa."

"I know," replied David, hugging him tightly.

"Thank you, Mom," announced David, as they exited the TV room. "That is the best gift I've ever received."

"Son," added David. "I have another matter to discuss with you. It's about Tina and the girls."

* * * *

David found Tina playing tag with the kids. He stood at a distance for five minutes, just watching her smiling and engaging every child.

He had a flashback of his deceased wife playing with their son, Mark, in the backyard when he was only five years old.

"Lord, if it is your will, I would be kind and faithful to this woman I see before me for the rest of my days," he prayed aloud.

* * * *

Joy and I toured the property on one of the newly acquired Indian motorcycles, taking care to protect her ankle. For the first time since we left our home, I felt like we as a group were safe.

We ran into David and Tina walking with Veronica and Suzie, exchanging hellos.

"I haven't seen Mike or Sheila since we arrived here," called Joy over the humming of the motor.

"I saw Mike get dinner for them both last night, but he brought it back to their vehicle and I haven't seen them since," David replied.

"I'm not sure what's going to happen with those two, but each of them brings something unique to our little group. I don't know how they are going to react to Mike at Saddle Ranch, though," I added.

Reaching the camp, David pulled me aside.

"Lance, Tina and I have been talking, and we think it would be best for her to stay here with our group when you all move on."

"I thought that might be coming," I replied, smiling and patting him on the shoulder.

"The girls also," David added, "as they are her family now and soon to be mine."

"Mark is OK with it?" I asked.

"He can't wait to have two sisters to look out for," replied David, with a big smile. "Oh...and I asked her to marry me."

"So, she is going to think about it for a long time, I guess," I said, joking with my old friend.

"Very funny. She apparently is not going to hold out, like Joy did the first few times you asked her!"

"Ouch," I said, both of us laughing.

* * * *

We watched Tina, making her rounds and talking with people, as Mark played tag with Suzie and Veronica.

"I think Mark needs this new family just as much as I do," stated David.

"My friend," I told him, "I am truly happy for you and your now-growing family. Your dad would be so proud."

"I know," replied David. "I talk to him every day, and he left Mark and me a DVD filmed a couple of months ago. He was dying of pancreatic cancer but didn't want us to know and treat him any different."

"That sounds just like the Dean I always knew and looked up to," I replied.

* * * *

Tina spread the news to the rest of the ladies, showing off an engagement ring Beatrice had given David last year to hold on to if he should ever need it.

The ring had been passed down for two generations but had gotten lost for several years and never made it on the hand of David's first wife.

David had asked Veronica and Suzie first about marrying their mom, to get their blessing, and David's mom was thrilled with the news.

Mark was able to get James VanFleet on the radio and let him know he could pick up his guns from Lance anytime.

"Sounds good," James told him. "We will be up for just a bit tomorrow morning, and tell your dad I have some other news about the area to discuss with him."

"Yes, sir," Mark told him. 'We will see you tomorrow then."

* * * * * * *

Chapter Two ~ Saddle Ranch ~ Loveland, Colorado

Mac, finishing his meeting with John and Bill, was still not sure how to proceed regarding the Miller boys, who were now nearly stalking him.

John advised that he review the perimeter security, suggesting that he and Bill inform Samuel about the new developments.

Jimmy was tasked with gathering the men on security for a noon meeting by the wood-shop, close to the western perimeter that had apparently been the breach site last night.

With a steady and confident demeanor, Mac started the discussion. With most having heard about the spray paint on his house and the earlier incident at the Millers' home, he wouldn't have to start at the beginning.

"OK, guys," he started. "Apparently, news travels just as quickly now as it did in the old-world. So, you all know that Dr. Melton took his life, with myself and Jimmy here as witnesses.

"Mrs. Miller, from up on the mountain, pointing to a ridge of pine trees two miles up Green Mountain, killed her husband and is trying to frame me for it. Thankfully, I was there with a few of my guys when we made the discovery. This fact will surely keep anyone from the Ranch or the West's property from coming to any false conclusions.

"However, the two Miller boys have only heard one story, and it's from their mother. They were here last night on our property. Not only on the edge of it but a full-on breach of our security allowed two teenage boys to advance to the center of our Ranch and my house.

"Those of you on security last night will be training this afternoon with Jimmy and me... On second thought, we will all train today after a quick lunch. Mistakes will happen, but this type of breach can't happen again.

"I can handle myself, as every one of you here can. Still, we are all responsible for protecting everyone else in this valley, and that includes our West neighbors. I have been in contact with both Bill and John on this matter and, for now, John wants increased security to be the top priority."

"I have a suggestion if it's OK?" Jimmy spoke up.

"Sure. What's on your mind?" asked Mac.

"Well, maybe a couple of guys and I could head up to the Millers' place—without you, of course—and try to talk to the boys."

"I'm not sure that would do any good, but I'll bring it up to John and Bill and see what they think," replied Mac.

"Are you worried about what might happen to me?" Jimmy asked.

"No. I'm concerned about what may happen to the boys," said Mac.

"I guess Mrs. Miller is single now," blurted out one of the guys.

"Is that supposed to be funny?" asked Mac in a serious tone.

"No, sir," the man stammered. "I'm sorry."

"Is that funny, Jimmy?" asked Mac to the young man who was smiling.

"I'm sorry, Mac, but after the few days we've had, it's a little bit funny."

Mac's glare turned into a slight smile. "Yeah, OK. I guess it's a little funny. Seriously though, you're a good group, and this job we have been tasked with will only get harder as the days and weeks roll on. Let's get lunch and meet back here in one hour."

Mac and Jimmy had lunch with Bill at John's house. Jimmy was eager to pitch his plan and was pleased to get a positive response. "It may be worth a try," said Bill, "but we might want to run it by Samuel, so that he's in the loop."

"Agreed," added John. "I would rather know where we stand on this matter sooner than later."

* * * *

"Bill!" came the call on the radio from the southern perimeter.

"We've got about 50-70 people out here, and they say they're from the city."

"What city?" Bill asked.

"From Loveland" came the reply. "And they want access to *their* lake," as they say. "What are they talking about?" the border guard asked.

"The reservoir," replied Bill, with a sigh. "The City of Loveland had it built more than ten years ago as a backup supply of water for the whole town."

"They just crossed the major Big Thompson River, with plenty of water, to get over to this side. So, I'm not sure what they want," the border guard continued.

"We will be down in a few. Don't let them through," said Bill.

"OK, boss. We will try to hold them off, but please get here as quickly as you can."

"What do you think, John?" asked Bill.

"They can get all the water they need from the river, so it has to be about our valley," John replied.

"This pristine valley is protected on all sides," added Mac, "with livestock and gardens, so it's a no-brainer."

All paused for what seemed like hours to Mac, until John finally spoke.

"We will let one man through to inspect the reservoir, whoever the leader is. Mac, you and Jimmy will escort him and do your best to figure out his intentions. You will only get one shot at this before we have a significant conflict on our soil, so we're counting on you."

"Yes, sir," they both replied at once, with Mac grabbing Jimmy by the shoulder and heading out the door.

"What was that about?" asked Jimmy, as they headed to their four-wheelers.

"I just didn't want to get pigeonholed into any more instructions we had to follow. Right now, it's simple. Show the guy around and then show him the door. If they all get on the property, it makes things much more complicated."

"I get it," replied Jimmy. "I guess the perimeter training will have to wait," he added.

"Let them know we will try to pick it up tomorrow, but I want the highest security tonight," stated Mac.

Arriving at the southern point, it wasn't hard to spot the man in charge. His name was Cory and he was the Chief of Police for the City of Loveland.

He agreed to come across alone, as long as his 15-year-old son could tag along.

"Why would he want to bring his kid over?" asked Jimmy in a whisper.

"Well, you only do that if you plan on staying," replied Mac.

Officer Cory was all business in front of the other townsfolk, demanding to get to the bottom of the lost reservoir issue.

Once across the line and out of earshot from his followers, he sang a different tune. "I used to come up to this valley with my boy Cameron here," he said, pointing to his son.

"We visited your church quite a few times over the years. His mom passed on a few years back, and well, we thought this might be a good place for us to start over."

"Just so we're on the same page," said Mac, skeptically but with respect. "You brought nearly 70 people out here to our valley to ask for refuge for you and your son?"

"No, not exactly," said Cory.

"The rest of them are townsfolk, with more than a few of them being turned away some days ago at your northernmost border. We tried to give them the slip, but they just kept following us. I was a good chief in the old-world, ask anyone, but now it's every person for themselves and I have a son to protect and raise.

"My position and badge mean nothing now, and everyone out there," he added, pointing across to his newly found entourage, "knows it."

"Why would we let you and your boy stay, and no one else?" asked Mac.

"That's a fair question," Cory agreed. "Most folks are just going along for the ride, but there is one guy goes by the name of Ralph and he's gathering a group of sorts to take this valley. Have you ever heard of him?"

"Yes," replied Jimmy. "He was hired at the same time as me, but he wasn't a good fit for either community here in the valley."

"This Ralph guy is dead set on getting rid of someone named Mic, I think," stated Cory.

"You mean Mac?" Jimmy asked, already knowing the answer.

"Yes, that's it," Cory said. "Something about stealing his wife."

"Cory, I'm Mac," he said, reaching his hand out. "I can assure you I have no intention of stealing his wife."

"I figured that much," Cory continued, "since he kept talking about having to correct his wife and boy with his fists when they didn't listen.

"In the old-world, I would have locked that SOB up and put him in front of a jury filled with moms and dads and let them decide his fate. Now it's a different world, and my job is to work hard and look after my boy."

"I get it," replied Mac.

"So, this has nothing to do with the reservoir?" asked Jimmy.

"No, not today," Cory replied, "but there are others in town concerned about it, and they are vowing to head out here in the next week or two to secure it. I'm pretty sure they are not expecting a blockade like yours, though."

"It certainly can't hurt to have a Chief of Police in our group," added Mac. "Let me talk to John and Bill about it before we move any further."

"You mean Bill the artist?" Cory asked.

"Yes. Do you know him?" asked Mac.

"Of course! We have a meal at his and Sharon's house every time we come out for a church service. They are good people and my boy Cameron here is an artist, just like their son Karl.

Together they draw the most incredible portraits of the Great Pyramid and Stonehenge. It's all math, apparently, and I don't understand most of it but it's still fascinating work."

Mac called Bill on the radio, and he immediately vouched for Cory and Cameron, citing he would have to run it by the council for approval. John was on board, pending the council vote.

* * * *

Mac, returning to the border patrol, was briefed about Ralph's challenge. It was a simple proposition. He and Mac would face off, man-to-man, in an old 1800s-style shootout draw. The victor would remain in the valley indefinitely.

Mac's initial instinct was to ignore the challenge, as he knew the council would never approve it.

"What's the advantage if I win?" asked Mac to the guards.

"Apparently, if you defeat Ralph, the rest of these people," one of the guards said, pointing across the crowd, "have agreed to move on their way and not return here."

"Can he shoot?" asked Mac.

"Nobody knows," replied the guard. "Can you shoot?" he asked.

"I'm not half bad," said Mac. "I grew up in Montana, and it's practically a requirement for citizenship up there, but I'm not sure this is what needs to happen here."

A call came over the radio from John.

"The council is behind you, Mac, whatever you choose to do," announced John.

"Let me talk with him first," said Mac. "Just me and Ralph."

After fifteen minutes and a neutral-free zone prepared by the perimeter guards, the meeting of the banished man and recently accused head of security commenced.

"So, you're taking me seriously now, since I have a large group facing your small numbers of guards. Right?" asked Ralph, smiling as if he already had the upper hand.

"I take everyone seriously all the time," replied Mac, "and my guys could take your group out in minutes, but only if they have to. We can all walk away from this bad scenario right now, if you choose. I not now nor have I ever wanted to steal your wife from you.

"On the other hand, we can't have 70 people gunning to take over this valley full of God-fearing people that I am proud to call family. So, if I have to meet you man-to-man to resolve this issue, then I will."

"You are underestimating me now," replied Ralph.

"I can assure you that I am not," stated Mac.

Mac called his men to get Dr. Melton on the radio and down here with her medical bag, if needed for either man.

Ralph excused himself, walking back to his newly formed group, taking two items from a forest green backpack lying on the ground.

He returned moments later with two old single-shot pistols, reminding Mac of the kind used in the Old West. As a boy, Mac had read every Western book by Louis L'Amour and had an idea of how a draw might go.

He offered one more time to Ralph to call it off and go on his way up the road, to no avail.

Ralph laid the pistols side-by-side in front of Mac on a small card table used for water distribution.

"You choose," said Ralph, with a grin.

Mac was reminded of a scene in his favorite movie, *The Princess Bride*. The villain, being chased by the heroine, switches cups of poison back and forth, before both rivals drink from them in a match of wits to the death.

Snapping back to focus, Mac inspected each pistol carefully, determining they both were equal in quality and each containing one round of ammunition.

He chose a weapon, as Sarah arrived with Samuel.

Grabbing Mac by the shoulder, she forcefully pulled him to the side. "Mac," she whispered, "you don't have to do this. I love you and want you to come back to me."

Mac, doing his best to keep his composure, told Sarah he loved her too.

"I wish it wasn't like this, and I'm so sorry about Bradley, but now I have no choice. I can't stand by and watch 70 people either get killed or ravage this pristine valley. It's worth risking my life for."

"Let's go, Mac!" yelled Ralph. "I don't have all day!"

"I think the good Police Chief here," pointing to Cory, "can go over some rules of an old-time duel," said Ralph.

Cory laid out the rules. "Each man will holster his weapon, standing back-to-back. You will walk ten paces on my count and will only turn when I say 'ten.' There is only one round in each pistol, and they may both be discharged before declaring a winner. Should both men miss their mark or one man be only wounded, another round will ensue. The victor alone will remain in this valley as long as they choose. Are there any questions from either man?"

"What time is lunch?" asked Ralph loudly, getting some laughs and cheers out of his group.

Mac remained silent, blowing Sarah a fist-bump kiss.

Meeting back-to-back, Cory announced the last rule.

"Any man turning before the agreed-upon ten paces will be disqualified and immediately forfeit all rights given to the victor. Understood?"

Both men answered, "Yes, sir."

Mac started to walk at count one, questioning his turn about. *Should I turn straight or duck down?"* he thought. *If one misses, the other has a clean shot*, he realized.

Ironically, he was walking one step at a time back towards the love of his life, nodding his head for her to get clear of the likely line of fire.

"Two," he heard...then "three" as the countdown continued.

Mac lost track of time for a split second, and the count was eight.

"Nine...ten...and they both turned fast.

Ralph shot first, three quarters into his spin, sending the bullet ten yards to the left, striking a large pine tree.

"Your shot, Mac," called the officiator, Cory.

Mac pointed the old pistol at his rival but didn't fire. The stunned crowd was silent, with some holding their breath. The two men standing 20 paces from each other breathed heavily. The tension was building as everyone waited for the shot.

"It's done!" yelled Mac, lowering his weapon, as Ralph turned to run down the road.

"All right, everyone!" called Cory loudly. "As agreed, it's time for you all to move on."

Some in the group were talking about why Cory and his son were staying behind.

"Good job, Mac," said Cory, as they met to talk briefly. "You would have been well within the rules to take your shot and be done with it, but you showed constraint and that says a lot nowadays.

"By the way, I know my son and I are still pending residency here, but I want to let that group get some distance ahead of us if we should have to go back that way."

"Sure," replied Mac. "Any company is not always better than none...

"Excuse me," said Mac, answering his chirping radio.

"That's great news!" he said, walking back towards Cory and his boy.

"You mind helping out with security around here?" Mac asked Cory.

Both Cameron and his dad had huge grins and a look of relief one only gets when they have put everything on the line and are praying for a miracle.

"John, Bill, and the council unanimously voted for you two to join our group, and John has asked me to add you to my security detail, Cory. We've got some things for you too, Cameron, if you're up for it," added Mac.

"Yes, sir," he replied eagerly. "Can I start now?"

"Hold on, buddy. Let's get you two settled first. We will find you some housing, and I'll schedule a property tour for tomorrow morning with Jimmy. After that, we will all be training on new security protocols, and I will be interested to hear your thoughts and suggestions, Cory."

"Absolutely," Cory replied. "You have no idea what this means for Cameron and me."

"We need good, hardworking people here, and not just more bodies," added Mac.

As the group from town settled down and cleared out, Mac caught a glimpse of Sarah off to the side. He walked slowly over to her, both smiling all the way.

"Is it my turn?" she asked, kissing him without a care of others around her, even Samuel.

"It's always your turn, Sarah. I just have to dodge an occasional bullet here and there first."

"She has chosen," said Samuel quietly to one of his perimeter guards.

Mac headed back to the Ranch to get their new guests settled in. He agreed to have Sarah up to the Ranch for dinner tonight. There would be no more hiding their relationship now, as they moved forward. He felt that this new-world could make anyone feel bipolar, moving from highs to lows and back, with little warning.

Mac made a brief stop at his house to inform his best friend about him and Sarah. Bo yawned from an afternoon nap and licked him on the hand. "I know you will love her, Bo, as much as I do," Mac said aloud.

Cory and his son settled into an upstairs three-bedroom apartment, recently refurbished before the lights went out. It was the very same apartment Lance and his family had occupied years before.

Cameron opted for Lance's old room, still with an above-room attic space and minus the air conditioning. Toilets were flushed with buckets of swimming-pool water, although the inground pool was running low.

Mac gave Rico a heads-up that Sarah would join him for dinner, not wanting him to make a fuss or prepare anything special.

"Of course not," Rico replied. "You are just two diners sharing a meal with everyone else now."

Mac borrowed a truck from the Ranch to pick up Sarah, as he felt his four-wheeler was a bit informal. He dressed up tonight—well, Mac-style dress-up, if he was honest. A long-sleeved cowboy shirt was paired with jeans and a nice pair of boots for his big date.

He met her at Samuel's place, and it felt a bit like a high-school prom date as he pulled up in front of the house.

Samuel answered the door on the first knock and told him Sarah would be down in a minute, with them both exchanging awkward conversation as the minutes dragged on.

Sarah strolled slowly down the stairs in an all-black form-fitting dress that rendered Mac speechless.

Her father smiled, proud of his daughter, and happy to see her confident and radiant once again.

Mac carefully took her hand in his and couldn't stop smiling. "You kids don't stay out too late tonight," joked Samuel, opening the front door.

Mac opened the passenger door for Sarah, as all men should, and buckled himself in on the other side.

"From this day forward," said Sarah immediately, "we will not speak of the tragedies of the past, and we will face the trials of the present and the future together. Are you in line with that, Mac?" she asked matter of factly.

"Yes, ma'am," he replied, thinking this would go down as one of his very best days.

I found the perfect one, Mom, he said silently. *I promise you I will do right by her and never hurt her.*

* * * *

Rico was up to no good as they arrived for dinner, sneaking a 2008 Gibson Bridge Pinot Grigio from a classic vineyard in Marlborough, New Zealand, on to their table. "This is a gift from my staff," he said, "to your very first true date."

"I think this is our third," replied Mac.

"No, no, no," interjected Rico. "I can see it in her eyes," looking directly at Sarah. "Tonight is your very first date of something very special."

She nodded her head in agreement, and Mac finally understood.

* * * *

"We will never forget this day, either of us," whispered Sarah to Mac, as they drove back to Samuel's home.

Mac kissed her good-bye and walked her to the door, feeling better than he could ever remember, and Samuel was relieved to have his daughter home by 11.

The Ranch was locked down tight this night, and those not on security slept soundly, even Mac.

* * * *

Morning came early for Mac, readying his men for security training and introducing Cory and Cameron to everyone.

Each man on security detail was happy to add a police officer to the mix. Cory was careful not to overstep his bounds and wasted no time in adding his expertise to Mac's training.

The nearly eight-hour training, only paused by a lunch break, was filled with both men and women, as well as a few of the older teens from both the Ranch and the West.

The northern and southern borders were operated by a skeleton crew, so that more could attend, making Mac nervous after yesterday's happenings.

While it was impossible to cover every perimeter of the nearly 500 acres between the two properties without an actual wall, they were able to identify the most likely breach areas.

It was clear to all that the days of the Ranch having just one nightwatchman and the West having none were over. Between the two groups, it was determined that most capable adults would do a one-night-on and three-nights-off shift for the foreseeable future.

Lookout posts with clear vantage points were marked, and every nightwatchman or -woman would have a dedicated radio until they ran out.

* * * *

The Ranch stockpile was in a large 1970s Faraday cage, kept in a cellar underground that had also been used to brew wine and beer by a few discerning members. There was a yearly summer Brew-off (adults only) during the annual Fourth of July picnic, with ribbons for the best beer and wine in various categories. Each winner had one year of bragging rights, until the next challenge.

The cage was regularly updated, with equipment added annually, including 22 radios, flashlights, lanterns, generators, and spare batteries of all sizes, from AA to truck, and even tractor, batteries.

There were a few odds and ends that didn't make much sense and sparked conversation among the members, including 26 kitchen timers with built-in clocks, and only four wristwatches. There were 12 Sony Walkman cassette players with stereo headphones and music cassette tapes, ranging from the former front man for the Commodores, Lionel Richie, to the 1970s rock band still making music up until recently, called Van Halen.

Rounding out the oddities were four navy-blue Razr flip phones, three original iPods, two handheld pocket video cameras, and five first-generation iPads (the thick, heavy ones in silver).

As an apparent joke, there was a small glass case containing a bottle of Johnnie Walker Blue, with two glasses inside and a miniature axe taped to the outside. The plaque on the front read "In case of emergency, break glass!"

* * * *

The security day ended with a welcomed visit and prayer from John, who was starting to get around a bit with Bill's help.

"Mac has told me about your training," started a confident John to his men.

"You have worked hard and taken our security here seriously, and I commend you on that.

You men and women are the lifeblood of our community and the entire valley. Without adequate security, we cannot protect what is most dear to all of us. You all are at the forefront of our fight to honor our Lord and protect his followers. Let us pray."

Dear Lord, we thank you for guiding our men and women on security training this day, and each day forward. We shall all work together to protect each other and this bountiful valley you have given us to watch over, Lord. We would ask that you continue to lead us in fulfilling your will in the days to come. It is in your name we pray. Amen.

John continued: "I am proud to know every one of you standing here today. We welcome Officer Cory and his son, Cameron, who I know will be valuable assets to our family."

Before departing, John and Bill pulled Mac and Jimmy aside.

"Can we borrow you for just a few?" John asked Cory.

"Yes, sir," he replied. "How can I help?"

Cory was filled in on the Mrs. Miller issue and asked if he had ever met the family.

"I know Mr. Miller...or knew him," replied Cory, "and I've met the boys a couple of times. They're all a piece of work, though, if I'm honest."

John asked Jimmy to run his plan by Cory and get his take on it.

"It just might work," said Cory, "but we're talking about a woman who killed her husband and it sounds like she's drunk most of the time.

"We will have to get those boys away from her to even have a chance at talking. Plus, we will have to show superior firepower to make sure they don't do something stupid out of fear or revenge.

"Those boys have their own issues, and I'm not saying we should invite them back here for supper," he added, "but they may not be as far gone as she is. They had to see something leading up to the killing of their father. But right now, they only have the one story."

"Jimmy is the lead on this," said John, "but can you help him get a plan together, Cory?"

"Absolutely, sir," Cory replied. I will help in any way needed."

Mac patted Jimmy on the shoulder, asking if he had this.

"We do, my friend, one way or the other. We will know where we stand soon enough. We can't risk you or Sarah being in the line of danger over a situation like this."

"Take five men, including a few witnesses from before, plus Officer Cory, and make a plan," said Mac to Jimmy. "I want it run by me, John, Bill and Samuel by noon tomorrow and executed right after, early in the afternoon if possible.

"You will need them separated from their mother," Mac continued, "but they spend most afternoons hunting off the property, so you may be able to talk with them alone—if you can find them, of course."

All Mac could think about was his next date with Sarah. It was tomorrow night at her house for "dinner and a movie," minus the movie, unfortunately.

Mac fell asleep quickly this night, having new confidence in his security team.

He was awakened at 2 a.m. with banging on his door. Bo barked and growled, leading Mac to believe it was the Miller boys back for more graffiti.

"Mac," one of his team called out. "We have a situation." Cautiously opening the door, Mac saw his man with a panicked look on his face.

"They burned the haystack for the cows, plus our woodshop!"

"Who did?" asked Mac, already knowing the answer.

"The boys...the kids did it...and left some warning signs too."

"All right," said Mac. "Let's get Jimmy and Cory on this also. I'll be up at the woodshop in a few minutes. Is it still burning?"

"They have the fire truck working on it right now," came the reply.

* * * *

Mac was at the woodshop in ten minutes, followed by Jimmy and Cory, all assessing the situation. The hay bales were totally burned, which would no doubt create an issue for the livestock in the coming days and weeks.

The graffiti was much the same as before, now being read for the first time by his security detail.

"This isn't going away," suggested Jimmy.

"No, it's not," replied Mac. "I'm hoping you can make contact with them tomorrow, before this really gets out of hand. On the plus side, our fire truck did excellent work on the woodshop. We will have to refill her tomorrow, though."

Mac could not sleep for the rest of the night. He hoped for a peaceful resolution, not wanting the Miller boys to get hurt or worse, but also wishing peace for this valley they all shared now.

* * * *

Meeting for a 7 a.m. breakfast of farm-fresh eggs, bacon, and potato wedges, the security team discussed the plan to be presented to John, Bill and Samuel.

Cory volunteered to go up the mountain in uniform, as long as he was backed up by Mac's guys. He was hoping to talk to the boys before this went any further. John, Bill and Samuel were all briefed and agreed the plan was a good start.

Readying their four-wheelers, Cory pulled Mac aside.

"I hope this goes well. If it doesn't, will you all look after my boy?"

"We would do that, and I would take the lead," replied Mac, praying silently that wouldn't happen.

Single file, led by Jimmy, they headed up the mountain, stopping first at old man Mac-Donald's place. Jimmy found him on the porch, smoking his pipe, just as last time.

"Any sign of the boys around here?" called out Jimmy, as he cut the motor.

"None that I've seen," replied the old-timer. "Saw you all had some fireworks down your way last night, though."

"We did," replied Jimmy. "You wouldn't know anything about that, now would you?" asked Jimmy in a respectful tone but still wanting answers.

"The boys are after Mac is all I know," he replied.

"Where did you hear that?" asked Cory.

"Hey, Chief," replied Mr. MacDonald. "It's been a while," he replied, without answering the question.

"Yes, sir, it has," replied Cory, then repeating the question.

"Chief, there are no more secrets up on this mountain than down on your Ranch. Everyone knows every damn thing about everybody else. Even those boys aren't entirely sure about Mac killing their father, but they only know what their mother told them."

"Why didn't you come down to the Ranch and tell us about this information?" asked Cory.

"Well, it's like this, I suppose," he answered, slowly exhaling a plume of smoke swirling into the otherwise clean mountain air. "Ain't none of my damn business...and besides, I figured you would all be up here sooner or later, asking a bunch of questions, like right now."

"Fair enough," said Jimmy. "Do you know where the boys might be about now?"

"I heard a couple of faint shots over the ridge yonder," Mr. MacDonald said, pointing behind him, "about a half-hour ago. Could've been them or someone else. I don't rightly know."

"Thank you, Mr. MacDonald," said Jimmy as they started the bikes, heading back toward the mountain.

"Single file, boys, and eyes open!" called Jimmy from the lead.

The message was passed down the line, like the classic children's game of passing the information from child-to-child and seeing how the instructions changed as they reached the end of the line. Thankfully, Jimmy's stayed the same throughout.

At ten miles per hour, they kept watch on the surrounding ridge. Keeping clear of the Millers' compound by two miles, the men canvassed the mountain.

Cresting a large hill with a vantage-point view of the valley, they heard the first shots. "Crack! Crack!"...a pause...and then two more.

"Take cover behind the bikes!" yelled Cory.

"I'm hit!" called out Jimmy, who was shot in the right knee and fell with a thump. He was on the ground next to his machine when the second bullet caught him in the right side of his neck.

"Return fire!" yelled Cory, pointing down to a large clump of trees 120 yards out, at the very end of the open field.

With no time to retreat, they all returned fire from behind their vehicles.

Cory yelled "Cover me!" as he dragged a panicked Jimmy behind his four-wheeler and out of the line of fire. Shots flew in both directions for the next minute, only drowned out by the sound of barking dogs.

"Cease fire!" called Cory, not hearing any more gunshots from the other side.

Seconds later, one man ran from the clump of trees, with two dogs following close behind, away from Cory and their group.

"Let him go!" Cory called out. "Nobody fire." They watched as the person ran down the road and out of sight.

Cory assessed Jimmy's wounds, wrapping his own shirt around Jimmy's neck in an attempt to stop the blood. He tasked two of the five men he now led with taking Jimmy down the mountain.

"You two go on one four-wheeler with Jimmy. Go straight to the West hospital as fast as you can, but don't dump the bike. I'll radio down now, and we'll get your other vehicle back later."

Cory radioed Mac, giving him details on Jimmy and the situation.

"I'll take care of things here and get Sarah notified about the incoming. Are there any more shot?" asked Mac.

"Not on our end," replied Cory.

"How about on theirs?" asked Mac.

"I'm not sure. We're about to check it out," said Cory.

"OK, guys," said Cory to the three men left with him. "Let's check out the shooting location carefully."

Scanning first with binoculars, Cory spotted one man down, just inside the tree line. With no movement and nothing else out of the ordinary, they slowly made their way down to the trees.

The younger Miller boy was shot multiple times and DOA.

"I'm sorry it came to this, son," said Cory quietly to the boy, carefully closing his open eyes. "I'll leave you here so your brother can come back for you."

Writing a quick note, Cory pinned it securely on the young man's shirt.

This was an accident and we only returned fire after being ambushed. Mac did not kill your father, and I would like to talk before anyone else gets hurt. Meet me tomorrow morning around noon at the apple tree [referring to the only one on the ridge, known by all]. We will talk, and I will personally guarantee your safety for the meeting.Cory Lerner, Chief of Police, Loveland, Colorado.

Piggybacking down the mountain, they got all the four-wheelers back to the Ranch.

Mac informed Sarah first about Jimmy, and she readied the hospital, gathering the other doctors and nurses, awaiting the arrival of their newest patient.

Mac briefed John, Bill and Samuel as he headed to the hospital. Helping to get a now-unconscious Jimmy on to the gurney, he was politely asked by Sarah to stay outside.

"We can't have any distractions inside," she told him.

Mac paced nervously, now regretting the entire plan Jimmy had engineered. *This is my issue*, he thought, *and people I care about are getting hurt over it.*

Mac had never prayed much throughout his life, but he did today. He prayed for Jimmy's recovery and thanked God for bringing Sarah back to him.

Cory met Mac outside the front of the hospital, filling him in on the Miller boy's death and his offer for a meeting.

"We can do that," said Mac. "But remember we're a team here, and we discuss things like this before executing the plan."

"I'm sorry. I didn't think about that. I'm used to giving orders, and I realize things are different now," replied Cory.

"We need to stake out the meet spot early tomorrow morning, in case he shows," added Mac.

"And one last thing. I want to talk to him face-to-face if he comes."

* * * * * * *

Chapter Three ~ Weston, Colorado

James and Jason each rode a four-wheeler, with Jason's leg nearly healed up, the 30 miles to the Raton Pass Militia's property.

The machines easily navigated the fire roads bypassing the former Keepers group, dropping down the back of the mountain.

* * * *

Arrival was approximately 9 a.m., just as the groups were finishing the morning chores.

Lance had the promised weapons already set aside for James, so the transfer was merely a formality.

James informed David about his new position as Mayor of Weston and spoke openly to his old friend about Sheriff Johnson and Judge Lowry, leaving few details out.

Mel was excited to meet James, as he had heard of James' greenhouses that kept producing through all four seasons, including the dead of winter.

After a nearly three-hour training, David and Mel felt confident in executing a plan for three greenhouses to be built over the next two months, with execution being near the top of priorities for the group.

Each would house different types of producing plants and small trees that complemented each other. When complete, the three inside gardens would produce enough food to feed 50 people year-round, with heirloom seeds being reused season after season.

Protein would now be high priority, including deer, elk, fish, and small game such as rabbits, squirrels and muskrats. Thanks to Tom Jones shooting three turkeys just days before, the group had been eating well, at least for a couple of days.

Adding Mel's provisions, including enough freeze-dried foods for a small army, canned goods that could fill a corner market, and enough pasta to last years, they were well set to wait out the next-world.

There was only one problem, as James pointed out. Could they secure it?

Two shots rang out in the distance towards the former Keepers group and their claimed property.

"What's going on over there?" Mel asked David.

"Well, they are either just hunting for food, or they have another new leader," he replied.

"I'm just glad Jason and I are headed the opposite way back home," said James, "and it's about time to head back."

James pulled his old friend David aside and told him of his growing family. "We may end up out on the road at some point if things get bad in town," he added.

"Can we look you up if it comes down to it?" asked James directly. "I have a growing family now and need a backup plan or two."

"Yes, I understand, as my own family officially doubled only one day ago," replied David. "And if your partners decide to expand the town another 30 miles, please let us know so we can be ready."

"I'll be sure to do that," replied James.

"Crack! Crack! Crack" came five shots in succession, each four seconds apart, from the old Keeper's side of the mountain.

Everyone ducked, including David and James, with no bullets coming their direction.

"That's not a hunter!" said David, "and I sure hope it's not what I think it is!"

"What are you thinking?" asked Mel.

"New leaders of violent groups have been known to show their power right away by killing multiple people who don't agree with them, execution-style. I think they have a new leader over there now, and they're not the kind of neighbors we want on our border," replied David solemnly.

"You want us to stick around for a few hours?" asked James.

"No," replied David. "I think this is going to be a slow build over days, or even weeks. The plans to get our guests back out to the highway safely may have to be changed, though."

"All right," replied James," but get us on the radio if you need help down the road."

"We will do that," said David, seeing them off.

* * * *

I met with Lonnie, Jake, Steve, Jim, and even Mike came out for a rare visit.

We had all heard the shots and agreed something had changed in the direction we would need to head through to get back to the highway in the next couple of days.

There was an old man in the valley that David and Mel had spoken to before, wanting nothing to do with the group. No one had seen a visitor at his place in years. However, he was known to nearly everyone in the area as a true mountain man.

The old man approached the camp cautiously and caught David's eye. "What's with all these people and the shooting?" he asked. "I like peace and quiet around my homestead."

"These are our friends from Texas, heading to Northern Colorado," David told him, gesturing with a sweeping right arm. "The shots, though, came from across those trees," he told the old man.

"Well, who's going over there to see what's going on?" the old man asked.

"That's a good question," answered David. "I don't know."

"Well, hell," said the old man. "I guess I ought to do it. I know damn near everyone on this mountain, and it looks like you all have little ones running around that you need to protect. I'm just one old fart headed to the other side of the sky, if it goes bad," he added. "I'll check it out, and if I don't come back, look after my dog, will ya? She's getting on in years, but she's a sweet old pug named Daisy. I'm sure the little ones would like her, at least. Anything you all want to know? You may only get one chance at this, and if I don't come back, then you will surely know what you are in for."

"Thank you for doing this. And yes, there are a few things we would like to know," replied David.

"1. What were the seven shots we heard earlier today?

"2. Who is the current leader of the group?

"3. Do our friends here still have safe passage out to the highway in a couple of days?

"4. How will we interact as neighbors moving forward?

"5. Will they respect our property line, starting just this side of the bridge, for the foreseeable future?"

"I'll do my best to get answers," the old man replied. "But in the end, we're all up here together, trying to weather the storm."

The old man headed toward the trees and the bridge. Walking cautiously, he took a rabbit with one shot on David's property. Stringing the nearly 4-pounder on his left hip, he not only had dinner but a believable guise of a rabbit hunter out for some food.

He was stopped near the end of the bridge by five men armed with semi-automatic weapons of varying makes and calibers, as near as he could tell.

"State your business, old-timer," announced the lead man.

"I'm just an old man, and I've lived just yonder for more than 40 years. I know just about everybody up here, so how is it I don't know you?" he asked.

The man laughed, saying, "You have no idea who we are? If you have been anywhere close to a radio, you would know we're from Topeka, Kansas, and this is the halfway point on our journey north into Colorado."

"What's in Colorado?" asked the old-timer.

"Our founder's hometown in Fort Col..." His radio chirped with instructions to leave the old man and return to base.

They told him to stay while they summoned their leader. Calling on a ham radio, they got hold of their superiors after several attempts.

"It's the Northern Scouts," he said. "Soldier number 459 reporting from Raton Pass, New Mexico. We have secured a post and 23 loyal followers, with seven deciding to go another way.

We also have an old man coming from the direction of land controlled by an outfit locally known as the Raton Pass Militia, and final numbers are unknown at this time."

After an interrogation of the old man, he was of no help gathering more information on David and his group.

"Back the way you came, old-timer," he commanded.

We all had questions for him as he returned.

"It's as bad as you are thinking," started the old man. "They kill all those who don't join them...well, except for me!" he laughed. "They probably thought I would slow them down.

You folks ever hear of an outfit out of Kansas?"

"I'm guessing you mean Topeka?" I asked.

"Yep, that's the one. Said they were headed to some fort in Colorado."

"What fort?" asked Jake.

"Something with a k or c. He started to say but got interrupted. Said their founder was from there."

"I hope it's Fort Carson, in Colorado Springs, and not Fort Collins, right past Loveland," I interjected.

Jim and Mark both got on the radios, hoping to learn more about the group from Topeka.

"They got here quicker than I thought," said Jim, remembering when we listened to the program back in McKinney.

"Well, it's about the same distance from Topeka to here as it is from McKinney," I pointed out. "I don't think their whole group is here yet...just some scouts, I bet."

"We need a plan," said David, "before they get here and we're outnumbered 100 to one."

"Where are they at now?" I asked the old man.

"About a mile and a half beyond the bridge. They've got some sort of camp set up, looks like."

I called a meeting of the adults, with serious questions for David and Mel.

"I know of three ways into this property," I started. "First, the fire road at the back that James and Jason came in on today. Second, the across-the-river route. And third, the bridge. One is easy to navigate, and the other two are not."

"No, no, no. Not so fast," said David, jumping up from a sitting position.

"It may be the only way," chimed in Joy.

"She is right, and we don't have a choice," added Tina.

"Hold on a second," called Mark, confused. "What are we talking about here, Dad?"

"They think we should blow the bridge," he replied, shaking his head back and forth.

"I don't see a way around it," said Jake. "If it's open, there may be a thousand Topeka city-folk-turned-fanatic-soldiers on this property in the next week. There are still two ways in and out, but the path of least resistance will be gone," he added.

"I'm not saying I'm in yet, but if we decided to, do you have any experience in demo?" David asked a smiling Mel.

"It just happens to be one of my specialties. I've literally been doing it for 20 years," Mel responded.

"I'll need a night to sleep on it," said David. "Once it's done, there's no going back. In the meantime, we need security on our side of the bridge tonight."

"I'll head that up," said Lonnie. "Can you help me, Mike?" he asked.

"Sure thing," Mike replied. "I've been bored lately and could use a change of pace."

"Take a couple of our guys and trade off shifts," said David.

Jake, David, Mel and I met briefly before dinner was served.

"I'm not all in on this yet," said David, "but I can see the point of it. Their group is headed somewhere else past here is all we know.

"I'm guessing they send scouting groups ahead to see what they are in for and to pillage supplies for their growing group. They will hopefully take the path of least resistance and move on towards their destination if we let them. Do you have a plan, Mel, if we decide to do it?"

"Yes, my friend. I still haven't shown you everything I have. I'm pretty sure we could take out our end of the bridge, and that's really all we need."

With Lonnie, Mike, and a couple more security on the bridge, they called it a night.

David stayed with Tina and the girls in their tent, not wanting to be indoors if he were needed quickly. Their first night together was anything but perfect. He worried about the group and dreamt of dark things.

All was quiet on the bridge, as men swapped shifts at four-hour intervals.

Mel was up for most of the night, with Tammy asking him to come to bed every hour.

"I'm sorry, honey, but I have to do this. He doesn't know it yet, but David is counting on me to figure out how to protect our group and provisions."

Mel had two ideas for a bridge collapse.

One of the cables had already snapped on Jake's trailer when crossing and had done damage to the bridge. There were five more securing this side and, once compromised, would drop the rest of the bridge into the river below, making a crossing impossible.

The other option was dynamite. Fast and effective, but far more dangerous than cutting wires.

Mel vowed to present both plans to David and the rest of both groups in the morning.

At 3 a.m., Mike and Tom Jones took a shift watching the bridge.

With Lonnie gone until morning, Mike told Tom to cover him as he slowly crossed the bridge.

One step at a time, Mike made the crossing.

He told Tom he was only going to do some recon on the bridge but, at the other end, he kept going.

Carrying his AR-15 and Glock 17 pistol and walking a little more than a mile, he was ready for a fight.

Around 3:40, he found the group camping haphazardly across an open field on the side of the road. Most had tents, but a few slept on the open ground. Two old military jeeps were parked towards the back.

Mike counted 23 tents, with another 8 people sleeping on the ground. The tents were a jumble of shapes and sizes. Three were army green and appeared to be canvas, all lined in a row at the front.

They all looked gray in Mike's night-vision goggles, but the shapes identified the new leader's quarters. His night goggles were worth their weight in gold this night.

Slowly creeping to the three soldiers' tents, Mike quietly dug into the small daypack he nearly always carried.

Next to the pistols, ammo, toilet paper, and Imodium was a roll of 12-lb. fishing line. Cutting ten small pieces with his Buck cadet pocket knife that he had carried every day since his eighth birthday, he snuck up on the lead tents.

Tying the pull tabs on the tent zippers in front and back of each tent, he froze, seeing the young girl of maybe 13 years staring at him in the dark.

She walked slowly towards him, careful to not make a sound. He could see she was unarmed, and against his better judgment froze while she advanced the ten yards towards him. Putting her mouth to his left ear, she whispered "Take us with you."

"I'm sorry, but I can't do that," Mike whispered back.

"You're a coward," she said, shaking her head side to side, "just like the rest of them." With that, she walked back toward her tent without looking back.

Mike had been called a lot of things in his life, but never a coward.

He slipped away quietly and could hear the faint barking of Ringo and Mini back towards the compound.

Mike observed the sleeping outfit for another 20 minutes and was surprised they had no night security.

The commotion started in the middle tent, as someone was probably trying to come out to relieve themselves. It started quietly as a confused and possibly intoxicated man trying to undo the zippers, and ended up stirring the entire camp.

Yelling and swearing ensued, as all three tents now shook with attempts to break out.

Mike observed from a distance until the first one was cut open with a large knife from the inside.

More yelling ensued, as Mike walked slowly away towards the bridge.

Two shots pierced the night, with more yelling. Mike returned to base with the sly grin of a teenager egging a house for the first time.

He used his time heading back to observe David's side of the bridge, should they decide to take it down. It wouldn't much matter for his group, since they had trailers too heavy to cross now; but for David and his group, it was something that couldn't be undone.

Mike didn't much care either way, as he was always up for a fight, but he would help David out if he could.

The quick shots woke up David and half the camp, with Mike and Tom not relating any news.

* * * *

Sunrise was incredible, as always, on top of the mountain pass.

"I'll never get tired of this," a groggy Mel told David before breakfast.

Having been up most of the night, Mel had made a couple of pots of coffee and brought them to the main camp in thermoses.

This morning the camp was bustling with the shots from yesterday and the secretly spread news of the bridge.

David was asked by several members what would happen, and his response was always the same. "We should all pray on it and make the final decision today. The good Lord will guide our hands and tell us what should be done."

"Will He really talk to us?" asked Tammy. "God, I mean? I've never heard Him before."

"I think He steers clear of coffee shops and trendy restaurants," quipped Mel. "Seriously, though," he added, "I watched my house burn to the ground and knew He was sitting right next to me, ready to point me in the direction of something much better," grasping her hand lightly in his.

"I think I get it," she responded. "We need to trust and not worry about understanding everything as it happens."

"Exactly," replied David. "The answers are there; it's just hard to see them right away sometimes."

"OK," said Mel to David and the rest of the future demo group. "We have two choices that I can see.

"Number one, we cut the remaining five wires and hope nobody gets hit as they snap.

"Number two, we dynamite our side of the bridge. Yes, I have tools for both scenarios, before anyone asks.

"Either plan, if successful, will drop our end into the river and cut off bridge access for the foreseeable future. We can still get in and out now, even with the trailers, but so can anyone else if they really want to."

"How exactly do you have dynamite, and where is it?" asked David, sounding concerned.

"When you demo land for twenty years, using dynamite on hand for the projects, it makes a man think about it when he decides to have an end-of-the-world-as-we-know-it house built in the woods.

"That's how I have it, and it was at my house until the fire. Now it's in an underground capsule of sorts a hundred yards out from our camp's northern border. It's probably the second choice, at best.

"My first choice is my portable bandsaw, starting from the outside cable on each side and working our way towards the center.

"Either way will be loud and draw unwanted attention, but both will likely get the job done."

David called a group meeting early that afternoon and decided on a vote.

"Hands up for disabling the bridge?" he asked, with most raised.

"Hands up for keeping the bridge?" he asked, with only a few raised.

"All right, Mel. When do we do it?" asked David.

"Tonight," he replied, "when everyone on the other side is asleep. We need all the surprise we can get."

Mike and Lonnie were back watching the bridge after Mike got a nearly six-hour nap.

"There's a man at the end of the bridge, waving a white flag," Lonnie told Mike. "It looks like he wants to talk."

Lonnie radioed David, and we all provided cover on our end for the soon-to-be meeting between the stranger and Mike, mid-bridge.

Lonnie was prepping a disinterested Mike about asking all the right questions.

Mike met the soldier halfway across the bridge, both unarmed, with rifles on both ends of the bridge.

"I'm Mike," he began, without a handshake.

"I'm Soldier Number 459, and we need to take inventory of your property."

"Inventory for what purpose?" asked a confident Mike.

"We're a growing group, as I'm sure you have heard. We will add you to our group of loyal followers, and your provisions will belong to our leader to distribute as he pleases."

"Why would we agree to that?" asked Mike, feeling anxious for some action.

"Everyone does, once they make the wise decision to join. Others don't fare so well."

"Is that so?" asked Mike, now clearly annoyed. "I heard a couple of shots last night over your way," he added. "What was that about? Maybe some pranksters infiltrating your kindergarten security? They didn't mess with your tents, did they?"

The soldier was fuming, as his face turned red. He looked over his shoulder, back towards his men.

"You need their help?" asked Mike. "Maybe you're man enough to settle this right here. The first one over the bridge is the loser. What do you say, Soldier Number 45?"

"It's Soldier 459!" he spat back.

Mike was anxious, being cooped up for a few days. A good fight might just settle him down, or maybe even a swim in the cool river below, although he doubted that scenario.

"My job is to purify the wicked," said the soldier. "Would that be you, Mike?" he asked.

"I'm pretty sure that's both of us," Mike replied, shoving Soldier 459 to gauge a response.

The man swung wildly towards Mike, getting a grin out of him. Mike landed a well-placed jab on the soldier's chin, knocking him back.

"Have you ever been to Brooklyn?" asked Mike, as he landed a punch to the gut, buckling him over.

"There is a lean and mean fighter who goes by the name The Great Bambino," Mike continued. "He taught me to fight, and do you know why?"

Dodging multiple punches, Mike occasionally let one land, just to feel something...anything.

"I learned to fight so I could protect women and children, like we have over in our group," he continued, picking his shots. Mike was careful not to knock the pseudo soldier out but wanted a slow beat-down in front of his men.

"I feel like my job, my only job, is to look out for them all," Mike added. "Your job, I assume, is to gather people and supplies for your boss, so you have a chance to make employee of the month. Is that about right?"

"We all share the same vision," the soldier replied, now spitting out blood onto the bridge floor, trying to take Mike in a double-leg takedown. Mike instinctively reacted with a sprawl and cross-face maneuver he had learned at the boxer's gym, although it was a classic young wrestler's move.

"Bullshit," said Mike abruptly. "I heard your leader on the radio, and he's a complete nut job. I met another guy like him a while back, named Ronna, and he was exactly the same."

"How do you know Ronna?" asked the soldier, now trying to pick his shots carefully.

"Ha! Now that's funny," replied Mike. "Now it makes more sense; I'm guessing he is your boss too?"

"Only recently, and I think we're done here," the soldier replied, lunging towards Mike's legs without a sprawl from an always-ready Mike.

The soldier lifted his opponent onto the side rail. Mike could have ended it with one well-placed punch to the chin but chose the other path.

"Let's make this interesting," said Mike putting his arms under the soldier's and locking his hands behind his back.

Leaning back, Mike took them both backwards over the bridge, falling the nearly 30 feet into the rushing river. Men on both sides of the river thought Mike was crazy for the stunt.

As they fell, Mike let go of the man, wanting to fend only for himself. Mike could swim and had paid for lessons for him and his twin brother, Arthur, when they were teenagers. The soldier, apparently, could not. He went under immediately after impact and never resurfaced.

Mike climbed the steep terrain back up to his side without a word.

"What was all that about?" asked Lonnie, as he reached out his hand and helped Mike up the last few feet of the dirt embankment.

"The good news is that I learned to swim when I was young," replied Mike, "and the bad news is we need to blow the bridge as soon as possible."

David, standing near as witness, agreed.

"Mel, let's get this bridge down. There's no point in waiting for the cover of darkness anymore."

"Let's give the bandsaw a try," said Mel, heading back towards his house.

Loading the saw onto a small trailer pulled by a four-wheeler, he made it back to the bridge site in 30 minutes.

"We will cut outside cables first," announced Mel. "And please, everyone steer clear. If you are hit by one of these cables as they snap, you are likely headed up to the Pearly Gates before the rest of us," he called out.

"If that doesn't drop it, then we dynamite the rest."

Mel went to work on the bridge, with Mike, Lonnie and Steve on guard.

Walking with my old friend David, we discussed the future of our groups.

His concern for the marching locusts from Topeka dominated the conversation, as it would likely affect us both.

"I'm guessing the group is large and adding members by the dozens every day," I said. "The good news is that they will most likely take the path of least resistance, following major highways and not veering too far off in any direction.

"That being said, they also have to feed everyone, and that takes adding any provisions they can get along the journey. My hope is that they will stop at the bridge, assuming we can get it down on our side.

"Should they make it over Raton Pass as a group, they will plow a hole through the center of Trinidad, Pueblo, and maybe even Colorado Springs and Denver. They could essentially be the rabbit for our group."

"What do you mean by *rabbit*?" asked David.

"Well, my father used to tell me on long drives in open country to find a 'rabbit,' or another motorist, going faster than the speed limit. Let them get ahead about a hundred yards, and they will typically draw the ticket, giving you ample time to slow down.

"They will essentially be our rabbits, clearing a path straight through any barricades or obstacles that would otherwise take us zigzagging around each city and town on backroads."

"That makes sense," said David, "as long as they don't spot you, but they are also walking and probably not too fast."

"Yes, that's true," I replied. "It's tricky for sure."

Jim and Mark motioned for us to come over.

"Sorry, buddy," Jim told me. "They're headed to Fort Collins. The camp is going to be headquartered at a place called Horsetooth Lake. Have you heard of it?"

"Yes, I know the area well," I told him, with a sigh. "It happens to be only about 12 miles from Saddle Ranch."

"I also have good news on that account," interjected Jim.

"We did get hold of Saddle Ranch, and someone is getting word to your parents, Lance. They should be on the line in the next hour."

"That's great news!" I told him. "Good job, guys."

Continuing to walk with David, we soberly discussed likely scenarios for both groups.

"Do you think either of our groups will ever be at peace?" asked David.

"I do," I responded, "but never like before. We all had it good in the old-world. Our biggest decision of the day was deciding where to eat out for lunch.

"The violence and uncertainty we see around us now were across the globe, in someone else's neighborhood. To them, it was normal and just something to deal with as a part of existing on this planet.

"Now we are in the same boat, and our normal will always be different than it was before. We are miles ahead of most other people in our great country, and we can make a good life for our families and all in our groups."

"That makes sense," replied David. "If I'm honest, besides losing my dad, of course, I have a better life now than I did before the lights went out."

"So do I, my friend. So do I," I responded.

"I know we are on different paths right now, but if we had teamed up, it would have been fun," added David.

"Let's check on the bridge progress," I said, heading back that way.

* * * *

"It's slow work," said Lonnie, "but Mel has two cables cut, and there's no sign of trouble on the other side that we can see."

"Snap!" came the sound from our left.

"Make that three cables cut," added Lonnie, as the bridge leaned further down, creaking under the remaining strained wires.

"Two more to go," announced Lonnie, hearing the first shot.

"Crack!" followed by two more came from just the other side of the bridge, with the first bullet ricocheting off a large Douglas fir tree just above Mel's head.

"Get low," called Lonnie, "and hold fire." We waited for more shots, but after five minutes none came.

"OK. Back up on the cables, Mel," called out Lonnie, half-joking.

"Oh, hell no," replied Mel, shaking his head. "I'm not getting shot today. We need a new plan."

David and I cautiously made our way to Lonnie and the guys, crawling on our hands and knees.

"What do we have?" David asked a shaking Mel.

"We...have...Plan B," is all he could get out.

We all backed away from the bridge, with Lonnie, Steve and Mike keeping an eye out from their vantage point in the trees.

"It's down enough so no vehicles can cross," I said to David.

"Yeah, but it's the foot traffic I'm worried about," he replied.

"You have to let me blow it, David," said Mel. "There's no other choice now."

"Can you do it without getting any of us killed?"

"I think so," replied a relieved and excited Mel. "You guys provide the cover, and I'll get it rigged. If it goes bad on our end, I'll be the first to know."

Twenty minutes later, Mel returned with a small metal box, asking for everyone to stay clear.

A distraught Tammy begged David to stop Mel from setting the charge.

"He's the best one to pull it off," David said, trying to calm her. "We can't have a hundred of the crazy Topeka guy's soldiers coming across our bridge. We just have too much to lose," he added, waving his arm towards both groups of men, women and children behind them.

Joy, Nancy, Tina and Lucy had everyone inside Beatrice's house, and even Sheila made a now-rare appearance, playing Legos with Hudson and Jax.

"I've got a steel plate half an inch thick that should shield you, Mel, as you set the explosives," said David.

"You're just now telling me about this?" asked Mel, sounding annoyed.

"It wouldn't have helped much with you cutting the bridge cables, and it's heavy as hell, but we can rig it up to a furniture dolly, and it might just work. It's about three foot by three foot, so maybe 185 pounds. I'm pretty sure it will stop any caliber of bullet and..."

"Just pretty sure, huh?" joked Mel.

"I think you should be more worried about the dynamite than anything else," added David.

"How old is that stuff, anyway?" I called to Mel, keeping a distance, as David was.

"Only a couple years," he yelled back, "so I think we're good."

Rigging the steel plate to the dolly turned horizontal, Mel was able to move it slowly towards the bridge, staying right behind it.

Jake and I offered to help Mel, but he refused, not wanting anyone else close.

"You owe me a tall Scotch, David, once this is done...and on the rocks!" called Mel.

"You got it, buddy," David replied, trying not to sound as worried as he was about his old friend.

"Let's pray," I told everyone, "but eyes open on this one."

OK, Lord, this is a big moment for both of our groups, and we know you are with us. We ask that you keep our friend Mel out of harm's way and give him the courage and skill to do what needs to be done and come back safely to us. In your holy name, we pray. Amen.

Mel rigged the charge and backed away slowly, using the metal plate as protection, although no bullets came his way.

Ensuring everyone was back safely, he detonated the explosives with a "Boom!", sending the remaining parts of the bridge on their side, careening down into the river below.

"Great job, Mel!" called out David. "It looks like you did it! We can check on it later, when we're sure it's safe."

"Or now," replied a smiling Mel, reaching into a large backpack.

"You're kidding me," said David, looking at the compact but formidable drone with its remote controller.

"I kid you not," replied Mel. "And just for the record, I still have a few more surprises I haven't shown you. Unless they shoot it down, it will give us a clear picture of the bridge status."

"Let's try it," I said, kicking myself for not having thought to put one in my Faraday cage.

Arcing up and over the area, Mel guided the aircraft high over the trees, giving back a perfect picture of the bridge dangling into the river on the opposite side.

"They are not crossing it now," said Mel, "and neither are we."

* * * * * * *

CHAPTER FOUR ~ SADDLE RANCH ~ LOVELAND, COLORADO

M ac waited outside the West's hospital for news on his new friend, Jimmy.

Sarah canceled tonight's date, just as Mac had expected.

"It's going to be a long night here," she told him. "Go home, and I'll radio you right away with any news." Blowing him a kiss, she disappeared in through the back door of the hospital.

Briefing John, Bill and Samuel about the incident and possible meeting at noon tomorrow, a weary Mac took supper home this night. Rico handed him a small bag marked for Bo, containing one juicy cow bone.

"You're a good man, Rico," said Mac, patting him on the shoulder.

"It's just what I do," he replied in his authentic Italian accent. "It's just what I do."

Under any other circumstances, a called-off date with the love of his life would have had him worried, but not tonight.

This night he would quietly read a book he had secretly acquired years ago and never opened. The title read *How to Treat a Woman*. He even let Bo sleep on the bed and hoped for a peaceful night.

Sarah's night was anything but peaceful, as they had to resuscitate Jimmy around midnight and keep a close eye on him until morning.

Bill was up early, talking with John, Mac and Cory regarding a possible meeting with the Miller boy.

Mac tasked three of his men with scouting out the perimeter of the apple tree from a distant vantage point. Each having a radio, there was nothing to report as of 8 a.m.

Just before noon, a cautious older Miller boy emerged from the trees, rifle in hand but pointed towards the ground. Mac and Cory observed from a distance with binoculars.

"He trusts us," said Cory.

"I honestly didn't expect him to show," replied Mac, now a little nervous.

"We need to talk to him," said Mac, "but not make him uncomfortable or scared."

"He only has one side of the story, from his mother, but his neighbor said he wasn't completely sure about the story she told," said Cory.

Cory approached the boy cautiously, with his hands held out in a neutral stance. He would call Mac over when the time was right and if all went smooth.

"I'm sorry about your brother," said Cory, as they came within ten feet of each other.

"How's your guy doing, Chief?" asked the Miller brother.

"I'm not sure," replied Cory. "He's bad off, far as I know."

"So, you remember me," added Cory, "when I used to come up to this mountain for a hike with my boy on an occasional weekend?"

"Sure, I remember, and everyone around these here parts knows you as a fair man. Seeing your name on the note is the only reason I done showed up here today."

"I'm sorry about your father, son. I'm sure you know we worked together years back at the precinct."

"Yes, sir. He would tell me stories about your cop days together."

"I also know Mac," added Cory, "and he had no reason to want to kill your father."

"I wasn't sure at first, when my momma done told me about it. Mac used to come up and do some handy work on our property sometimes. She swears he killed my pops right in front of the house where we found him."

"Mac heard three shots up on the mountain that day and went up with three of his guys to investigate," replied Cory. "They saw old man MacDonald before heading up to your place. Your daddy was shot three times in the back, and he lay face down, away from your front door. Did you know that, son?"

"Yeah, I knowd it. Didn't seem right at the time."

"Do you think three men are going to just stand around while another shoots a retired police officer in the back?" asked Cory.

"Well, I guess not, but Momma was sure he done it."

"Did your momma kill your daddy?" Cory continued.

The Miller boy stood silent, working some kind of formula or idea in his head.

"They used to fight a lot about her drinking and all the money she spent on booze. He was always around guns, though, and I can't see how she could have done it, even if she wanted to."

"It's not too hard to shoot someone in the back as they are walking away," replied Cory.

"Can I talk to Mac?" asked the boy.

"Yes, you can, but I'm staying right here," said Cory matter of factly.

Motioning for Mac to come out from the trees, Cory told the boy to stay calm, with no sudden movements.

A cautious but confident Mac made his way to the meet spot.

"Did you kill my papa?" the boy asked right away.

"No, I did not, and I have three other men I trust that will tell you the same. Your mother was drunk and told me she killed him because she was tired of him getting on her about the drinking.

She told you boys I did it, since somebody had to be blamed.

"Just so you know, I would never shoot another man in the back or try to take advantage of another man's wife."

"I believe that, Mac, and I'm sorry about the paint on your house and the fires. It was my brother's idea, but I went along with it."

"How did you get on to our property and down to my house without being detected?" asked a curious Mac.

"My dad taught me to hunt, evade, and not be seen. You all have a lot of holes need pluggin' if you're gonna keep people out.

"My momma wasn't too happy about me coming here today, and we just buried my brother next to pops this morning."

A single shot rang out from the direction of the Miller compound. The boy winced, closing his eyes slowly...

"Rest in peace, Momma," he whispered, bowing his head. "Now I got nobody," he wept.

Cory hugged the boy tightly and promised he would check on him in a few days, asking if he needed anything.

Mac headed back down to the Ranch, feeling better than he had in a while. With the exception of Jimmy, Mac thought things were beginning to look up again. He and Sarah were solid, and the Miller situation seemed to be resolved.

Mac would even admit, if only to himself and maybe Bo, that Cory had resolved a major conflict in only 24 hours with the stroke of a pen. He filled in a relieved John, Bill and Samuel on the details, giving Cory most of the credit.

The rest of the afternoon Mac spent checking the maintenance on the trailer-sized freezers supplying the Ranch with more than a year's supply of food. He made a mental note to get with John and Bill to discuss how long the generators could power them.

Exiting the large freezer, wearing his heavy winter gear, he was flooded with the heat of the summer afternoon. Many residents sat at the long string of picnic tables, shucking peas and snapping green beans for canning. Mac pitched in for the last hour, happy to have some easy work and light conversation having nothing to do with security or issues.

The topic of conversation at the tables was favorite TV shows of the '80s. Rounding out the top ten were *The Cosby Show*, *The Facts of Life*, *Mash*, *Cheers*, *Magnum PI*, *The A-Team*, *Married with Children*, *Full House*, *The Dukes of Hazzard*, and his favorite, *MacGyver*. *Seinfeld* would have made the cut, first airing in 1989, but most people voting considered it a '90s sitcom, grouping it in with the *Friends* era.

* * * *

Riding his four-wheeler, Mac stopped at the West hospital and was able to get a few minutes with an exhausted Sarah.

He was thankful to see Jimmy, if for only a few minutes. He was awake but could not speak.

Mac did all the talking, thanking him for saving the lives of the other men and reassuring him that his old job as second-in-command of security would be waiting for him when he was better.

Jimmy was able to squeeze Mac's hand once for yes and twice for no, at Sarah's instruction.

Mac told him about the meeting with the older Miller boy and assured him he would recover and be back on his four-wheeler in no time.

Sarah kissed Mac as he left the hospital, promising a true dinner date the following evening.

All slept well that night...except, of course, for the Miller boy...

* * * *

Sarah had gotten a full eight hours of restful sleep and was happy to have the other doctors in the hospital to trade shifts with. Besides checking in on Jimmy, she had the entire afternoon off.

Sneaking up to the Ranch in Samuel's truck, she told Mac's guys not to ruin her surprise for him.

At 1 p.m. she entered the Ranch Pavilion, as the last of the lunch crowd cleared out. Sarah had a meeting this afternoon with the head chef.

"This time it's my turn," she said to a smiling Rico. "Can you help me make the most special meal tonight for my guy?"

"Leave it to me, Dr.," he said, smiling.

"If you don't mind, I would like to help since I have the afternoon off," she offered. Rico's eyes lit up.

"We will need something very special for my favorite couple," said the chef.

Removing his apron, he announced to his shocked staff that he would be taking the afternoon off. "He hasn't taken a day off in six months!" they whispered to each other.

"Don't be troubled, my students," he told them. "I'll be back for the final check before dinner tonight."

* * * *

Taking Sarah by the hand, they headed down the dirt path to one of the main freezers.

"Did you know, Dr., that I have been head chef here for ten years?"

"No, I had no idea," she replied, adding "and please call me Sarah."

"Yes, Sarah, it shall be. Anyway," he continued, "about six months before that day I had a dream, or maybe just a feeling, that change was coming. I took an entire Saturday off, creating panic amongst my understudies, to gather some special items from the surrounding cities. A few I even had to get flown in from halfway across the world, and the Kobe beef was a nightmare to acquire.

"Please put on this jacket, Dr...I mean Sarah."

Both wearing heavy jackets and gloves, they entered the freezer through the back door. The cold hit her warm face like a slap.

"I've never been inside a walk-in freezer," she admitted. "It's not what I expected."

"Over here, Sarah." He led the way, shining his flashlight halfway back into the cold, dark trailer. Just ahead was a large red metal cooler with 'Rico only' written in Sharpie across the top.

Sarah wasn't sure what to expect when he opened it, but she was intrigued and felt oddly safe with this man under these vulnerable circumstances.

Opening the heavy lid, following a few light strikes with Rico's wooden mallet, she could see inside. Nine compartments were equally divided and labeled accordingly.

"Gulf Jumbo Shrimp" read the first. "Atlantic Scallops, Australian Lobster Tail, Colossal Bearing Sea Red King Crab, English Truffles, French Escargots, Canadian Foie Gras, Japanese Wagyu, and Kobe Steak."

"I hope you like seafood and beef," Rico said, as more of a statement.

"My two absolute favorite foods!" a delighted Sarah exclaimed. Each compartment held seven bags with their respective contents.

"One of each it is," announced Rico, adding each bag to the smaller cooler he had brought.

"Are we going to cook this in your kitchen?" she asked.

"Not a chance," he replied. "If my students learn how to cook each of these delicacies, they won't want to make an ordinary dinner ever again."

"Do you think Samuel would mind if we used your kitchen at the West?"

"I'm sure it's not a problem," Sarah answered. "And besides, I have someone I want you to meet," she said, with a wink.

"Oh, you mean a lady? Why does everybody always want to fix me up? Do I look lonely?"

"Just meet her and say hi, that's all I ask," Sarah continued.

"OK. For you, I will meet the woman, but that is all. Agreed?"

"Agreed," said Sarah, with a devious smile.

* * * *

"I've never prepared truffles before," said Rico, as they walked into the West's kitchen.

"I have," said a woman overhearing the conversation.

Rico turned to see a confident and radiant Patty. He was taken aback by her deep green eyes and thought her classically beautiful.

"Hello, Chef," she said, with a smile.

"Do we know each other?" he asked, smiling back unintentionally.

"We have met twice," said Patty. "The first time was when I was just a week into training as a prep cook. The head chef was out sick, and you ordered escargots at my restaurant. I recognized you from the cooking magazines you were featured in.

"My manager made me prepare them, although I never had before. You sent them back, asking for something, anything, else prepared by a real chef. I cried myself to sleep that night, and the next morning I was determined to become a great chef.

"Three years later I would be Head Chef at the Catacombs restaurant in Fort Collins and would serve you again. It was the best escargots you have had, you told my manager. So, thanks to you for making me Head Chef of one of the finest steakhouses in Northern Colorado."

Rico blushed, embarrassed. "Please accept my most sincere apologies. I don't remember either incident. But back then, I got caught up in the life of a celebrity chef. And with a cocaine problem, I have been told I was kind of a jerk. I got clean and opted for a slower life here in this valley.

"I am still tough on my students, but now I encourage them to be exceptional at their craft with positive reinforcement."

"Apology accepted," Patty replied. "Now, are you going to let me help you two or not?" she asked, still smiling.

Rico paused as Sarah asked, "Well, Chef. Are we going to work together here?"

"Of course! We all have something to learn, I'm sure, and I need help with truffles, to start."

Patty, pulling four black truffles from a heavy freezer bag, looked them over closely and put one to her nose.

"These are English Autumn, also known as Burgundy truffles. They are fungi originally found by pigs and now by trained dogs. The prized fungi lie just beneath the ground near beech, hazel, birch, and oak trees in rich soils.

They can be prepared and added to a variety of dishes. I would suggest a classic truffle risotto with a light cream sauce. The truffles will be sliced, shaved and grated."

"You know your truffles, Patty," said an impressed Rico.

Reaching into the cooler and pulling out a two-pound bag, he asked, "What do you know about Kobe beef?"

"You mean the beef from China?" she asked, baiting him for a response.

"Actually," started Rico, "it's from Japan, and it's their most expensive meat."

"Do you mean the Wagyu beef from the Tajima strain of Japanese Black Cattle that are raised in the Hyogo Prefecture? The Kobe raised and slaughtered according to strict rules set out by the Kobe beef marketing and distribution promotion, and it makes up the top approximately 1% of the meat processed."

Taken aback, Rico smiled at the exchange.

"I may have met my match," he told a surprised Sarah, raising his wine glass to toast with Patty.

"Don't even get me started about Bearing Sea Red King Crab or Canadian Foie Gras," replied a confident and sassy Patty, who hadn't felt like her old self in quite a while, she realized.

"What are you doing for dinner tonight, Patty?" asked Sarah, as she pulled bag after bag out of the cooler.

"Nothing, I suppose, since Joshua is spending the night at his new friend's house."

"How about you, Rico...I mean besides your quick final check on your students? There's far too much great food here for just Mac and me," Sarah said, with a smile and a wink at Rico. "With two pounds of meat in each bag, we could feed a small village."

He started to protest until Patty spoke up, saying, "It might be nice to talk shop with someone over a nice dinner and some wine."

"OK. OK," said Rico. "I suppose I have nothing to lose."

"Would you mind, Rico, if we put just a little of each dish aside for my father? I know he would love a treat like this," continued Sarah.

"Absolutely," he replied. "I have calculated a plate for both Samuel and John, as well. Maybe you can deliver his while I deliver John's and check on my students."

"Can I meet them...your students, I mean?" asked Patty.

"Sure. Why not?" agreed Rico. "We will prep everything first and prepare it right after we return."

With all three working, course prep took just over an hour. With an additional 30 minutes to prepare Samuel's and John's plates, the three split up, with Sarah lending the truck to Rico.

Samuel was thrilled with the lavish meal, as was John.

Rico returned to his kitchen to a frantic but competent staff pulling off a classic meatloaf meal, complete with butter-smashed potatoes and green beans au gratin. Paired with a loaded garden salad, and banana cream pie for dessert, he stood proud as he introduced Patty.

One of his newer students smiled at Patty flirtatiously. Pulling Rico aside, he asked what her situation was. "She's spoken for," Rico replied flatly, surprising even himself.

"What was that all about?" asked Patty, as the trainees all resumed their work.

"Oh, nothing," he replied. "It just seems a few of my students noticed how pretty you are!"

"Are you saying I'm pretty, Chef Rico?" she asked bluntly.

"Do you always just say what's on your mind?" he replied.

"Yes, pretty much always. That's who I am," said Patty.

"Well, Ms. Patty, who is both pretty and always speaks her mind, would you please help me pick out some special wine for tonight's dinner?"

"For tonight's *dinners*, I believe you mean. Of course. I would be happy to. What do you like, Chef?"

"Rico. Please call me Rico, and surprise me with your choice," he said, leading her to the wine room.

Her eyes widened as she saw hundreds of bottles lining all four walls of the large room.

"Where did all these come from?" she asked, recognizing the labels on a few bottles she had already pulled out.

"Gifts mostly, from wineries across the globe hoping I would mention them in an interview or article I was featured in."

"Do you know how snobby that sounds?" she blurted out. "Oh no, I'm sorry. That wasn't fair. Sometimes I put my foot right in my mouth."

"No, that's OK. You're pretty much right," Rico replied. "Back then, I was the snob you are referring to. When people bend over backwards to give you lavish gifts, at a certain point one starts to think they have actually earned or deserve it.

"Some people get caught up in drugs or alcohol, sex or money, but my vice was recognition and praise, with some coke mixed in, and I consumed it like a heroin addict.

"None of that matters anymore, but I think we are looking at one of the most diverse fine wine collections anywhere in the world, especially now."

"I would agree," she replied, as she paired each dish with its proper wine.

Patty smiled, remembering a scene in one of her favorite movies, *City Slickers*, starring Billy Crystal and Jack Palance. Fellow ranch guests Barry and Ira Shalowitz, loosely portraying Ben and Jerry's ice cream founders, have a showdown where Ira claims to be able to pair any meal with the correct ice cream.

She would never forget the classic response from Ira when Crystal's character asks him to pair a flavor with beans and franks. "Scoop of chocolate, scoop of vanilla. Don't waste my time."

"Ever see *City Slickers*?"

"What's that?" asked Rico.

"Never mind," she said, now concentrating on each categorized shelf.

She chose a Sauvignon Blanc to pair with both the meat and seafood.

Pulling a bottle at random, she gasped. "This is a Screaming Eagle Sauvignon Blanc from Napa Valley, bottled in 1992, their debut year. It's over $6,000 a bottle!"

Quickly putting the bottle back on the shelf, she asked if there were any others more reasonably priced.

"Why does that matter now?" he asked. "In this next-world," he continued, "a Screaming Eagle carries no more weight to people than an average box of wine. It's just wine to them."

"I know you appreciate it. And Patty," he continued, smiling, pulling back out the bottle and another identical one just below. "Wait until you see their Cab! This is why I don't let just anyone come into the wine room.

"What is the price of good company and engaging conversation?" he asked, holding up each bottle.

"We shall serve this wine at exactly 47 degrees, if only to preserve a small amount of snobbiness from the old-world."

Patty was feeling happy around a man...for the first time in a while.

If she was honest, she didn't miss Ralph at all. The love she had for him started to wane long ago with her very first abuse at his hand. Once he started hitting her son, it disappeared altogether, never to return.

Still not sure about Rico, she enjoyed the conversation around her passion for food and drink.

* * * *

Meeting back at the West's kitchen, Sarah was instrumental in getting a newly hired Patty off the dinner shift for the night.

With the food prepared, Mac showed up at Sarah's house at 7:30 p.m., as instructed. She had asked him to bring Bo in the truck, leaving Mac only to think he would be spending the night.

Dinner by candlelight was the norm now and still kept its charm. Mac loved the dinner, admitting he couldn't spell most of the items he consumed.

He made love to her that night, confident and gently, leaving her no doubt she was choosing wisely.

Rico and Patty thoroughly enjoyed their evening at his home, talking of culinary things most would find trivial.

He walked her home, kissing her on the cheek, and thanked her for the best night he had had since he could remember. "What did you think of the wine?" he asked.

"Mmm, it was just OK, I guess," Patty replied, with a wink and a smile.

"Yeah, right!" replied an excited Rico, laughing. He drove back to the Ranch, again borrowing the truck, with a smile and renewed faith in his place in the valley.

* * * * * * *

Chapter Five ~ Weston, Colorado

James and Jason made it down the mountain the way they had come.

Pausing for a moment at the same spot on the road where they had first met, Jason gave a silent prayer for how much his family's life had changed in a short period of time.

The rest of the short trip was uneventful, with both keeping a watchful eye for anything out of the ordinary.

Pulling in to Second Chances Ranch, the men were met with the happy screams of children and a now semi-mobile Chance.

"What have you all been up to?" asked Jason, lifting little Jenna and tossing her playfully in the air. She squealed with delight.

"My turn," said the other girls, as he switched between them.

"Can I get a turn, Daddy?" asked Billy to James. "Sure, son," he replied, winking to a shocked Janice and Lauren.

"Whee!" cried Billy, as James swung him around. "More, Daddy, more!" he called out. James, always having had a good sense of people, and especially his wife, took advantage of the opportunity, telling Billy, "OK! Mommy's turn," as he handed him to Janice.

Swinging him in a large circle, he cried out, "Faster, Mommy! Faster!"

Hugging him tightly, she whispered, "I love you, son."

"I love you too, Mommy," he replied without hesitation, running off to play with the girls.

* * * *

David got on the radio with James in the early evening, relating the new information about the Topeka Kansas group headed their way.

"Well, we're a little over 20 miles west of the I-25 Interstate, so I hope they will not veer that far off the beaten track, but we will be prepared in case they do," said James. "Thank you, my friend," he added, "for the update. How's it going on your end with the bridge?"

David relayed the story of Mel using the bandsaw, as well as Mike's little stunt on the bridge. "It's down now, the bridge that is, thanks to Mel and a few sticks of two-year-old dynamite."

Signing off, James and Jason prepared for their first official day as Mayor and Deputy Mayor of Weston, Colorado.

Arriving at the Sheriff's office at 8 a.m., they were shown the office area on the second floor of the courthouse, designated for their positions.

Each had a small room with plaques on their respective desks, announcing their titles. "It's a bit quieter without the phones, computers and fax machines," noted the Sheriff. "But that just gives you more time to be out amongst the townsfolk of our fair town."

"Great," said James. "Where do we start?"

"You have a meeting with the newly elected city council at 1 p.m. today," replied the Sheriff.

"OK," replied James. "Do we have an agenda?"

"Of course..." Then, following a long pause before the Sheriff walked out the door, he added, "I'm sure you two resourceful men will come up with one."

"Pen to paper, Jason, but this time without the scotch," said James, laughing. "The city council works at the pleasure of the mayor's office," he added.

"Yes, and the mayor's office serves at the pleasure of the Sheriff's office and the court-house," replied Jason.

"It's the circle of life, I guess. Now let's get down to business," suggested James. "We have four newly elected town council members: two previous ones and two new ones. They will, of course, have their own ideas of where this town is headed and how to get there. I want them on our side if it ever comes down to it. You and I are never going down like Mr. Grimes, I can assure you.

"One more thing, Jason. There can be no more comments about the Sheriff or the Judge in front of anyone outside our Ranch. Are we agreed?"

"Yes, we are. I understand it's our families first. Nothing matters more."

* * * *

The council meeting at 1 p.m. was anything but tame, with the longstanding members reserved at first and the two new ones shouting conspiracy theories about Mr. Grimes.

He was apparently their choice, and they seemed to have the story about right concerning his early demise.

James gave Jason a look that said, *Don't agree. Just listen*, as the veteran councilmen looked on.

"The council serves at the pleasure of the Mayor, and I serve at the pleasure of the Sheriff and Judge Lowry," stated James, not believing the words were coming out of his mouth.

Forgive me, Lord, for not standing up for injustice now, as David stood to Goliath, James thought. *I will, in good time* he prayed silently.

The veteran council members nodded approvingly, and James worried about the futures of the new ones.

Topics of the day ranged from clean water, hygiene, safety, and food, including a community garden that got James' attention.

"I'll donate a variety of heirloom seeds, meaning we can reuse year after year to get the garden started," James announced. He and Jason would make gathering the supplies for five initial greenhouses a priority for the week.

* * * *

Presenting the idea to Sheriff Johnson and Judge Lowry, James and Jason were given one acre of land in the middle of the town for the project, but not before being grilled about the meeting with the town council, wanting to know everything.

"Just town talk about how to help citizens with clean water, hygiene and food," replied James.

"Everyone seems on board to get things done," he added.

"That's good to hear," announced Sheriff Johnson.

"We need loyal people we can trust to watch over the good people of *my* town," interjected the Judge, getting a look from the Sheriff.

"There is one last thing that Jason and I did not discuss with the councilmen," James said. He relayed the information of the Topeka group, telling them that he had overheard it on his radio while at the ranch. He was not about to give up any information about David and his outfit, and a look to Jason told him to keep quiet.

"I will consider *my* options," said the Sheriff, "and have a plan, just in case they make it all the way up here"—this time getting a cross look from Judge Lowry.

"We'd best be getting back to work," said James, with his hand on Jason's shoulder.

* * * *

"Were getting in the middle of some crap here, aren't we?" Jason asked as they walked back across the street to their new office.

"Like it or not, yes, we are," replied James. "Those two men will have it out eventually, and if it's a fair fight I'm pretty sure the Sheriff will come out on top. I just don't count on the Judge fighting fairly is all. We need to be prepared for either outcome, though."

The rest of the afternoon was boring by next-world standards.

"We will start on the community gardens in a couple of days," said James. "I'll bring the tractor, but the Sheriff and Judge will be paying for the gas."

There were three gas stations in operation within the town limits when it went dark. Judge Lowry and Sheriff Johnson made it clear from the third day that all gasoline from the three stations would belong to the town, and any remaining fuel would be distributed at their discretion.

The gas station owners were agreeable, as they seemingly had no choice. Getting the gas out of the large underground tanks proved difficult at first, having to be siphoned by the gallon.

With the Sheriff nominating a few local ranchers, they were able to set up a foot-powered pump capable of pumping nearly four gallons a minute into five-gallon containers.

Nobody knew exactly how many gallons were in the ground beneath each station, but the station owners had an idea, with each checking their written logs. All agreed it should last a while.

* * * *

James and Jason headed home about 5:30 p.m., according to the town clock.

Going home to anxious children was nothing out of the ordinary to Jason. For James, it meant everything this night.

He imagined, as all dads do, that their young child would greet them at the door with a hug and hopes of games to be played. He would not be disappointed this night, as Billy ran across the large open living room and jumped into his arms, telling him everything about his day.

"Sorry," he said to Janice in a whisper.

"No worries," she replied. "He's been glued to my side all day." Her smile said it all.

Dinner tonight was ribeye steak from their own steer, slow-cooked over the traditional charcoal barbecue grill. James would have commandeered the grill, had he been home, but both he and Jason were impressed by the outcome.

"You ladies did a fine job on the steaks," said Jason.

"I'm a grill guy, as you know, Janice," said James. "But I'm not sure I could have done a better job. What's the secret?"

"A mix of ketchup and steak sauce," announced Janice, just poking fun.

"That belongs on a burger and nothing else," replied James, now slightly annoyed but in a playful tone.

"I told you he was serious about his steak," said a joking Janice to Lauren.

"I'm just kidding, honey," she added, looking at James. "I would never do that to your steak or mine.

"The secret, though, is slow cooking over 1/3 of the coals for four to five hours... Don't tell the media, though," she added with a wink.

James relaxed, feeling bad about his outburst. "How do you like your steak, Billy?" he asked in a jovial tone.

"I've never tried one," he admitted, "but it smells good." With only one bite, Billy was a bonified carnivore, asking if they could have steak every night for supper.

Billy was now settling into his own room, but each of the girls took turns sleeping beside him until he got comfortable being by himself. If it were up to Janice, her son would sleep with her until he was 13.

James argued that he needed some space and that the girls would keep him from being alone.

* * * *

Up at dawn, today was a work day for all.

Chicken eggs were collected by the children, with the girls showing little Billy the ropes.

James and a nearly full-functioning Jason checked on the still and then focused on the perimeter fencing.

Janice and Lauren took to the greenhouses, tending the plants and testing the automated watering and filtration equipment.

For Janice, this was where she shined. Her years of indoor gardening gave her insight few could replicate on the care of food-producing plants.

* * * *

It was determined that James and Jason would erect the greenhouses in Weston, while Janice, with Lauren's help, would plant the seeds that would eventually feed many in town.

Sheriff Johnson was feeling content, having disposed of his rival, Mr. Grimes, and in front of the whole town. For a while, he was OK with being the second-in-command, and actually considered Judge Lowry a friend.

His thoughts were now of grander things. *With a competent Sheriff at the helm, does a new-world town even need a Judge?* he thought.

His latest girlfriend was a genuine resident of Weston, having lived here all her life.

"Judge Lowry can't even decide what sex he wants to lay down next to at night. How is he possibly qualified to make big decisions over the town?" she would say often. "You're the one they trust," she told him. "You're the one to lead this town now."

Sheriff Johnson had stayed true to the Judge, but if he were honest, his loyalty was waning.

He replayed Judge Lowry's remarks to James earlier, about it being *his* town, over and over in his head. *Will the next hanging include a masked man that used to be a Judge?* he thought.

* * * *

While scouting out the new property designated for the town greenhouses, James and Jason were making quite a stir with the townspeople. Most were thrilled with the idea of growing food for the citizens, with only a few openly skeptical about how it would be divided up.

Sheriff Johnson stopped by to get some face time with his constituents and carefully took most of the credit for the idea.

"When the town votes for a Sheriff like me and a Mayor like Mr. VanFleet here," he said to the growing crowd, while putting his hand on James' shoulder, "well, this is what you get. Several greenhouses to be used to grow food for the entire town all year long."

"Are there any volunteers to help?" called out Jason.

"Nope," yelled a large man in front. "Just let me know when to come and pick up my free share."

The Sheriff recognized him from the last hanging, when he was shouting about Mr. Grimes possibly being the hooded man in the execution line.

"I forgot about you, big boy," he said under his breath. "You will surely be the star of my next hanging."

"This will have to be a community effort," James continued, ignoring the last comment.

"Food will grow, but not without careful guidance and daily monitoring. Anything worth having is worth maintaining," he added.

"We will post a signup sheet with various shifts in front of the courthouse for volunteers to start work next week. Rest assured, we will be working side-by-side with you the days Jason and I are in town, until these greenhouses are up and running."

Most cheered upon hearing this and seemed eager to help.

"My jail cells are all empty," said Sheriff Johnson to James, as they walked back the quarter-mile to the office.

"That sounds like a good problem to have," interjected Jason, overhearing the conversation.

"It's just too quiet is all. I prefer the conversation of the condemned. And if I'm honest, I kind of miss having Mr. Grimes under my roof. You should have seen his face when he realized where he was. It was priceless, like those old credit card commercials.

"Your opponent is out of town when the world goes to shit $10,000. He returns a week later, $1. He crosses the sitting Sheriff and ends up hanged in front of the entire town. Priceless! He fought till the end, though; I'll give him that." *I wonder if the good Judge would be so feisty?* he thought, not daring to say it out loud.

"You're kidding, of course?" asked Jason.

"I'm not really a funny man," replied the Sheriff, with a glare.

James could tell Jason was getting worked up, and Sheriff Johnson was getting annoyed. Putting a hand on Jason's shoulder, he said, "We have some work to do. I think Jason and I will spend some time spreading the word about the new greenhouses around town, Sheriff."

"Sure, James. It's always good to give them something to look forward to. Just don't forget to tell them I donated the land and gave you two the task of getting it done."

"We'll make sure they know," replied James, now wondering if Jason would blurt out something and cause a scene.

Headed downtown on foot, Jason asked if he did good.

"Are you being sarcastic?" asked James.

"Oh, maybe," replied Jason. "Or maybe I just have a better handle on the big picture now. I'm pretty sure the Judge and Sheriff will have a showdown soon, and we will eventually have one as the victor for control of the town."

"I think you're spot-on with that," James replied with a sigh.

"I'm not sure the good Lord will let this abuse go on for too much longer without sending us into the lion's den with spears," James continued. "Our job now is to win the support of both the city council and the townspeople. When it goes down, we will have the proper backing to see this town move forward and prosper once again."

Weston Grill and Tavern was hopping today, leaving James wondering how many of the townsfolk could afford to buy a meal.

"We take certain items on trade days," said the owner of the restaurant. "Everyone has something valuable in their possession. Maybe it's not worth what it used to be, but I still find value in certain things. This watch is a genuine Rolex, kept in a Friday cage, I'm told."

"I think you mean Faraday cage," replied James. "It just keeps things from getting zapped. How do you know it's real, though?" asked James, not wanting to be rude but genuinely curious, having never seen one up close.

"Well," said the restaurant owner, "it can be tough sometimes to spot a fake. Here's what I look for," he added, handing James the watch. "What do you notice?" he asked.

"It's impressive," replied James. "It feels heavy and solid."

"What about the second hand? Is it ticking or sweeping?"

"Sweeping, I guess," replied James.

"Exactly! All true Rolexes have hands that sweep and don't tick, although there is a school of thought that the ticks are so fast that it appears like a sweep. The last and most important thing is removing the bracket to view the serial numbers at either end. It's still not 100% accurate in spotting a fake, but if it's that good of a knockoff, then what do I care anyway?" he said, laughing.

"So, they trade a Rolex for one meal?" asked Jason, sounding annoyed.

"No, no. Don't worry; we are trading fairly. The former owner of this watch has quite a few prepaid meals in his future," assured the restauranteur. "Who knows, this watch may be worth a few steers down the road," he joked.

Loud voices came from the outdoor patio as a group of maybe 25 men and women were apparently arguing. Three of the town council members were there, with one being a veteran member and the other two new. James could hear that the topic was Mr. Grimes.

The two new councilmen were half drunk by the looks of them and engaging the rest with conspiracy theories, although surprisingly accurate James and Jason concluded, even down to the false-flag explosion at the last trade days.

The veteran councilman was quiet and distanced himself physically from the other two.

"Why, there's the Mayor right there," one of them spat, slurring his words. "I'm sure he can tell us all what really happened."

"Councilmen," said James in a commanding voice. "I think it's time you went home. We have a lot of work ahead of us to ensure the survival of this great town, and this type of behavior is not a good start."

Sheriff Johnson pulled up in his official truck, only hearing the last words from James.

"What's going on here, gentlemen?" he asked. "Can I help you two with something?" he asked the councilmen.

"No. I mean no, sir," one of them replied, stammering.

"Stop by my office, both of you, first thing in the morning," he added, as the two left the restaurant in a hurry.

"What do you know?" he asked the veteran councilmen.

"I only know that I'm not a part of their opinions about you or this town," replied one of them.

"Let's take a ride," said the Sheriff to the terrified councilman.

James and Jason were successful at quickly turning the conversation to the greenhouses and new food supply, also getting the restaurant owner's interest.

When they left 30 minutes later, everyone had forgotten about the earlier conversation and were now talking planting strategies, with the old-timers leading the way.

Sheriff Johnson drove the veteran councilman back to the station, grilling him on what happened at the restaurant. After a full confession regarding the two new posts, the Sheriff told him to have them at his office first thing in the morning with their resignations in hand.

"I can't have elected city men publicly intoxicated in *my* town. I need people I can trust around here," he said. "Can I trust you, councilman?"

"Yes, sir, without a doubt."

"What do you think about James and Jason?" the Sheriff continued.

"Well, I've known James for a long time, and he's a straight shooter. I'm not sure about the other guy, though."

"I want you to be my eyes and ears out there. Can you do that for me?" asked the Sheriff.

"Yes, of course, Sheriff. You can count on me."

As he left to deliver the news to the newly elected men, he was happy just to be leaving in one piece.

* * * *

Early the next morning, the new councilmen arrived at the Sheriff's office.

The first one, apologizing, placed a folded resignation letter on his desk, quietly walking out the front door.

The second cited a list of reasons a councilman may be removed from his elected post. He clarified that public intoxication was not among them. "You're stuck with me, at least until the next town election," he said, laughing as he headed towards the front door.

"Stop and on your knees," commanded a red-faced Sheriff, not believing the gall of this man to defy his orders in his own jailhouse.

Drawing his Glock 22 from his right hip holster, it took everything he had not to shoot the man in the back.

Sliding an equal pistol across the smooth tile floor to him, Sheriff Johnson gave instructions.

Holstering his own weapon, he continued. "I'll make this fair. The first one down after a count of three wins.

"One," he said, as the councilman begged.

"No! No! I don't want any part of this." Gone was the smug man from just a few minutes ago.

"Two," said the Sheriff, as the man began to sob.

"That's enough, boys," called Judge Lowry, coming through the front door.

"Stand up, son," he said to the councilman.

"Sheriff, I can see you're flustered. Did you know that anger and sobbing are only slightly different? Both are uncontrolled emotions that don't move *my* town forward. Are you going soft on me?"

"No, sir. I'm OK. Just got upset is all," replied the Sheriff, shocked at himself for explaining his behavior to another man, even the Judge.

"I won't let you kill him," said Judge Lowry, "but I'll let you lock him up for a while. Let's check on the townsfolk and make sure they know about my greenhouse plan. I may even buy you breakfast."

* * * *

James and Jason had the day off, at least from official town duties.

A rancher is always working, minus a few hours on Sunday for church. The girls were excited about going to church this coming Sunday, as they had not been in quite a while.

For Billy, it would be his first time attending any church, and he could hardly wait. Everyone picked out their best outfits, with Billy still in need.

Janice met up with a close neighbor, only a few ranches down, that she hadn't seen in a while. She remembered her having two young sons a few years ago and stopped by her place for a chat.

The woman had three nearly full bags of clothes in Billy's size.

"How much for all these?" asked Janice.

"Oh, they're hand-me-downs. You can just take them."

Janice, always trading fairly and knowing the woman could use some help, traded a good amount of beef, eggs, fresh vegetables, and honey.

Billy was happy with the new old clothes and felt more comfortable each day. James and Janice made a point to talk about his father every day, not wanting him to forget. It was the perfect match. Billy needed a caring mommy and daddy and James and Janice needed a sweet little boy to love and raise.

The girls constantly fought over who would be sleeping next to, or playing with, little Billy. Chance, now on the mend, took turns sleeping in the kids' rooms most nights.

* * * * * * *

CHAPTER SIX ~ RATON PASS, NEW MEXICO

With everyone back at camp, congratulating Mel on the bridgework, Tammy was the most relieved. She finally had something she really wanted and didn't want to lose it all in an instant.

The topic on everyone's mind now was the next step for our group.

For this, we had every adult in attendance, including Mike and Sheila.

"There are a few ways to look at this," I began, getting everyone's attention.

"This is only the halfway point to Colorado, and the rest of the trip has to be done in the summer months. The winters can be harsh here and are not conducive to traveling as we are. So, we either leave soon or wait an entire year. We have obstacles either way," I added.

"First, we know there are at least 20-30 people across the downed bridge, and some with firearms."

"Unless the soldiers disarmed the citizens," called out Jake.

"Exactly," I agreed, "which is likely, considering their MO.

"The only way out with the trailers is through the river, where we came in, and back across the ten miles of potentially hostile roads to get to the main highway again. There is the barricade at the end we are supposed to have a lifetime passage through, although that can change at any moment.

"Second, the group from Topeka, Kansas, is massive, we believe, and growing every day. They will likely travel ten miles from this very spot over Raton Pass and plow a hole through any city or town that the I-25 highway intersects.

"They will no doubt be moving slowly, as many of the people they add to their group will be walking. We are looking at about 285 miles to Saddle Ranch. At 3 miles per hour for 8 hours a day, they could make it in about 12 days walking. Add in a couple of weeks for unseen issues, with roadblocks or other hostiles along the way, and we're looking at a month."

"That's also assuming they are close to here now, and traveling in a straight line," added Lonnie.

"Their final destination will be less than 15 miles from Saddle Ranch, but that is an issue for another day," I added.

"So, the choices..." said Lonnie. "We clear the area across the bridge, up to the main road, before traveling with the children, and prepare to leave in the next day or two. But we will have to tiptoe around towns and cities, just as we did getting here.

"Or we try to figure out when the main Topeka group will be coming through and follow a safe distance behind them. The downside is getting a later start by a couple of weeks, maybe more."

"They may have scouts following the group, but they will most likely not expect an attack from behind, unless it's military," added Mike.

"Let's discuss the options tonight and reconvene in the morning over breakfast," I said.

I pulled Lonnie, Jake, Mike and Steve aside for the last bit of information, not wanting to worry the rest of the group.

"The Topeka group," I started, with a noticeable sigh and clenched teeth, "have a few ways to get to their final destination at Horsetooth Reservoir.

"One stays on I-25 into the city of Fort Collins, after blasting a hole through the northern border of Loveland.

"The other two bring them through the center of Loveland, and at least one probable route brings them within one mile of Saddle Ranch.

"I'm quite sure they have the entire four miles across the valley secured by now, but the marchers could go right past the northern border of the valley, only 100 feet away.

"This is my biggest concern, not only for my family and the others residing in that valley but also for our group as we try to start a new life."

"Lance," came the call on the radio from Jim. "I've got your parents on the line."

Quickly heading to Beatrice's house, where he had the radio set up in Dean's workshop at her insistence, I was excited to hear their voices.

"Hello!" I said, with Joy and the boys gathered around. "We're all here," I announced as she and the boys said hi.

"Great, honey," replied Sharon. "I've got Dad and Karl here as well. I'm sure you remember John," she added.

"Of course! How are you, sir?" I asked.

"We're hanging in there," John replied. "Your parents were able to give us a fighting chance, thanks to the information you had told them over the years about power outages and EMPs.

How many are in your group?"

"We're about 20 men, women and children now. We're at the halfway point at a location I won't mention over the radio for obvious reasons. A few have decided to stay here; however, the rest of us are headed that way if that's all right."

There was a long pause, and I was getting nervous. Had I promised something I couldn't deliver? Were we not welcome there, after all we had gone through to get this far? Joy looked at me, questioningly.

"Hello," I said, now just wanting an answer.

"We lost them," said Jim. "Hold on, and I'll try to reconnect."

Ten agonizing minutes later, we were back on.

"Sorry about that," said John. "We lost you for a bit. I'm not sure what happened. How many did you say are in your group, Lance?"

"About 20 men, women and children."

"Well, that sounds fine to me," replied John. "Your parents told the council and me you would likely be headed here with a small group. We were actually prepared for up to 30 of you, so there shouldn't be any accommodation issues, even if you pick up a few strays along the way. How long until you get here?"

"Well, we're not sure just yet," I replied. "At the soonest, it would be about a week or two; at the longest, hopefully a month.

"There is something you should know, and I'll relay the information as best I can without giving away any locations.

"Dad, do you remember where we used to go hiking, maybe five miles northeast from the general store my friends and I would ride our dirt bikes to during the summer?"

"You mean the place with the rock, near the water?" Bill asked carefully, not to give a name to the location.

"Yes, that's it," I told him. There is a large and growing group from the Midwest headed to that very spot, as we speak.

"My best guess is that their main body is about 3-5 weeks out, but they have forward observers scouting out the way and looking for supplies to be confiscated. They are on the main interstate as best we can tell, and I'm not sure if they will turn when they get your way or not. Does that make sense, Dad?"

"Yes, I know what you're implying, and we will take the necessary precautions, just in case.

And just so you know, we are working closely with Samuel now."

I was interested to hear about their progress on security and provisions but didn't want any details going out that could jeopardize the community.

I knew they had likely secured the entire valley, since they were working with Samuel.

Taking with my mom and brother Karl, I kept the rest of the conversation light, giving the boys a chance to talk to their grandparents and uncle.

* * * *

Most of us took the night off, with a couple of people volunteering to stay on security detail.

The kids watched the classic baseball movie called *The Sandlot*. My boys always loved the part where the kid called Squints put himself in a near-drowning state by jumping into the deep end of the pool, even though he couldn't swim. The lifeguard that they all had a crush on, named Wendy Peppercorn, saved him and was giving him mouth-to-mouth resuscitation when he winked to his friends and tried to kiss her. He gained respect from his friends that day, while getting them all banished from the pool for life, and he would eventually marry the very same girl.

"They're going to miss the movies for sure when we head out," I told Joy.

"About that," she said. "What do think we should do?"

"Well," I told her, "I vote to let the Topeka group pass and follow a safe distance behind. One, it eliminates the guaranteed fight with those across the bridge and doesn't present a new fight with the rest of them.

"Two, should they try to breach this property, David and his group are going to need our help and firepower to defend them.

"Three, it's the path of least resistance, straight up the middle of the state. If there is a major roadblock, we won't be the first to encounter it. We will know which way they are headed, once they get to Loveland, and we can warn the Ranch if needed.

"I'll present my views when we all meet in the morning and see if anyone has another idea. One thing is for sure—we can't wait another year to go."

The boys wanted to sleep in Veronica and Suzie's tent. David, setting up another, gave him and Tina some alone time and the same for Joy and me.

Mike and Tom were on perimeter patrol again. For Mike, it was calming, quietly waiting in the darkness for something, anything to peak his interest. He would not be disappointed this night, as the bushes next to the river road shook side to side.

"A hog, maybe," said Tom, "or possibly a bear. Either way, it's good meat."

"Hold on," whispered Mike, half hoping it would be a zealous soldier he could face, one-on-one.

All at once, everything was still. There was no more movement from the side of the road...only silence.

"If you are going to shoot me, then get on with it," came a female voice, as a figure emerged from the second bush back.

Mike, seeing a young female in the road through his night-vision goggles, called to Tom, "Hold your fire."

"I'm with you on that," he replied, seeing the same image.

"We're not going to shoot you," called out Mike, "but come up here nice and slow, hands out to your sides."

The young girl did exactly as instructed, and as she neared he could see she was no more than 13-14 years old. Her jet-black hair, long and straight, hung in her face. Seeing her face as she brushed her hair back, Mike saw a beautiful girl that had both innocence and battle scars.

"What's your name?" asked Mike,

"Katie," she replied. "Now you," she stated.

"I'm Mike, and this here is Tom."

"Who else is with you?" asked Tom.

"What do you mean?" she replied.

"Listen, lady. I'm a hunter and a darn good one. I can tell by the movement of the bushes that you're either hiding another person, or an animal that could feed our group, and I never fire on something I can't see. So, which is it?"

"Come on out!" called Katie. "It's my little brother, Jonah. He's only six and really scared."

"We're not going to hurt you," said Mike, "but we need to talk a bit if that's OK?"

"OK," Katie agreed. "But no one takes my brother from me, not ever!" she screamed.

"Katie, it's OK," whispered Mike. "You're safe here. I was a police officer only a few weeks ago, and I protect children. Do you understand?"

"Yes," she replied, still reserved, but starting to come around.

"It's just those men, those bastards that killed our mom and dad. I want them to die!" she shouted, rage turning to tears as she put her head on Mike's shoulder, sobbing.

Frozen, Mike was out of his element. Emotion was not on his list of attributes, but today, at this moment, he felt something he couldn't describe. It started as anxiousness as she embraced him, quickly turning to something resembling compassion, and finally vengeance as he plotted to avenge her parents' death.

Jonah, grabbing his sister's leg, was shaking and crying while calling for his mommy.

"Are you being followed?" asked Mike.

"No, sir. I don't think so. The guards across the river were drunk and asleep when we left."

"How did you know to come over here?" Mike asked.

"Well, we saw someone the other night come across and do something to the tents of the bad men. He looked like you," Katie continued, "but it was dark, so I'm not sure."

"How did you see me that night?" asked Mike. "Weren't you asleep?"

"I'm always up now, since it's just my brother and me... Anyway, the next day we saw you fighting one of the head men on the bridge, and I knew we had to find you."

"What about your parents?" asked Mike.

"The day your people first came across our camp, I saw you shoot the Keeper. My parents said you were bad, and I believed them then.

"But that man called the Keeper was really bad. He hurt people...women...and even my...I mean...our mom," she added, hugging her brother. "I'm glad he's gone. The second guy was nicer, but nobody listened to him.

"When the bad men came, they got us all together and took all the weapons. They told us we could join their group or go off on our own, and they divided us into two groups.

"I counted nine of us choosing to head out on our own and the rest wanting to join their group. Only they were lying, because we didn't have a choice. They went down the line, shooting everybody on our side, one after another, even our mom and dad.

"In the end, Jonah and I were the only two left. I begged them not to hurt him, and the head guy said he would keep us alive because I looked pretty. He told me I would belong to him from that day forward."

"Did he hurt you?" Mike asked, already fearing the answer.

She paused, looking off into the night sky.

"He won't anymore," she finally spoke. "When I saw you were fooling with their tents, I knew there was another way. During the commotion, my brother and I ran out of the camp with some food we grabbed from our tent and went into the woods. We saw the bridge fight from down on the river bank, hiding in some bushes. I watched you throw that monster over the rail, but I still wasn't sure you were good. You almost stepped on us when you climbed out of the river," she added.

"Where have you two been since then?" asked Tom.

"In the forest, hiding. We drank from the river and ran out of food earlier today. Now we're here. Should we move on?" she asked bluntly.

"No. Not so fast, Katie," said Mike. "I have someone I want you to meet. Stay with Tom here for a few minutes, and I'll be right back."

A nervous Katie consoled her brother and last family member of the new-world.

"Sheila," Mike called quietly, shaking their tent.

"What's wrong?" she asked. "Is your shift over?"

"Not yet," Mike replied. "Get dressed. There are some people I want you to meet."

"Can it wait until morning?" she asked, laying her head back down on the pillow.

"Nope. It's a now kind of thing."

Tammy dressed and made the 1/8 mile walk back to the security post with Mike.

"Katie and Jonah, this is my girlfriend, Sheila," said Mike.

"What do you know about kids?" Katie asked her, matter of factly.

"Not much, I'm afraid," a surprised Sheila replied.

"That's good to hear," said Katie, lowering her defenses just a bit.

"So, do you even like kids?"

"Sure, I do," replied Sheila. "I used to visit my nieces and nephews back East a few times a year before...well, you know. Are you two OK?" she asked.

"We're tired," admitted Katie. "Can we sleep somewhere my brother will be safe?"

"Sure, sweetie," replied Sheila. "You can sleep in my tent, and our strong man Mike will watch over us for the rest of the night."

Katie agreed, exhausted from the past few days, and kept Jonah close to her side.

* * * *

Morning came early, with talk from both groups about what should be done moving forward.

With a groggy Mike and Tom following the night shift, nobody knew yet about the new additions.

Having all of the adults in attendance, including Sheila sitting where she could watch for the still-sleeping children, we submitted our plans.

I opted to go first, hoping to get some agreement up front and then just talk logistics.

I gave the same ideas I had given Joy last night, adding that staying through the winter would put an unfair strain on David's group, as ours would run out of food before then.

"We also need to make a stop in Trinidad to check in on our friend Vlad," I continued. "As most of you who know him are aware, he was in bad shape arriving at the FEMA camp in Amarillo. We were told that he would lose his leg to infection, and he was transported to Trinidad by helicopter for the operation."

"Vlad is much of the reason we have made it this far, and he is our friend. He may not have survived, or he may be able to continue our trip with us. I promised him a life of peace in the Rocky Mountains in exchange for his guns. I will do everything possible to keep that promise."

Mike was the only one up for taking out the guys across the bridge but didn't care if we waited a few weeks after that.

Thankfully Lonnie spoke up, agreeing with me that it would only pick a fight with the larger group, forcing them to retaliate.

"Best case scenario," added Jake, "they just move on past, not wanting to bother with a detour and river crossing to try and take our supplies and guns."

"If they do come on to the property from the highway, there is only one way in, across the river," added David, "and a show of firepower might turn them back."

"There is no perfect scenario," I ended with, "but let's vote anyway.

All in favor of waiting 2-4 weeks, until they pass, raise your hands.

Nearly all hands raised, including women and men.

"Those opposed?"

Only Mark raised his hand, adding, "I would like you all to stay for a year or more."

David smiled, feeling proud of his son's generosity and strength to stand for his beliefs.

"Thank you, Mark," I told him, "but we need to keep moving. Besides, with a few more weeks here, we can help build your greenhouses and beef up your perimeter security."

It was decided that Jim, Steve and Mark would rotate radio shifts and monitor 24 hours a day for the most updated information on the Kansas group and any other news we needed to know about.

Jim added that the President would be giving a State of the Union speech today at 5 p.m. Central Time, and it would be broadcast from an unknown location.

It was settled and, God willing, we would shortly be following close behind the largest and most deadly group we knew about in the next-world.

Greenhouses were the topic of the day, along with the upcoming President's speech.

Many theories of the President's address we're flying around. Some thought it would be a repeat of the last one, slightly edited to make it appear new. People in this camp thought the government had completely abandoned its citizens and flew or took ships to other ally countries to wait it out. Once the food ran out at the FEMA camps, it would be a repeat of the first day.

Others considered the President, Vice President and Cabinet, along with members of both the House and Senate, with everyone's families in tow, to be hiding in a lavish bunker somewhere on the East Coast. They would be waiting to reunite the country, just as soon as the power could be restored.

The last camp considered the government selling the country's land for the exploitation of its raw minerals, petroleum, timber and vast farmland to overpopulated countries like China, Japan or India, using the citizens still alive as modern-day slaves and only providing crude room and board in exchange for hard work and absolute loyalty.

These options, along with a few others further down the crazy train tracks, encompassed aliens and fully automated androids at the helm.

I could picture Jerry Garcia and Ozzie Osborn on board the crazy train, yelling to the conductor "Faster, Casey! Faster!"

Next came the discussion of retaliation for the country involved in the EMP attack.

Many considered we had wiped North Korea off the map, including millions of hard-working citizens who were likely only caring about their families and the next meal.

Another view was a regime change in that country, replacing Kim Jong-un with Dennis Rodman, an over-the-top former professional basketball player from Chicago.

"James would love this," David said, whispering to me. "He's a Chicago Bulls fan through and through."

I found it funny, knowing that Rodman had called the North Korean leader his friend and visited his country more than once.

The third, and most plausible to me, was offered by Jake and Nancy.

"An EMP is an act of nuclear war with no fallout or contamination to another country's air supply," Jake began. "For that reason, it kind of gets a pass in the nuclear war rules. It's not a good thing to do in the eyes of other countries that may be allies, but it's also not a full-scale nuclear bombing, sending a mushroom cloud of toxic chemicals into the jet stream that may harm other countries.

"Think of our likely allies of South Korea, Japan and Australia, with both Japan and South Korea in the immediate nuclear aftermath zone of such destruction. Do you think they are going to want to aid a former ally who has put their citizens just outside the direct line of fire?"

"I don't think they will, and all those ships with aid that the President spoke about on the last radio address would reverse course and head back home," continued Nancy.

"I agree, guys," I said aloud. "We may have hit them with an EMP or attempted a regime change, minus Rodman, if we're being realistic, but there's no way we nuked an entire country. The risks are just too high.

"When people, and even entire families, can be executed or put into hard labor camps for saying something bad about the regime, it doesn't seem unlikely that they would appear to support their leadership unconditionally during public ceremonies and parades.

"If I'm honest, I'm glad we likely didn't destroy millions of men, women and children to fix what has always been a regime problem."

I saw many from both groups shaking their heads in agreement, although I knew there would likely be some folks in each camp.

"Maybe we will get some answers with President Obama's speech today…and maybe not," added Lonnie, seeming to agree with Jake and Nancy's logic as well.

"I hope they're bringing over some South Korean barbecue beef," said one of the adults, getting a few laughs.

"Either way," interjected Joy, "any help from a foreign country will most likely arrive by ship, and in a port far away from New Mexico or Colorado. I doubt any aid will make it past the first few FEMA camps near the coast."

Most agreed with her on that theory.

"Let's shelve this until we hear the President's address," offered Lonnie.

"Now, on to the greenhouses," announced David. "I think Mel has something to share with us."

"It took me half the night, but my adrenaline was still kicking from the dynamite yesterday. You never really know how that stuff will play out," Mel said jokingly, getting a stern look from Tammy.

"Anyway, I created some drawings," he continued passing out a few pieces of computer paper with exact dimensions and materials listed.

"You did this yesterday?" asked Lonnie, surprised.

"Well, actually last night," replied a smiling Mel. "I bet you were expecting it to be done by hand and not a computer draft!"

"That's right," replied Lonnie. "The Faraday cage again, am I right?"

"Yes, sir," replied Mel. "The computer and printer and copier. And before anyone asks, I do not have access to the Internet, although it seems possible, given that it's worldwide and hosted by satellites."

"Are these renderings accurate?" asked David.

"Down to the last screw, my friend," replied Mel.

"You all have had my Mel up half the night two days in a row," shouted Tammy in a playful tone. "He's mine tonight" got a cheer from the other ladies and a few of the men.

Mel, blushing, said, "Can't argue with that!"

"You've done a fine job over the last couple days, Mel, helping both of our groups," said David in a serious tone. "You have my vote for a night off *only* to catch up on your sleep," he added, breaking his demeanor as a smile crept in.

"You've got my vote too," I said, laughing as Mel blushed just a bit more.

A raid of Dean's workshop revealed many of the parts needed for the project, including boards, nails and screws, and hand tools such as hammers, levelers, saws, screwdrivers, and an impressive amount of power tools that could be run on a generator.

"The rest is in the other shop," said David getting a look out of both me and Mel. Even Mark looked surprised, hearing this from his dad.

"I've been up here a long time, Dad, and I don't see another shop."

"Are you sure you don't see it, son?" asked David, pointing to a large rock sitting in front of a large pile of dirt.

"I see the rock, but that's it," said Mark.

I was looking at a rock nearly 10 feet by 10 feet in an area with no other rocks close to that size.

As we walked closer, David knocked on it with his closed right hand.

"That thing sounds hollow," said Mel.

David slid the 50-pound rock that should have weighed 10,000 pounds aside to reveal a metal door painted earthen brown that was only visible by the round rusted handle.

Unlocking the padlock with the key from his pocket, he swung open the large metal door, revealing a dark room dug into the side of the mountain.

Shining his flashlight, David entered the wide-open space, with the rest of us following closely behind.

"I haven't been in here since it happened," said David, trying the light switch with no luck. "I figured it was worth a try since the whole thing is technically in the ground."

With the rest of us adding our flashlights, we were able to see inside clearly.

"Over there are the rolls of plastic my father saved, hoping to one day build greenhouses of his own," pointed out David.

The sheetrock walls were covered with exceptional paintings of Beatrice at every stage of her life since they met all those years ago.

"Those are incredible!" I called out. "Why are they not in the house?"

"She has never seen them," said David. "All the years they have been married, he had done one portrait every year for 42 years, and she had no idea."

I wanted to ask why he didn't show her when he knew he was dying of cancer, and suddenly realized he probably would have if he had lived just a little longer.

I was relieved that observation didn't slip out in front of Mark, but I wondered if he was thinking the same thing.

"Can we show her now?" an excited Mark asked.

"Not yet, son," replied David. "It's the sort of thing that needs to be revealed in a certain way. Let me think about it for a day or two.

"In the meantime, we need to get the building supplies over to the main workshop, so everything is in one place."

We opted to get all the materials over ourselves, so as not to have anyone else see the portraits.

"Lance," called Mark's friend, running from the house and out of breath. "Jim has something on the ham."

"OK. Tell him I'll be right there."

Without running all of the possible scenarios through my head of what he could be referring to, I ran to Beatrice's house.

"I've got news on Topeka," said Jim. "They're coming."

* * * * * * *

CHAPTER SEVEN ~ SADDLE RANCH ~ LOVELAND COLORADO

Sarah brought Mac into the hospital in the morning, no longer caring what anyone might think. Jimmy was improving and could speak quietly. He wanted to know what happened and Mac gave him an abbreviated version of what he knew.

"You did a good job, Jimmy. All the guys, are grateful to you for saving their lives."

"I'm not sure about that," Jimmy whispered, "but I'm glad they are all OK."

"Your idea put an end to the Miller boys' issue, and that means a lot for the community," Mac continued.

"Thanks, Mac," replied Jimmy in a hoarse voice.

"That's enough for today," stated Sarah, touching Mac on the shoulder. "He needs his rest."

"You're two for two," Mac told her as they left the room. She raised a questioning eyebrow. "You saved two of our guys from certain death."

"Well, he's not entirely out of the woods yet. But yeah, I'm kind of a thing around here, in case you haven't heard," Sarah joked.

* * * *

Cory and Mac took a few guys for a ride up to the Millers' place before lunch to check on the boy. He was sitting on the front stoop, with a rifle on the ground in front of him.

"How are you holding up, son?" asked Cory.

"OK, I guess. Just got my dogs now."

"Where are they?" Mac asked, looking around the perimeter.

"I put them up," he replied. "It's not hard to hear five ATVs coming up the mountain."

"Do you need any help with the burials?" asked Cory.

"No. It's done."

"Do you need anything?" asked Mac.

"Yeah, I guess so. I need something to do. I like to hunt, but it don't take much to feed just my dogs and me. Plus, I think I need more than just meat to survive up here."

"I understand," replied Mac. "I'll check with our people and see if there may be a position in security in exchange for some food."

"Should we stop at old man MacDonald's place?" asked one of Mac's men as they headed back.

"Not today," Mac replied. "From what I hear, he already knows everything anyway."

* * * *

"Mac!" came the call over the radio from the southern border.

"We've got some guys over here on horseback, demanding to talk with Chief Lerner."

"Who are they?" mouthed Cory to Mac without a sound.

"Where are they from and what are their names?" asked Mac, now holding the radio so both he and Cory could hear. "Also, what do they want?"

After gathering the basic information, Mac told the man on the checkpoint he would get right back to him.

They were apparently part of the Loveland City Council and Sanitation Department, and Cory knew all of their names. "They want to secure the reservoir. They say it belongs to the City and they are challenging our right to have a barricade blocking their access," he added.

"Well, this should be fun," said Cory to Mac. "Do you want to come with me?"

"I wouldn't miss it for a root canal," joked Mac, still feeling great about his new life.

* * * *

Ten minutes later, they arrived at the checkpoint. There were 14 men on horseback, including the Mayor of Loveland, who they had forgotten to mention, plus most of the City Council and a few of Cory's former officers.

"I'm surprised. Most of these guys even know how to ride," said Cory quietly to Mac. "Except, of course, for my old officers."

"This is getting a bit more complicated than we thought," remarked a now-serious Mac.

"I'll speak to the Mayor first, and then the officers present," called Cory to the border guard.

"What about the Council?" the guard asked.

"Nope, not today," replied Cory, getting an approving nod from Mac, understanding the idea of "divide and conquer."

Mac was reminded of a night when he was maybe 17 or 18. He and his buddy were joyriding around town, drinking a few beers.

When the police pulled them over, they interviewed them separately before deciding on the validity of their stories. Either way, they both spent a night in the drunk tank and his truck was impounded, with everyone in the small town knowing what happened. It was thankfully enough to learn his lesson for good.

"I'll only deal with Chief Lerner," the Mayor spat.

"Let him across," called Mac.

Cory reached to shake the man's hand, addressing him as "Mr. Mayor." The handshake was not returned but, rather, replaced by a demanding glare from a man who clearly did his talking with his mouth.

"You will be talking to both of us, sir," said Cory, still trying to be civil.

"You abandoned your post, Chief Lerner, and left the rest of us to pick up the pieces," he said angrily.

"Really?" asked Cory. "Is that what you're telling the other guys with you? Those three," Cory continued, pointing to his old officers, "know the truth. They know that after everything happened we tried in earnest to gather the leadership of the City, and you, sir, were nowhere to be found. Your City Council only wanted a free pass of food and protection for their positions but were not willing to work for it. Nobody stepped up to lead the city, and after meeting several times with all of my men, we unanimously decided to each go our separate ways and take care of our families.

"That being said, just in case it needs to be stated clearly, I, Cory Lerner, Chief of Police of Loveland, Colorado, hereby surrender my post, effective immediately."

Border security led an agitated Mayor back across the line and brought three more men over to Cory.

"How are you guys holding up?" asked Cory, smiling. These three were all good officers, and he wondered how they got caught up with the Mayor.

"We're OK," said one. "It's good to see you, Cory. The Mayor got all worked up about the reservoir out here, and since Fort Collins, next door, has already secured their water supply, he was embarrassed, I guess, for not having done it sooner."

"You mean Horsetooth Reservoir?" asked Mac.

"Yes, the whole valley up there was secured only days ago, with the help of the local FEMA guys, and of course Fort Collins."

"FEMA, huh?" asked Mac.

"Yeah, they have a camp up that way, and apparently they are interested in the water supply."

Mac and Cory had spoken briefly to John and Bill over lunch, learning about the Topeka guys planning to settle at Horsetooth Lake.

"That should be interesting," Cory said to Mac, recalling the earlier lunch meeting.

"Are one of you looking to be Chief of Police now?" asked Cory respectfully to his old friends. "Is that why you're out here today?"

"No, sir. We all talked about it," said another, "and none of us want to be in charge or work under the Mayor. We just heard you were out here with Cameron and, well, we just thought...well..."

"Just say it!" said another officer.

"Well, we wanted to know if our families could join out here and work with you again."

Mac's mind was turning. He had heard earlier that Lance's group would be half of what John and the council had allotted for. *Could I get three more highly trained security added to my team?* he wondered.

Mac pulled Cory aside, asking the men to sit tight for a few minutes.

"I want to talk to John, Bill and the council," Mac told him. "These families are 20 miles outside of town already, and if we wait on this, they will likely find somewhere else to help out. I know it's already afternoon, but let's see if these three—just your old officers, I mean—can stick around for an hour or so. I'm sure they don't need the Mayor's help to get back to town."

Cory and Mac headed up to John's house, radioing ahead.

John and Bill were about to meet with the council briefly before getting Mac's opinion on the Horsetooth Reservoir situation.

"Are we agreed, Cory, that adding a few of your old men with their families is a smart move for our community, needing as much trained security as we can get?" asked Mac.

"Absolutely," replied Cory. "There has already been a need, and that is about to increase tenfold in the coming weeks and months, maybe even years."

* * * *

Entering John's house, Mac took the lead in addressing the group.

"John, Bill, council members," he started. "I believe most of you have met Officer Cory Lerner, former Chief of Police for Loveland." Most heads nodded yes.

Mac continued: "We were paid a visit about an hour ago, on our northern valley border, by the Mayor and City Council of Loveland. As head of security, it is my responsibility to maintain

a safe and secure valley, including both our and the West's properties. With more than 500 acres to monitor, it can be taxing on our security detail. We learned firsthand recently that our borders can be breached, as the Miller boys showed us.

"Officer Lerner, or Cory, as he likes to be called, was instrumental in resolving the Miller situation. Three of his former officers, two males with families and one single female, have inquired about a position on our Ranch. I'll let Cory speak to their character before we step out to give you all time to discuss it."

Cory stood in front of the council, a little nervous. He was used to talking in front of a room full of officers, but this was somehow different.

"First, thank you for approving residency for my son, Cameron, and me. We will work hard to earn our place here.

"As for my former officers, all three were on the force for more than five years, each with impeccable records. I would trust my life to any one of them. One has a wife and two girls, ages four and six; the other married officer has with one son, age three, I believe. The third never married and has no children. If you are looking to add more highly trained people to your group, these are the three, in my opinion."

"One last thing," said Mac. "The Miller boy is alone up on the mountain now and is asking to help with security here in exchange for food."

"Mac, can you guys please give us about 15 minutes?" asked John.

"Of course," replied Mac.

Cory and Mac talked outside, awaiting an answer.

"What do you think?" asked Cory.

"Well, John and Bill both have seen firsthand how important security is," said Mac, "and I think the council realizes that everything we have means nothing if someone else can just take it. Samuel's group learned that recently with their mountain community."

"Come on in, guys," said Bill, stepping out the front door.

"We have discussed both ideas presented," announced John, "and have come to a near-unanimous conclusion. The Miller boy can help out with security as you see fit, Mac, but he will not reside on our property. We had some issues with those boys a few years back, as you know.

"As for your former officers, Cory, we unanimously agreed to add them to our group. The spouses will be expected to contribute to the whole with fitting jobs.

"Mac," continued John, "you have done a good job as head of security so far."

Mac's head was spinning, as he wondered if he was being demoted.

"You have amassed a good group and trained them well," John continued. "We would like you to appoint Cory, and Jimmy as soon as he is able, as your supervisors. They will each lead a team that you pick, and report directly to you. We would also ask that you update us weekly, at the very least, on the security of the entire valley, including the West property and both border stations. Obviously, anything needing immediate attention, such as today, would qualify for a quick gathering of all present here. How does that sound, Mac?"

"Great, John. That's just fine by me."

"Cory, are we agreed on your end?" asked John.

"Absolutely, sir, and thank you for the opportunity," replied Cory.

Both left the meeting feeling much better than when they arrived.

"Are you going to be OK working under me, Cory?" asked Mac.

"I already do," Cory replied, smiling. "And it's much more than I ever expected for me and my boy when it all went to hell. So yeah, I'm good...better than good."

Mac, feeling like the kid who finally busted open the piñata, couldn't wait to tell the officers the news.

* * * *

All three were thrilled with the news, and the Mayor changed his demeanor for only long enough to ask for a spot as well.

"We're all set on leadership here," said Cory, maybe feeling a little bad that he took pleasure in turning his old boss down, whose weekly motto had been "The Chief of Police serves at the pleasure of the Mayor and can be terminated at any time." If he was being honest, he didn't feel bad at all.

The three officers vowed to come back with their families in three days' time.

* * * *

Mac couldn't help but make a stop at the hospital to tell Jimmy the news about his new position as soon as he was better. He wouldn't mind seeing Sarah for a few minutes as well.

The small hospital was bustling with activity as Mac and Cory entered through the front door.

"What's going on?" asked a concerned Mac, as Sarah rushed passed him in a near run.

"Back outside, both of you!" she commanded.

They did as they were told and were filled in about the happenings by a front-desk receptionist on her cigarette break.

"The guy in the back had a stroke," she said, without emotion.

"You mean Jimmy?" asked Mac.

"I think so," she replied, "if he's the one who got shot a couple of days ago. The name sounds right."

"Oh no!" said Mac, asking if Jimmy would be OK.

"Do I look like a doctor to you?" she asked, followed by a perfect smoke ring that only an accomplished smoker could pull off.

Mac held his tongue and waited another 45 minutes before sending Cory home to his boy.

"I'll stop by later and let you know what I find out," said a concerned Mac. A reluctant Cory headed back up to the Ranch.

A full hour later, Sarah opened the front door of the hospital.

"I wasn't expecting you to stay, Mac," she said, smiling only a little.

"Jimmy had a stroke. It was an unforeseen complication of the neck wound, and the left side of his body is paralyzed. We're doing all we can, and he is stable now."

"So, what does *that* mean?" Mac questioned in a loud tone.

"Mac," she said in a low voice, putting a hand on his shoulder. "It means if all goes well, he will survive but will likely have limited use of his left arm and leg, at best."

"No, no," said Mac. "He's supposed to be one of my key security leaders. Please...just fix him."

"We're doing all we can," she restated. "He's lucky to be alive at this point."

"I'm sorry, Sarah," he replied, calming down. "Of course you're doing everything possible for him. I know that."

"Do you?" she asked.

"I do," he insisted, hugging her tightly. "He's my friend, too, and Lord knows I don't have many of those."

"I know that," she replied. "You're all he's talked about the past day, since he could speak."

Mac continued: "I just don't get it. When something good happens, it seems something bad is right around the corner."

"It all depends on how you choose to see it," Sarah replied. "Your men brought Jimmy to my hospital half dead, shot in the neck up on a mountain and brought down on a four-wheeler with a T-shirt around the wound.

"In a fancy city hospital, even if he were shot in the front lobby they would still be lucky to save him. We did save him and he had a complication, as many in that state do. It may not be the last one, either. He is still alive and will hopefully leave this hospital down the road."

"But if he's paralyzed he won't be able to lead my team," replied Mac.

"That's where you're wrong, Mac," she stated confidently but respectfully. "People with disabilities of all kinds go on to lead exceptional lives. The guy with prosthetic legs in the Olympics; or the brilliant physicist Stephen Hawking; or the Governor of Texas who was jogging and had a tree branch fall on his back, paralyzing him from the waist down. What was his name?"

"Greg Abbott," said Mac, without thinking. He knew politics back and forth, not that it mattered

much anymore.

"OK, Sarah. I get your point. And if he can make it and stay alive, I will make it my mission to help him run his post. I had forgotten about Hawking, but it goes to show that the mind is far more powerful than the body... Can I see Jimmy now?"

"Not a chance," she said flatly. "It will be a long night for me, so go home and dream about us," she said, kissing him. "I'll radio you if there are any changes."

* * * *

Mac returned to the Ranch, stopping by Cory's place to fill him in.

"We'll take it a day at a time," Mac told him. "Hopefully your officers will make it back with their families and we can start dividing up the teams. I'll want your three split up to balance everything out."

"I think that's a good idea," agreed Cory, "and just let me know what you want to do with the Miller boy."

"I had forgotten about that, with everything going on," acknowledged Mac. "We can discuss it tomorrow. I'm getting supper-to-go and going to bed early tonight."

Bo was happy, as always, to see Mac come home, waiting on the front porch of their small cottage.

* * * *

That night Mac dreamt of unpleasant things he couldn't put his finger on. He was reminded of a dream he had each year on his birthday, from age 8-13, he guessed. The dream was always the same—an indescribable force consuming the land, like locusts rolling across the open countryside, crushing everything in their path. Was this the same dream? He couldn't remember.

Waking up in the middle of the night, he called out her name, "Sarah!" over and over. Bo barked twice, snapping him back to reality. He realized he was sweating, with the top sheet kicked off

somewhere in the dark room.

Not being able to go back to sleep, he dressed quickly. He left Bo inside and ran a check on his overnight security detail, getting as close as he could without getting shot. He was surprised he hadn't thought to do this before, but now it excited him to be the intruder in his own camp.

It didn't take long to find the first security man asleep at his post, hunched over a crossword puzzle titled "Devas from the Nineties."

"Madonna," whispered Mac, as a few of the letters were already filled in. The clue read "What pop singer living in New York City in the 1970s claimed she lived mostly on popcorn?"

Mac shook his unsuspecting man side-to-side, getting a scream out of him.

"Go home," Mac commanded. "If you're going to sleep, then you might as well be in your bed."

Walking the property, he saw most of his men doing their job, although he still moved undetected.

Only one was found listening to a Walkman stereo from the Faraday cage. His headphones were on and Mac could hear the loud noise at 20 yards. Walking up behind him, not having to be quiet and seeing the man's weapon laid haphazardly on the ground several feet away, Mac made his move.

Wrapping his right arm swiftly around the man's neck, Mac squeezed just enough for the scare of the man's life. With the headphones knocked off of his head, the music was even louder.

Mac could tell it was an old cassette tape of a band called Aerosmith as the high-pitched lyrics to the hit song Dream On invaded the otherwise silent night.

Letting the man up, Mac asked how he could possibly be effective on security while listening to music. He sent him home as well, frustrated that even after an eight-hour training only days ago, he would find two of his men ineffective at their posts.

That settled it. Mac would be up for the night.

* * * *

Cory met with an agitated and now tired and grumpy Mac at breakfast.

Relating the night's events to Cory, he questioned his own training of the men.

"That's not it," replied Cory. "I was there, and I know you did a great job. I've been involved in hundreds of training sessions over the years, and yours was top notch. No, the problem is training men who didn't ask to be on security. It would be like me hiring a random civilian to join the police force. You can train them, sure, but if they don't have a passion for the job, or at the very least an interest, then you get two guys like you saw last night. They are just going through the motions, punching the clock. They will shine like a quarter when they know you're watching but will settle back into the bare minimum standards when left alone."

"That makes a lot of sense," replied Mac, feeling better about things.

"I'll bet there are some men and women working other jobs who would love to trade for a security position," added Mac.

"When the three return from Loveland, what would you think about a recruiting period for those interested in joining or staying on the team?" asked Cory. "You could even have me try out, as an example to the others."

"It's a great idea, minus the part about you," replied Mac. "John, Bill, and the council have already decided your and Jimmy's positions, as well as my own, so I don't want to waste any time proving loyalty to the cause. With your help, however, we can run a weeklong boot camp and see who really wants the job."

"What about the two guys from last night?" asked Cory.

"Well, before our little talk, I was going to fire them both this morning. Now I think I'll give them a chance to earn their way back if they really want it. Everyone deserves a second chance."

"And if they don't?" asked Cory.

"They will have to find another job here to contribute, and then it's out of my hands. Let's see if Dr. Melton will let us see Jimmy this morning," added Mac.

* * * *

"No news is good news, I hope?" Mac asked Sarah, coming out to meet them in the lobby.

"He was treated with an anti-clotting medication within minutes of the episode," she told them. "This greatly increases his chances of a near-full recovery, with some deficits still possible. You guys can see him now for a few minutes, but don't get him riled up. He needs his rest."

"Yes, ma'am," said Mac.

"This sucks," said Jimmy, as they entered the room.

"What's that?" asked Mac.

"The whole thing, being laid up here while everyone else is working."

"I understand," said Mac, putting a hand on Jimmy's shoulder.

Tears filled Jimmy's eyes. "What's next?" he asked. "I just lay here and let people wait on me hand and foot?"

"No, it's not like that at all," Mac told him. "John felt the same way when he was here, lying in this very same bed. He took the time to recover, and now he's back in his old position, getting things done.

"You have a new position waiting for you but only when you're ready. If you try to short-cut your recovery to come work with me, Sarah is going to kick my ass."

That got a smile out of Jimmy. "I get it," he said, with a long sigh. "It still sucks, though."

* * * *

Mac and Cory headed up the mountain to talk to the Miller boy and found him walking the road with his dogs.

"All right, son," said Mac, cutting his motor. "We don't have any extra room at the moment, but you can help out on security in exchange for food and general provisions. You will need to be present for all security meetings and carry this radio at all times," he added, handing him a bright red walkie-talkie.

"Yes, sir. You can count on me to do whatever needs done, plus I can't be no worse than your two guys last night."

"How did you know about that?" asked Cory, surprised by the remark.

"I don't sleep good...never have. So I wander at night—without my dogs, though," the boy replied.

"Well, that settles it," said Mac. "You'll officially be added to the night crew. You'll have to pull a three- to four-night-per-week shift, if you can handle that?"

"Only need Sunday off," the boy replied. "It says in the Bible it's a day of rest. I'm good for the other six, though. That's for sure."

"All right! Just keep your radio close, and we'll replace the batteries as needed," said Mac.

As they rode back down the mountain, pausing just before the cattle-guard at the end of the

road, Mac commented to Cory, "That's a kid who's trying to earn a security position."

"I'm just glad he's on our side now," replied Cory.

* * * *

Mac called an all-valley security meeting at 11 a.m. Physical attendance was mandatory, with the exception of Jimmy and the border crews, all listening in by radio. With everyone in attendance, he began.

"This here is Garret Miller from up on Green Mountain. His father, as some of you may know, used to work under Cory in the Loveland Police Department. He will be competing for a security detail position over the next week, as will each of you."

Pausing for a minute, he and Cory listened to the grumbling and whispers among the group, exactly as they expected.

"Who has a question?" Mac asked, wanting to know who would step up and ask the obvious.

"Why do we have to compete for a job we already have?" asked the man wearing the headphones last night.

Mac couldn't believe what he was hearing and looked at Cory, shaking his head.

"Would you mind taking this one?" asked Mac in a near-whisper, doing his best to hide his anger at the man's question.

"Speaking with Mac earlier about this very subject," said Cory, "we realized that most of you were chosen for this position early on, without being asked if you felt confident in your ability to uphold the responsibilities of this most important job.

"Two of our men, only days after an eight-hour training course, were not able to perform even the basic tasks of security last evening and had to be relieved of their posts by our leader, Mac, who had the night off."

He paused, letting the men talk amongst themselves.

"We have three of my former officers from Loveland, who should be here in a couple of days, two males and one female. They, too, will be competing for their positions. Unlike our beloved Denver Broncos—man, I'm going to miss football," he joked—"who only have a limited number of

positions open each season, we have enough for any man or woman who works hard and earns their spot."

"Mistakes will happen," chimed in Mac. "But anyone falling asleep or listening to music while on duty, as we saw last night, will only be given one chance to reverse course. Our fellow community citizens across the valley deserve to sleep each night peacefully, just as we all

did for decades before, when our strong and capable military kept bad things outside our borders.

"Every able-bodied adult in the valley has a job. If you feel another calling more suitable to your talents, now is the time to look into that. Current shifts will remain unchanged until training begins in a couple of days. That's all for now. Enjoy your lunch.

"Thanks, Cory, for taking over; I was about to go off on the music guy," said Mac.

"No worries, boss. He would have had it coming, for sure."

"'Mac,' just 'Mac.' None of the 'boss' stuff, please?"

"Sure thing, new friend."

"Let's grab Cameron and get some lunch," suggested Mac.

The lunch menu today read: "Pacific Northwest Krab Cakes, paired with Turnip Blossoms and a loaded Garden Salad."

"They misspelled crab," said Cameron, pointing to the menu.

Rico was excited to have Patty and her son, Joshua, up for lunch today. He couldn't wait to see what she said about the menu.

Greeting them at the front door of the Pavilion, he tried hard to keep a straight face as she read today's menu.

She paused, saying each line out loud.

"Sounds good," she finally said. "Where do we start?"

Rico was taken aback that she hadn't mentioned anything about trying to pass fake Krab off as the real thing.

Did she even notice? he began to wonder, as they sat down with other diners at a communal table.

Taking a small bite of her meal, Patty said, "Mmm. This is wonderful, Chef Rico! Where ever did you find authentic crab for this most special lunch? It must be a secret family recipe."

All at the table agreed, with "Hear! Hear!"

Leaning over and whispering into his ear, she said, "It's killing you to know what I really think about your Krab with a K, isn't it?"

"Yes!" He smiled, covering his mouth to contain a childlike fit of laughter. "I'm dying over here, wondering if you didn't get it."

"Did you know," she said to Joshua quietly, so only he and Rico could hear, "that Surimi is the art of disguising one type of fish for another and dates all the way back to the 12th century in Japanese culture? The cheaper white fish is ground and molded with paste to resemble real crab legs. Both Alaska and Oregon were large producers of Krab, spelled with a K, for the last at least 20 years.

"Mmm, just incredible!" she said aloud, taking another small bite and winking at Rico.

Rico was grinning from ear to ear, now confident he had finally found the perfect blend of beauty, intelligence and sarcasm he had been looking for all these years.

"You haven't touched your Krab cakes, Chef. Is everything OK?" she asked loudly so several tables could hear.

"Oh yes! Everything is fine," he said, taking a large bite and nearly choking with laughter, turning most heads at the remaining tables.

"I told you I'm not the same snobby guy from the old-world," he said, so only she could hear.

Clanking spoons on glassware, as was the norm, quieted the lunchroom. Today's prayer was offered by an elder woman of the council.

Lord, we thank you for this bountiful land we have been given to watch over and ask you for the safety of our fellow countrymen across this great land. We also ask you to continue healing our dear friends Jimmy and John, and we thank you for this most excellent meal that is almost as good as the real thing. It's in your name we pray. Amen.

"The jig is up," whispered Patty.

* * * *

"Mac," came over the radio. "It's Sarah. I need you down here right now."

There was sadness in her voice—not panic or fear but the absolute opposite of happiness.

He responded to a dead radio, walking quickly out of the Pavilion, waving at Cory to follow.

* * * * * * *

CHAPTER EIGHT ~ RATON PASS, NEW MEXICO

"Where are they now?" I asked Jim.

"Well, the scouts are here, as you know, and some even further ahead, near Trinidad. The main body is held up in the Comanche Grassland, on the southeastern tip of Colorado."

"That's interesting," I said, calling Lonnie, Steve, Jake, David, Mel and Mike on the radio to come over.

"Let's wait a few minutes for the rest to make it over," I suggested. "Can I see your map?"

"Sure," replied Jim. "They are right here." He pointed out a small section of the large grassland area.

"I was there a long time ago as a kid," I said. "I think it's a few hundred thousand acres or more, if I remember correctly."

Each man showed up, with a groggy Mike taking up the rear.

"OK, guys," I started. "Jim here has news on the Topeka group and says they are currently held up right here," pointing on the map at the Comanche National Grassland. "It's in southeastern Colorado. That's all I know so far, so I'll let him finish."

"Well, we now know more, thanks to Mike's guy from the bridge the other day. They are working with Ronna. The interesting part is that the two leaders have never met. Ronna's group is also growing, although not quite as fast as the other.

"The Topeka group is led by a man calling himself Colonel Baker, and I'm pretty sure he doesn't hold that rank—or any other, for that matter. Baker, as I'll call him, is headed to Capulin, New Mexico. That's the same place we stopped for the night. They should arrive there in about five days.

"As for Ronna's group, they pretty much followed our path to a T, and they should be there in a day or two at the most. After that, it's straight through Raton and right up I-25 to we all know where!"

"This could get very interesting before they even get close to here," I said.

"How so?" asked Jake.

"We've got two new leaders, both as crazy as they come and power-hungry. They've never met, yet they are already working with each other so closely? With that many people, there can only be one leader.

"Do they draw straws, fight it out bare-knuckle style? Maybe the Baker guy gets it automatically since he has more followers, or perhaps it's a setup of one side or the other."

"One way or the other, though, they will all be right past this property in two weeks or less," said Lonnie.

"I have something to show you guys in my tent," interrupted Mike, "and then I need to get some sleep."

"Is Sheila OK?" I asked.

"Yeah, she's fine. It's something else."

"You didn't get a pet turtle, did you?" joked Lonnie.

"No, not that either. Wait here a minute, guys," he said, as he poked his head into the tent. Everyone was awake and dressed.

"I've got some people for you to meet. OK?" said Mike to those in the tent.

"Are they good like you and Ms. Sheila?" asked Jonah, speaking for the very first time since they met.

Mike opened the tent wide.

"Whoa!" said Lonnie. "Those are not pet turtles!"

"This is Katie and her brother, Jonah, from across the bridge," said Mike.

He then spoke to the children. "This is Lonnie, Lance, Steve, David, Mel, and last but not least, Jake."

"Hello, kids," we all said, not sure how this all happened.

"Give me a couple of hours' sleep, Lonnie, and I'll fill all of you in on the details," added Mike, zipping the tent from the inside without another word.

"Where did they come from?" asked Jake aloud as we walked back to Beatrice's house.

"I don't know," replied Lonnie, "but I'll bet they know what's going on across the bridge."

"Should Mike be trusted around kids?" asked Steve.

"I'm not sure there is a choice now; but I, for one, have no concerns about him around women or children. It's only the men I'm concerned about," I spoke up.

I got a "Second that" from Lonnie, but that was it. "We're putting the cart before the horse anyway," he added.

Lunch was fried-egg sandwiches with mayonnaise on Beatrice's homemade bread, along with canned sliced pickles.

Sheila came out for four plates, engaging more with the other ladies but not talking about the new additions to their tent.

Near two o'clock, Mike met us back up at the radio station that Mark was now manning.

"The kids," he started, "are Katie and Jonah, ages 13 and 6. They came out of the woods on my perimeter shift last night around 2 a.m. They are from the other side of the bridge and told of what happened to their parents."

He relayed the rest of the story as Katie had told it, leaving out the part about him messing with the tents.

Only Tom knew anything about that, and of course Soldier 449, located somewhere down river, and maybe even miles away by now.

"They do not want to go back and, as far as I can tell, the other group doesn't know where they are."

"So, what now?" asked Lonnie. "You and Sheila adopt two orphans and call them your own?"

"No, no. Hold on now. All I did was give them a place to sleep and some lunch. I never said anything about adopting them... Besides, I don't know the first thing about kids."

"You did a good job with my Hendrix," I said, loud enough for all to hear. "You were calm and confident, and he really likes you now."

"There's a big difference in helping a kid out of a jam and taking on the responsibility for them until they are grown!" Mike replied defensively.

"Yes, there is," I replied. "But it's not that much of a stretch to make it happen. You just agree to love them and help them out of jams from time to time, until they tell you they've got this. Then you're there when they need you."

"I don't want to send them back, but I can't do it," said Mike. "I just can't."

"Just can't what, Michael?" came a voice from behind, catching us all off-guard.

Turning to face Sheila, with the kids on each side of her, Mike turned red.

"Sheila, I didn't see you there," said Mike, fumbling.

"I know. You were too busy finding one excuse after another not to step up and do the right thing."

We all froze in awkward silence, like when a couple argues at a family gathering.

* * * * * * *

Chapter Nine ~ Raton Pass, New Mexico

"So, you don't want us," said Katie. "Is that what this is about?"

I felt bad that he was getting it from both sides, but I knew they were right. When Joy and I found out we were having twins, we stepped up, put our adult pants on, and bought two of everything.

Others, hearing the commotion, gathered around with Tammy, now standing next to Mel. She whispered in his ear, and he blurted out, "We'll take them!"

"Now, wait just a minute," called out Sheila. "We found them first."

It was the strangest thing I had seen in this next-world, and that was saying a lot.

"OK, that's enough," intervened Lonnie before it went any further.

"Mel, you and Tammy wait over here in those two chairs. Mike, you and Sheila over there," pointing across the dirt road, "and I'll talk with everyone in due time."

"Lance, you're with me," called Lonnie, without asking.

We started with the kids, as Lonnie asked a series of cop-type questions, not far off from those Mike had asked Hendrix in the valley. After hearing their story firsthand, we both agreed they had to stay.

"There seems to be more than one couple interested in caring for you, but I will talk with both of them first," spoke Lonnie. "Without telling you who is from where, I will say that one part of the group is staying on this mountain, and the other is moving to Northern Colorado in a few weeks."

"I hate it here," screamed Katie, crying. "All I have is bad memories of my mother being hurt and my father not being able to help her. Then both of them were killed like animals by those bastards."

"There's another boy my age still there," said Jonah quietly. "They took his mother to their leader to marry but left him."

"We tried to bring him with us, but he was too scared to run," added Katie, starting to calm down now.

"What's his name?" I asked.

"It's Javier, but he goes by Javi," said Katie. "He's so sweet, but he's scared all the time. I want to be as far away from here as we can get," she added.

"It's OK, Sissy," said Jonah, hugging her. "It's OK."

"I was not expecting this today," Lonnie told me, as we headed to Mel and Tammy.

"We overheard what she said," Mel spoke up, "so I guess that puts us out of the running, huh?"

"We don't know anything yet," said Lonnie. "Hang tight," he added, as we went to meet with Mike and Sheila.

"Mike has something to say to you both," said Sheila. "Go on, Michael," she prodded.

"OK, guys. I'm sorry about that earlier. I just panicked. You two know me better than anybody else around here, and I think you both understand I would do anything to protect the children.

"It's a long story, but back in Brooklyn, years ago, I made a vow to protect any woman or child in need, even if it cost me my own life. I can tell you honestly, I have never broken that vow.

"Now here we are, with two children in need of a place to call home. I'm sure Mel and Tammy would make an excellent home for those two, and I would be happy to see that. Sheila would also make a fine mother, I'm sure. And, well, I am willing to see it through with them both if that's what needs to happen."

"Maybe we should give it a few days, with each couple spending some time with the children, and see if the answer gets any clearer," I suggested to Lonnie.

"It's not a bad idea at all. Sort of a trial period," he agreed.

The kids, happy to be anywhere this side of the bridge, agreed to spend the first two days with Mel and Tammy, and the next two with Mike and Sheila.

The four headed back to the tent to get the two small backpacks carrying everything the children owned.

Once feeling comfortable, they told Mike and his girlfriend everything about their old life. It sounded nice until the day the Keeper quickly secured the area, recruiting a few armed men to help with his agenda.

Every story, from the Keeper forward, was worse than the last, and most included little Javi.

"Where is he?" asked Mike, feeling flushed, like when Dan struck Sheila.

"He's over there," replied Jonah.

"What I mean is, what does he look like and where does he stay?" asked Mike. "What tent does he sleep in? Is he ever alone?"

"Slow down... What are you getting at?" asked a curious Sheila.

"I'm just asking in case we run into him on the way north," replied Mike. He got the answers he was looking for from Katie. He played it off in front of Sheila and the kids, but his mind churned as he calculated a plan.

* * * *

"Let's get you two up the road to Mel and Tammy's place. They have a house you will like," said Sheila. "Mike and I will have a house when we get to Colorado. This tent is just temporary."

"We know," said Katie, smiling for the very first time.

* * * *

Jim called out over the radios: "The President's speech is in 30 minutes. All wanting to hear it, come on up."

Nearly every adult was present, and the children were told to stay inside Beatrice's house for a while. Her famous no-bake oatmeal cookies were enough to keep them occupied with Suzie and Veronica, both helping make a large batch.

"No-bakes," as Hudson, Jax and Hendrix called them, were a staple in the Ewing house. The perfect blend of peanut butter, cocoa and rolled oats made them hard to pass up.

"Do you want to hear the speech?" David asked his mother.

"No, son. I have everything I need right here," she replied, kissing both Veronica and Suzie on the forehead.

At exactly 5:30 p.m., according to Mel's watch, the announcer came on.

"It is my great honor to give you the President of the United States."

There was some crackling, followed by a pause.

"My fellow Americans, this is your President. By now, if you are hearing this message, you have either taken our advice and reported to the nearest FEMA shelter in your area or have dug in and found a way to gain this transmission.

"As previously mentioned, we recommend that any citizens of this great country who have not already taken advantage of the safety and convenience of our FEMA facilities, complete with food, electricity, and even hot showers, do so immediately following this broadcast. Everyone is welcome, with no exceptions, for a limited time.

"As far as the aggressor, North Korea, I have decided a regime change would be the most effective military response to such an act of war.

"We have united the countries of North and South Korea once again, with the help of our allies in the Pacific and beyond. South Korea's President, Park Guen-hye, has been instrumental in the reunion of the north and south. She and I have been in contact daily, as events unfold in the region.

"As previously noted, our allies across the globe have already begun delivering aid by ship to our major ports of call on both the eastern and western coasts.

"Our government has assembled a team of people, both locally and abroad, to start the challenging process of restoring power to the states affected by the outage.

"Listen closely. We need to stay strong as a country now, and I want you to all know that your government is working hard to restore our great nation and return it to its proper status once again as a world leader.

"Progress will be updated as news becomes available. I will address you again using these and additional outlets, as needed.

"Stay vigilant; stay strong. May God bless you and the *still* United States of America."

After a pause and static, the announcer returned. "That's it, folks. Remember to stay tuned to this channel daily for breaking news. Now stay tuned for a note from our sponsors."

I looked at Jake, and he had the same expression, wondering who could possibly be sponsoring a radio program now.

A semi-familiar jingle started to play, but I couldn't remember the words.

"If you're tired, if you're down, FEMA will turn your life around. Hungry, sweaty, walking for hours, we've got both good food and showers. So, let's hurry, and don't be late. Get in now before we close the gate."

The entire jingle was sung in a 1920s style by a woman sounding like Marilyn Monroe.

"Awe, crap," said Jake. "The worse the song is, the more it gets stuck in my head. This one's going to be there for a while."

"Of course!" laughed Lonnie. "Who were we expecting the sponsor to be—some auto dealership or personal injury attorney? I would like to sue the United States government, along with 350 million other Americans, for the mental pain and suffering we have undergone so far," he joked.

"The interesting thing is that both the President's speech and the little jingle eluded to a timeline for the FEMA camp admissions," I interjected.

"Sounds just like they are creating a sense of urgency to conduct a proper census for when the power is restored," chimed in Mel.

"Bullshit! And pardon my language, ladies. They're just rounding everyone up, so when China buys the country (if they haven't already) they will know exactly where to find their new workers," said Tom, now clearly in the America-has-been-sold camp.

"I guess we'll find out soon enough, when we check on Vlad," said Jake.

* * * * * * *

Chapter Ten ~ Raton Pass, New Mexico

Joy, Tina, Lucy and Lonnie's wife had been working on a spaghetti dinner for everyone. Nancy had the venison ground with a hand-cranked grinder Beatrice had used for years. Most of the tomato sauce had been canned by Beatrice and Dean more than a year ago. It was just enough to feed everyone—when stretched with ketchup. Nobody knew... Even Joy, who had come up with the idea, couldn't taste the difference.

"That's the last of the tomato sauce," announced Beatrice.

"Only if you don't like freeze-dried!" called out Mel.

All cheered, with most not aware of how many provisions Mel actually had tucked away.

* * * *

Mike volunteered himself and Tom for another security night shift. David didn't mind, knowing that it would all fall on his shoulders soon enough.

* * * *

"I was kind of hoping to get some sleep tonight," said Tom, as they began their shift at 9 p.m.

"Not tonight, buddy," said Mike. "I've got something important to do, and I know I can trust you to keep it secret."

"Are you going to go spy on those guys again?" Tom asked. "You *do* know the bridge is out."

"Yes, and yes," Mike replied. "There is a young boy named Javi over there, about your little girl's age, whose mother was taken into slavery. He's alone and scared and needs to be on this side with us."

"How is that our responsibility?" asked Tom, yawning.

"It's not," replied Mike, pretending he didn't see the yawn. "It's just the right thing to do. If it was your little girl, would you want me to go over and see if I could help?"

"Of course," he replied, "but that's..." Tom paused for a moment, working something in his head... I guess you're right, but aren't you afraid of getting shot?"

"Nah. Everybody dies, but not everybody lives," Mike said, grinning.

"You really like this danger stuff, don't you, Mike?" Tom continued.

"I always have...well, at least since I was 14."

"Fourteen?" replied Tom. "What's that got to do with it?"

"Everything," said Mike. "That's the year I became a man, but that's probably a story for another time."

"I'd really like to hear it, unless you're leaving right now," Tom replied.

"Nah. I want it to get nice and dark first," replied Mike. "This is between you and me, though, Tom. You didn't say anything about me going across the bridge last time, so I'm going to trust you again to keep my business confidential."

"Of course, Mike," Tom replied, now excited to hear the story.

Mike relayed a story of his twin brother and how he became a man the summer of his 14th year on earth, sticking up for his brother and best friend, Arthur.

"It's going to take me about an hour to get over there, since I have to cross the river now. If I'm not back by sun-up, don't send anybody over looking for me. It would just be a waste of time and energy. Oh, and Tom, no more yawning. And don't you dare fall asleep on me!"

That last statement from Mike was absolute and sent a chill down Tom's spine. He wouldn't be sleeping tonight, maybe not even tomorrow.

With a small daypack, night-vision goggles and his AR-15, Mike made his way down to the river. At the bank, he walked slowly down, looking for a suitable place to cross. He half expected to trip over his old foe, Soldier Number 449, lying somewhere in the thick brush.

His rifle and pack were raised above his head as he carefully traversed the rushing river. He counted four times he was pushed downstream several yards before regaining his footing, never getting a drop of water on his gear.

Mike grinned, getting a flashback of all the sayings he learned on first moving to Texas about not spilling your beer.

He guessed the camp would be in the same place as before, or at least close. Katie had given him a good idea of where Javi may be sleeping, but he knew it could have changed since their escape.

Staying just off the road, he could hear the camp guards bumbling around, shining flashlights in all directions. His first thought was that they had spotted him, but after observing for ten minutes it was obvious they were just trying to look like they knew what they were doing.

Their flashlight pattern appeared random at first but synced up the more he observed. It was a crude security detail, like in the movies when the bad guy times the automatic sweeps of the light perfectly and enters the building undetected.

It was 10 p.m., according to the wristwatch given to him by Mel while on security. He counted four men on security, with one stationed in each direction.

The camp was quieting down, with only a few people walking around and occasionally ducking into the trees near the back border, probably to use the bathroom, he thought.

Thirty minutes later, after all was quiet, the guards grouped up on the west side, passing around a bottle of something. It had to be strong, he thought, because they were daring each other to take more than one drink at a time.

"That's it, boys," said Mike in a whisper. "Get drunk and stupid."

According to Katie's recollection, there were approximately 20 people, with nearly half being children, and an additional five guards.

Javi was staying in the back tent, on the far east side of the camp, with a few older kids.

Mike slowly made his way over to the tent she had described, being the last one in the row and slightly off-center, due to a large rock stuck in the ground that nobody wanted to sleep on. He overheard talking coming from several tents, as both adults and children were settling in for the night.

"Stop touching me, Javi," he heard from the last tent. "But I have to go pee," the boy replied.

"Just go then, and stop bothering me," came the voice of clearly an older boy.

"I'm scared to go out by myself," Javi cried.

"Then you'll just have to hold it until morning," came the reply.

The back tent zipper opened slowly, and out came a young boy, shaking as he walked.

"Make sure you go far enough away from the tent," called the other boy loudly.

"You boys keep it down now," came an angry voice from one of the drinking guards, "or you'll get the switch."

Mike knew all about the switch from his younger days, before his father left them. It was a thin tree branch used for swatting or spanking.

Little Javi walked right past Mike, concealed in a bush, and another ten feet to do his business. He was crying quietly, looking around quickly with every forest sound.

* * * * * *

Chapter Eleven ~ Raton Pass, New Mexico

M ike knew he had only two choices, and the easier one would probably backfire.

He could stop the boy and tell him who he was and that he was there to help. It was the easiest of the two possibilities, unless the boy screamed out or ran back to camp. In this scenario, a second attempt tonight, or any other, would be many times more difficult.

Option number two was a hostile and swift abduction to remove him from the immediate area as fast as possible. This option would instill more fear, at least for the short term, and possibly traumatize him in the future.

Turning to head back, little Javi paused as if he felt something was different. Mike still had not decided on an option, with only seconds to make a final decision.

A guard yelled, "Boys, you better shut up!" although Mike heard no more talking from the tent. "That was your last chance!" the guard continued, throwing the bottle he held to the ground with an empty clang.

"Oh, no," said Javi, as the soldier stormed in his direction.

Sorry, buddy, but option number two is the only way, Mike said to himself, grabbing the boy with one arm and covering his mouth with his other hand.

Javi struggled, kicking his arms and legs and trying to scream, as he was carried at a full run through the trees.

Mike slowed to a walk two hundred yards closer to home and in a low, calm voice said, "Your name is Javier, but you like to be called Javi. Katie and Jonah told me where to find you, and they are waiting to see you again. My name is Mike and I won't hurt you, but you can't scream when I take my hand away. OK?"

Javi answered yes by nodding his head.

Mike was prepared for a scream anyway, as he removed his hand slowly from the boy's mouth.

There was no scream, no speech at all, just the rapid heartbeat and wide-eyed panic of a frightened child.

The river crossing had a typically confident Mike feeling anxious.

"Javi, do you know how to swim?" asked Mike.

The boy shook his head no without saying a word.

Mike briefly considered going the three miles downstream to cross where they had with the trailers not long ago.

Looking down, he realized he was making tracks in the soft dirt that even a two-year-old could follow.

"Over here!" came shouting from the camp. "Over towards the river!" they called. Three gunshots rang out, with the last one hitting a pine tree just above Mike's head.

"This is it," Mike said aloud. "Sorry, kid, but we have no choice now," jumping into the rushing water. Raising the boy and his rifle over his head, he didn't worry about his pack getting wet.

Losing his footing on only the third step, Mike regained his stance 15 feet down the river.

"That's was close, buddy. We almost got..." There was a loud thud as Mike was hit square in the back, taking his breath away. Gasping for air, he saw the large log that had struck him in the back careening past him.

"Javi," he yelled, as the boy and his weapon plunged into the river.

His eyes locked on the boy. "Grab the log!" he yelled.

Little Javi's head was bobbing up and down, with his arms frantically slapping the cold, rushing water. Mike let the current take him—forcing his head to remain out of the water.

His eyes locked on the boy, and nothing else mattered. The strap of his rifle had caught in the log that inspired the drama. Javi clung to the same log at the far end.

Passing up the rifle and instincts to retrieve it, Mike lunged for the boy, grasping the collar of his shirt.

Barely keeping the frightened child above the surface, Mike grabbed the log with his other arm, slowly steering it towards the right bank and kicking frantically with his feet.

"Are you OK?" he asked the scared boy over and over, with no response.

The river slowed as Mike navigated to the shore. He wasn't sure how far downriver they had traveled, but he was determined to complete his mission.

I was the first one to make it to a wide-eyed Tom.

"Where's Mike?" I asked. Tom didn't say a word but pointed down towards the river in the direction of the gunshots.

"He went back for the boy, didn't he?" asked Mel—"the one Katie was talking about."

Tom nodded his head yes, still not saying a word. As long as he didn't speak, he felt he could still be trusted to keep a secret.

"You ready, Lance?" asked Mel, straightening his night-vision goggles.

"As I'll ever be," I replied, doing the same.

There's an odd feeling you get, I realized, when you're voluntarily running towards gunfire.

I guessed it was just second-nature to a soldier on the front line, or a veteran police officer who had likely seen this type of scenario before. To a civilian like me, however, it went against every bit of common sense I had. But Mike was down there, and likely a little boy needing help.

"Cover us, Tom, and don't let anyone pass," I said, looking behind me to see many from our group running towards us.

Voices yelling could be heard from the other side of the river.

Standing for the first time since entering the river, Mike had Javi in his right arm and could see the strap of his rifle hooked to a branch on the far end of the log. Tugging the strap pulled up a water-submerged rifle, which he put over his other shoulder.

"Let's go, Javi," Mike told him, as the voices got closer. Mike carried him at a full run into the woods, away from the river, still with no sounds coming from the boy.

"Over there!" shouted one of the men, firing his weapon.

Mike thought about stopping to return fire but kept running.

Mel and I met Mike, carrying the small boy on our side, near the river bottom.

I called out to him, as he nearly ran straight into us. "It's Lance and Mel!" I yelled.

We all met for no more than ten seconds, with me taking Mike's pack and rifle while he kept the child.

"Crack! Crack! Crack!" came the sound from across the river. Javi cried out in pain, grabbing his left arm.

"Hold on, buddy; we're almost there," I told him, returning fire randomly into the dark for the very first, and hopefully the last, time.

"Let's go!" called Mel, as we all turned to run.

Now more cracks from the other side. I counted eight when I felt a thud in my left hamstring, followed by burning, like a fire poker had been put into my leg.

Mike fell forward, tripping over a fallen log, clutching little Javi as a football player may stretch out to catch a ball in the end zone in a close game.

The shooting continued as bullets careened around us. I ran, limping, with Mel helping me along.

"It's going to be OK," Mike told Javi. "They won't cross the river."

He was right, and with the shooting stopped, we slowly headed back to camp.

"Are you OK?" Mike asked, with no response from the frightened boy. He was grazed on his left arm. There was blood, but Mike could tell the wound was not deep.

Reaching Tom, who was now standing surrounded by members of both Raton groups, he dropped Javi into Nancy's waiting arms.

"I think he's OK," said Mike, out of breath, "but please look him over."

* * * * * * *

CHAPTER TWELVE ~ RATON PASS, NEW MEXICO

Lonnie, Jake and David were all present, having heard the gunfire.

"Lance, were you hit?" asked David, noticing the limp but not seeing the blood in the dark.

A flashlight directed by Lonnie told the story.

"Nancy, we need you over here," called Jake. "Lance has been shot."

Tammy took over with Javi, cleaning and dressing his wound, requiring no stitches.

Nancy cut my left pant leg, already torn by the bullet and more than one bush I had run through.

The entrance wound was clearly visible in my left hamstring.

"It missed the femoral artery, thank God," she said, "but there's no exit wound. When the bullet hit you, did it burn?" she asked.

"Like crazy," I responded, "but I just kept running."

"Exactly where did you feel the burn after impact?"

I pointed to a spot towards the front of my thigh. "It was about 30 seconds, I think, before it stopped. Now it just stings."

"Jake," she called. "Get my medical bag. And Tammy, I'm going to need your help. We've got one shot at this while the wound is open, and Lance, this is going to hurt," she said, looking me in the eye.

"Is Javi OK?" I asked.

"He will be just fine," responded Tammy.

David and Jake, grabbing two four-wheelers, took Nancy, Tammy and me up to Beatrice's house. Beatrice drew a warm pot of water and got clean towels for the event.

The morphine kicked in near the start and I smiled, knowing we had done something really good.

Mike wouldn't leave my side until he knew I was all right.

"Lord," Mike spoke silently, "we both know I'm a bad man, but today I did something right. I helped your little boy, and he will be safe for the rest of his days."

After thirty minutes, the slug was removed successfully from my leg, and the stitching process commenced.

"We've done everything possible to keep this wound clean," said Nancy. "The rest is up to you, Lance. I want you to see me twice a day until I say you're good. Understand?"

"Yes, ma'am. I'll do just that," I responded gratefully.

* * * *

Javi was scared and wouldn't speak to anyone. With Katie and Jonah fast asleep, the group wasn't sure how to proceed. Sheila tried speaking to him, but he only wanted Mike.

Lonnie drove an exhausted Mike back to the tents, where little Javi was waiting.

Introducing him to Sheila, the boy calmed quickly. "She is my girlfriend, Javi, and she stays in my tent. Do you understand?"

"I think so," Javi replied. "You mean she will help me like you did?"

"Yes, Javi, she will."

"I'm so tired," he said, starting to cry.

"Would you like to sleep next to me?" asked Sheila.

"Yes, ma'am," he replied, scooting towards her and melting her heart.

"I'll just be over here somewhere," joked Mike.

"You're a good man, Michael," said Sheila, "and I'm a lucky girl. Good night, my love," she whispered, giving him a kiss.

I'm going to get hammered tomorrow by everyone, I'm sure, he thought, *but it will be worth it.*

"You brought him back," said Katie in Mike's dream that night. "You brought him back!"

I lay next to Joy and our boys, dead tired but content.

I felt good tonight, knowing the dawn would come soon and bring the inevitable pain of fading morphine.

I woke up four hours later, with the sun staring me in the eyes. The pain in my leg was dull as I looked down at the blood-soaked dressing.

Lonnie picked me up on the four-wheeler for the unavoidable meeting to come.

Mike, a few tents down, was looking across his own tent at a sleeping Javi, cuddled tight to his new girl.

Is this it? he thought, not taking his eyes off of them. *Is this my new life, my way forward?*

"Are you going to tell me what happened?" asked Sheila in a whisper.

"It's complicated," replied Mike. "I knew there would be some that would be upset about it, maybe even you," he continued, "but I had no choice. It was either me by myself or nobody. I would do it again, just the same."

Lonnie, Jake and I were being peppered with questions about Mike and the little boy. Tom was still asleep following his shift, but would no doubt be interrogated soon enough.

"Time to face the music and get this out in the open. I'll be back soon and fill you in on everything, I promise," Mike told Sheila.

* * * *

"Here he comes," said Lonnie, pointing at Mike walking up the road.

We all waited for him, and even Katie and little Jonah were up, arriving with Mel and Tammy.

"How did they do last night?" David asked Mel.

"We did great!" replied Katie, before Mel could answer. "We haven't slept in a real bed for a while, and Mel and Tammy are really nice."

Katie didn't know anything about Javi yet, having slept right through the gunshots and commotion last night.

"All right, Mike," pressed Lonnie. "What happened last night?"

"Good morning, guys, ladies," Mike started, as the whole camp seemed to gather around. "Hi, Katie. How are you and Jonah holding up?"

"Really good," she said. "That was the best night's sleep I've had in a long time," she added, yawning.

The air was tense, with the obvious conversation about to make it front and center.

I didn't have the full story, but I had heard Katie and her brother talk about little Javi and how he needed help.

Joy and I had discussed it early this morning, looking at both sides. On the one hand, a boy was taken from the very people we were trying to avoid a conflict with in the near future. This could bring unwanted attention to both groups.

On the other, a scared little boy whose mother had been trafficked was rescued from a group with only bad intentions.

"We should have discussed this, Mike, as a group," said Lonnie. "It may have consequences for us all down the road."

"Let's say you're right, and I told you all of my plans yesterday. Would you all, or any of you, have agreed to move forward with it?" Mike responded.

To my surprise, Joy raised her hand. I was proud of her, as the only one to do so, with our boys looking on.

"Me too," I said with conviction, raising my hand.

A few more hands raised, including Mel, Tammy, David, Tina, Nancy and Jake.

"What are you talking about, Mike?" asked a confused Katie.

"Javi," he replied. "We're talking about Javi. I rescued him last night, with Mel and Lance's help, and didn't ask anyone's approval first."

"Is he here?!" she asked excitedly. "Is he OK?"

"Yes, he is here, and he will be fine," Mike answered.

"So, let me get this straight," said a sassy Katie, "just so us kids can understand. Every adult that didn't just raise their hand thinks that Mike should have left a defenseless and scared six-year-old boy to rot over there with those animals?" Her voice grew louder with each word. "Am I hearing that right? What's *wrong* with you people?!" she screamed.

Mel put a hand on her shoulder, which she quickly knocked away. Jonah tugged her arm as he started to cry. "It's okay, Sissy," he said, looking up at her.

"No, it's not," she replied. "Come on, Jonah. Let's go." Grabbing his hand, she walked back towards Mel and Tammy's house.

* * * * * * *

Chapter Thirteen ~ Raton Pass, New Mexico

E veryone was quiet, and the silence was deafening. Even the other children didn't say a word.

"I'll check on them," said Mel, excusing himself.

"She's right," said Lonnie, feeling bad he had not raised his hand. "Sometimes, the right thing to do is the hardest to justify. Mike, I would not have supported you on this yesterday, but I do now."

A few others nodded their heads in agreement, without speaking up.

"Thank you for saying that," replied Mike. "I should have brought it up yesterday, but I couldn't stand the thought of him being over there all alone after Katie and her brother told us the story."

"You're bleeding through the dressing," Nancy told me. "Let's get it changed now, unless anyone has anything else."

Veronica raised her hand. "Yes, sweetie?" said Nancy.

"When can we meet Javi?" she asked, with the other children nodding in agreement.

"He's with Tammy right now," interjected Mike, "and he had a long night. As soon as he is awake, you can be the first to meet him, Veronica."

She smiled at Tina, excited to be picked first for this important opportunity.

"To answer your first question, friend," said Mike, looking at Lonnie. He retold the story in its entirety, realizing it sounded like something out of a Rambo movie.

"Weren't you scared?" asked Hudson.

"Only when I lost Javi in the river," he replied.

"Will they come looking for him?" asked Jax nervously.

"I don't think so," Lonnie responded. "He will be safe here with us."

Mel entered his home to find Katie packing their belongings.

"Where are you going?" he asked, concerned.

"I don't know," she replied angrily. "We're not going back, and we're not staying here."

"Can we talk for just a minute?" he asked quietly, hoping to calm her nerves.

"Jonah is my responsibility now, not theirs," she said, pointing back towards the group just down the road, "and not yours either."

"I understand that," he replied, racking his brain on the next step. Never having children of his own, and not recalling any recent experience with them, he was at a loss. *Think, Mel. Think!* he told himself.

"Katie, do you miss anything about your old life? I mean," he stuttered "besides your parents, of course."

"Do you mean like my friends and school?"

"Yes, kind of," Mel replied.

"Well, I miss movie night. We used to have pizza, microwave popcorn, and a movie every Friday night. It was my brother's favorite day of the week."

"What was your favorite movie?" he asked, hoping it was one he had on hand.

"My favorite movie, well both of our favorites, is called *The Princess Bride*," she said, pulling the DVD out of her small backpack. "We can't watch it anymore, but we know most of the lines anyway."

"I'll make you a deal," said Mel. "You and your brother agree to stay here one more night, and I'll figure out how to let you eat popcorn and watch your favorite movie."

"Yes, Sissy!" said an excited Jonah. "I want to watch our movie!"

"It's not true," she told him. "He's just feeding us lies, like the last guys," she added, shaking her head.

"Hold on for just a minute," said Mel, realizing that this was an opportunity that would not come around again. "Can I see your DVD?" he asked.

"Why not," she said, sarcastically handing it to him. "It's not like you can hurt it now."

He handed her the remote and asked if she knew how to work it.

"I did before," she replied.

"Press this button," he showed her, and as she did the 70-inch television turned on, showing a black screen.

"That's not possible!" she said, staring in amazement.

"Now this button," he showed her, opening the DVD slide.

Setting the disc carefully inside, he closed it with a finger. Moments later, the large screen was filled with the opening title of the nearly 30-year-old movie.

"Sissy! Sissy!" said Jonah, pointing at the screen. "Look! It's Andre the Giant and the Montoya man."

"Hello. My name is Inigo Montoya. You killed my father. Prepare to die." Mel said out loud, spouting a popular phrase from the classic movie in his best Spanish accent, realizing too late it's exactly what happened to their dad.

"Oh, forgive me," he said to Katie, with a face that said he was truly sorry.

"It's OK, Mel. It happens to be my favorite line in the movie, followed by Wesley saying, 'As you wish' to the Princess Bride."

"Is it true?" Jonah asked her.

"I think so," she replied, smiling at Mel. "If you can make popcorn, we will stay."

Tammy came back inside as the first smell of microwave popcorn wafted through the small three-bedroom, two-bath house.

"So, you bribed them?" she asked Mel in a whisper, looking at the packed belongings on the floor.

"Yes, I did," he replied, "and I'm not ashamed of it. They have had a tough time, and she needed to see that an adult could keep their word. I have done that today, and we have at least one more night with them under our roof."

"I'm proud of you, my sweet Mel," she said. "You stepped up again today, like you always do. In another life, we could have ruled New York City together."

"Oh, you know it, babe," he replied, putting his arm around her as they watched their children lost in the opening scenes of their favorite movie.

Mel slipped out to talk with the rest of the group about Katie's outburst and them wanting to leave. He didn't want Mike and Sheila to think he was trying to bribe the kids to stay with them.

Sheila had little Javi up and about, with Veronica getting the first introduction, as promised.

Mel pulled a few of us aside, including Mike and me, along with David and Lonnie. He explained the movie and popcorn, hoping they would understand.

"I get it," said Mike. "No worries, my friend," putting his hand on Mel's shoulder. Mike had come to like Mel, having an appreciation himself for a willingness to get in harm's way and still get things done.

"I think it's just God's plan," said Sheila, overhearing the conversation, with Javi in her arms. "These children need a home, and we all need these children. Mike and I will take care of Javi, and I know you and Tammy will be great parents to Katie and Jonah."

Mike nodded in agreement and smiled.

"As long as you can keep them here," said Lonnie.

"Don't worry about that," replied Mel, grinning now with the realization that he would be a parent after all these years.

"Thank you, Sheila and Mike; you have no idea how happy this will make Tammy."

That's two good things I've done in as many days, Lord, thought Mike. If he was honest, it felt pretty good.

Javi was making friends quickly as he opened up, seemingly more each hour. He told of his experience in the river and proudly showed his bullet-grazed arm.

"Mike is going to teach me to swim in the lake," he added excitedly.

He was referring to the lake where David and Mel reunited only a short couple of weeks ago, and members of both groups had been using it to bathe every two to three days.

"Every child should know how to swim," said Mike aloud. "Anyone else need to learn?" To his surprise, nearly half of the children, and a few adults, raised their hands.

"OK. OK," I interjected. "Keep your hands up for a minute. All right, now lower your hands if you do not want to learn to swim in the next week or two?" Only one hand lowered.

"Mom?" asked David, surprised Beatrice's hand was still raised.

"What, son?" she asked. "Am I too old to learn a new skill?" The kids cheered her on, and the rest of us followed.

"Well, I guess not," replied David.

The list of students grew, as some wanted a refresher course. Eight adults, including myself and Joy, were tasked with helping to teach, with Mike in the lead.

"We will spend one hour learning or improving our swimming skills each afternoon, after working on the greenhouses," said Lonnie.

Katie and Jonah were in kid heaven. Katie reconsidered her opportunity for them both here and was worried Mike and Sheila would be upset that they wanted to stay with Mel and Tammy.

"Is this the only movie we have?" asked Katie to an attentive Mel.

"No, we have a lot more," he remarked, opening the TV cabinet, revealing the rest of the formidable list.

"We never expected a movie and popcorn," she told him, "and I knew you wouldn't have pizza."

"Just you wait until next Friday," he told her, both judging her reaction to staying another week and because he knew he could deliver on the promise again, and this time including the pizza!

"OK, OK," she said, after a whispered conversation with her little brother. "We'll see about next week."

"Yes!" replied Mel loudly, raising his right arm in a victory stance. Tammy looked at him, raising an eyebrow.

"It's all good in the hood, honey," he said, smiling. "We've got them for another week."

Katie and Jonah walked with Mel to see their friend Javi. Katie greeted him with a hug and a smile.

"My new dad is going to teach me how to swim," Javi said, beaming.

"How's it going with Mel and Tammy?" asked Sheila, hoping the answer was good.

"It's good," replied Katie. "They have movies and popcorn, and they're really nice."

"Are you OK about staying with them? I mean, you and your brother, of course, while Mike and I take care of Javi?"

"I think that's a good idea," replied Katie. Jonah was agreeing with a head nod.

"And Mike is teaching swim lessons if you're both interested."

* * * * * * *

Chapter Fourteen ~ Raton Pass, New Mexico

"Guys," came the call on the radio from Jim.

"We've got something on the ham that's important. There has been a development with Baker and Ronna. Baker apparently offered Ronna the second-in-command position, and it didn't go over very well. Ronna refused, as far as we can tell, and has been taken captive."

"That's crazy," I said aloud.

"Oh no," added Jim. "That's only the beginning. Listen to this!"

"Ronna called someone right before he was taken captive. I'm not yet sure who, but they are high up in the military, and he requested backup. Four helicopters, six all-terrain vehicles filled with troops, and two fricking tanks show up three hours later."

"For Ronna?!" asked Lonnie, not believing what he was hearing.

"Yes, exactly—at least as far as Mark and I can tell," said Jim. Mark nodded in agreement.

"What happened?" asked Jake. We were all on the edge of our seats now.

"I don't know," said Jim. "That's the odd part. I hear a lot of chatter, but I still don't know who's in charge."

"The military is always in charge," said Jake.

"Stay on the radio, guys. Good job," said Lonnie. "We need round-the-clock information about this. I want to know exactly what's coming our way and when."

Perimeter locations for the greenhouses took up the rest of the day. With all pitching in, they were making progress.

Freeze-dried Chili Mac was on the menu, along with a rabbit, thanks to an early afternoon hunt by Tom.

"Do you think the kids will eat the rabbit?" Joy asked me.

"Absolutely! Just don't tell them what it is."

Movie night was at Mel and Tammy's, with another favorite—the 1985 cult classic Steven Spielberg movie called *The Goonies*. Every child got a bowl of popcorn.

Mel held Tammy close. "This was a great day," he whispered.

"One of the best I've ever had," she replied.

Even Ringo and Mini enjoyed it, joining the kids spread out on the floor in the living room, quickly gobbling up random pieces of dropped popcorn.

* * * *

With the radio monitored through the night, there were various accounts of what happened between Ronna and Baker, with none sounding official or completely accurate.

"This time, I'm going to ask someone about it when we check on Vlad," I told Mike.

Mike and Tom had the next two nights off of perimeter duty.

The next morning was buzzing with talk of swimming lessons that afternoon. Nancy adhered a waterproof bandage to Javi's arm and forbade me from entering the water above my knees.

Nearly everyone showed up to swim after a long day of work. Mike started by defining basic strokes, including the crawl, breaststroke, sidestroke, backstroke, and if all goes really bad, the doggy paddle.

"Mini likes the water but not Ringy," observed Hendrix.

"Aren't they both labs," asked one of the adults? "I thought all labs loved water."

"Maybe 50%, seems like," added Katie, deciding to bring Jonah for some lessons.

After 15 minutes of theory, there were 45 minutes of practice, with a few of the children backing out at the last minute.

I did as instructed, and even sat in a chair on the shoreline with my new old crutches close by that David kept for years after his knee surgery.

Joy, with the other adult helpers, was entirely in the water and counting heads with each passing minute.

As a lifeguard in Southern California, I had a few rescues under my belt. The scenario for me and the other guards was typically the false sense of security when parents fit their child who cannot swim with improperly fitting safety wings, floats and vests. Even way before cell-phone days, the parents were completely distracted or disengaged, assuming the float device was foolproof.

I was used to counting heads, but I used to sit high up on a tower, and now we were head-level with all of the swimmers. Each child did great, with all levels of expertise and manner of dress accounted for.

Beatrice had never owned a swimsuit, but she managed with yoga leggings and a T-shirt. She always considered herself a gym rat, only the kind who worked out at home. Joy taught her how to float on her back in only ten minutes. "Dean would be so proud," she told Joy. "He tried to get me swimming for years." Floating peacefully on her back, she winked up at the sky, positive that he was watching her.

I was feeling stressed for the first time in days, watching everyone, but it kept me on my toes.

"OK, that's all for today," called out Lonnie at exactly one hour. There were groans, but only from the children.

* * * *

After dinner, we discussed the Ronna/Baker situation, with Jim and Mark having listened to the radio for the entire day.

"This reads like an old soap opera," said Jim, now letting Mark tell some of the story.

"OK," said Mark. "What we knew before has changed, but we're not exactly sure why or how. It appears that after the military show of force, both Ronna and the Baker guy (who I think we all knew is not a real colonel) are working together with equal leadership powers. The military has left and Ronna is free—we know that for sure."

"As for the Ronna/military connection," interjected Jim, "it's still a mystery. They have to be using him for a bigger agenda is all I can come up with. The bottom line is that they are all still headed past here, just like before, and not much else has changed."

"In the old-world, this story would have gone viral," added David. "An ex-coffee barista amasses a formidable group in just weeks and gains the backing of the United States Military."

"Just a few weeks ago, even a well-established country couldn't do that so quickly," I added. "Unfortunately, it does change things."

"How so? "asked Steve.

"Well, with a small or medium-sized group just looking to pass through here, a show of firepower could be enough to keep them moving. Add in military backing, and we get outnumbered and overpowered quickly. I, for one, don't want helicopters, vehicles, troops, and tanks pointed at our kids."

"What are you saying?" asked David.

"I'm saying," looking at Mike nodding his head in agreement, "that Mike and I need to take a trip to see the Colonel from the FEMA camp sooner than we had planned."

"How soon?" asked Joy, now clearly concerned.

"Like tomorrow," I told a shocked group around us.

"No, no, no!" shouted Joy, with Sheila agreeing. "It's too risky."

"What's risky," replied Mike, coming to my rescue, "is the thought of trying to defend the group, both of our groups, against the US Military."

I was a bit surprised to hear this from a guy who was always up for a fight, no matter what the odds. Then it hit me. He now had his own child to protect, and that changed everything for him.

I spent that night talking with each of my boys and tried to explain why I had to leave. I silently gave us a 50-50 chance of pulling it off and a 60-40 chance of ever making it back alive.

Joy wasn't excited about the idea, by any stretch, but she at least understood it. After explaining why it had to be Mike and me, since we were the only ones having a good rapport with the Colonel, she understood.

I was both nervous and excited about the trip. On the one hand, I may never see my family again. On the other, I felt that a private conversation with the Colonel could be eye-opening and reveal information that could be useful.

I had read somewhere that when a new President is about to take office, they are quarantined for a matter of a few days and informed by the various government agencies, both public and secret, on all matters sensitive to private citizens.

I thought, growing up, that it would be fun to be the President, just to find out about Roswell, New Mexico, and the possibility of alien life, or what really happened to JFK in Dallas by the grassy knoll.

As I got older, I would hear people complaining about how President Bush spent too much time "vacationing" at his ranch in Crawford, Texas, or how much time President Obama spent golfing.

Neither of these arguments ever got my vote, as I watched both Presidents age considerably in less than a decade. I knew full well that, regardless of whether they were in the White House, on a ranch, or a golf course, there was no vacation to be had.

I always believed that, besides sleep (which I imagined was interrupted often), a so-called vacation would come with at least hourly updates and spur-of-the-moment decisions about both domestic and foreign conflicts, completely derailing any sense of a normal family getaway.

The problem was, do we go back to Amarillo, where we saw the Colonel last, or go the shorter route to the FEMA camp in Trinidad and possibly find out information on Vlad at the same time.

A look at the map made the decision easier. Amarillo was 230 miles back the way we came, and Trinidad was only 30 miles up the road. The question of the moment was how to get back across the river and safely to Trinidad.

Mike and I were both up early the next morning, planning our next great adventure, with Joy offering to let Sheila and Javi sleep in our tent if Mike and I were gone more than one day.

* * * *

Packing light firearms, just as we did on the last trip with Vlad, neither of us wanted to lose any more than we had to for the group if things went bad. One AR-15, a pistol each, and 300 rounds between us would have to do.

Loading what all considered now as Lonnie's truck, we each had a backpack, in case we lost the truck. Packing my new old crutches, Mike would be doing all the driving.

"You can take the backroads here," pointed David on the map, "following the same route as James and Jason but veering back towards the highway in time to see if your group really has a lifetime pass on that side. It's the only way to avoid the guys across the river."

"That sounds like a plan," I told him, wanting to get started, as my leg was already hurting.

Saying our goodbyes, Mike took the truck slowly over the ridge. "How's your leg?" he asked.

"Well, the bumps in the road don't help," I said.

"I'll bet; hopefully, we'll be on the pavement in 15 miles or so. Anyway, you and Mel really stepped up last night and helped me out. Sorry about the bullet wound."

"It's fine. You saved that boy, and that's always going to be worth some trouble. Plus, now I'm not the only one in my family who didn't get lost or injured. It's weird, but that was making me feel bad. Does that make sense?"

"Oddly, it does," replied Mike.

The winding fire road was clear of large rocks and ran through the tree- and bush-covered landscapes of the backside of the mountain.

Slowing every 50 yards to navigate large ruts in the road, Mike thankfully was mindful of my leg and did his best to keep the ride smooth.

"Your boys...they are respectful and tough. How did you manage that?" Mike asked.

"All of this," I said, waving my arm around at the surrounding land, "makes them tough. Everyday training keeps them respectful."

"Did you know I'm a twin?" asked Mike.

"No, I've never heard that." I was surprised, since one of the classic, usually true, stereotypes of having twins is that anyone else who has a twin, is a twin, or knows a twin, will always tell you so when they meet yours.

"Boy or girl?" I asked.

"Arthur. His name was Arthur, and he died in our senior year of high school."

"I'm so sorry," I replied, not having a clue of what it would be like to lose a twin.

"He was my best friend," Mike continued. "Do you want to hear about him?"

"Sure," I said.

"By the way, I know you kept our last conversation, when we were going to get Hendrix, confidential, since I would have heard about it if you hadn't. This story is the same, if you want to hear it."

"Of course. And yes, I didn't tell anyone about the last one."

"My dad left my mom when we were young, making it hard for her to make ends meet, and I had no choice but to step up and take care of my twin brother and sister, Lily. In middle school, the kids teased my brother and me about our shabby clothes. Arthur was slow, and nobody knew what was wrong with him, but the other kids were brutal. It started with name-calling, and it wasn't too bad at first, since Arthur didn't understand it. I was an awkward, skinny 14-year-old when it got bad. The bullies beat my brother up almost every week. I wanted to help but was too scared. I tried to tell them to stop, but they wouldn't.

"Two weeks before the end of the school year, I finally got up the courage to fight back. It was a Friday after school, and the bullies surrounded Arthur, just as always. Something was different today, and I had had enough of the teasing and hitting and watching my brother cry himself to sleep every night. This day I snapped. Screaming and crying, I swung my arms wildly, connecting with the meanest bully's face and torso, striking him over and over.

"Arthur smiled at me, with blood pouring from his mouth, and said thank you as the rest of the group beat us down. The blood from both of us when we got home was enough for our mom to bring us to the church that very night.

"Father Corraso listened patiently to her pleas to tell God to make it stop. The good Father pulled me aside and told me I was brave for standing up to those boys. "They will most likely leave you alone, now that they know you will fight back," he told me.

"That didn't happen, and the last two weeks of school were littered with nearly daily beatings for us both. On the following Sunday, after mass, Father Corraso introduced Arthur and me to a friend and longtime parishioner of the Church."

"Have you ever heard of the Great Bambino?" asked the priest to us both.

"Yes, sir," I replied. "He's the greatest baseball player of all time."

"Yes, he is," Father Corraso agreed. "But I mean the other one, the boxer. What's happening to you and your brother is not right. Be assured that God is with you, and He has brought you here. Joey, also known as the Great Bambino, is the best boxer to ever come out of Brooklyn, and let's just say he feels like he owes me a favor. I never considered taking him up on it until today."

"I met the gigantic cruiserweight with a fist bump."

"If you want to learn how to protect yourself and your brother, be at my gym every morning, Monday through Friday, at 5 a.m. sharp," he told me.

"I'll give you an hour before I start training each day. Miss a day, and the training is over. Understand?"

"'Yes, sir,' I told him, with more excitement than I can ever remember since.

"With the help of Father Corraso, they convinced our mother that the training was necessary to protect Arthur at school.

"I showed up at the gym every day before 5 a.m., walking the five long blocks, with Arthur tagging along as a spectator most days. Even when I was sick or tired, I never missed a morning.

"Day by day and week by week, I learned to fight. Changing my diet, with the help of Joey's trainers who took a shine to my always-smiling brother, I added 30 pounds of muscle and grew six inches that summer.

"At the start of our freshman year, I was no longer weak or afraid. On our second day back, the bullies targeted us like before, but I wasn't the same scared kid from the last school year. Facing off each bully, one by one, I protected Arthur for the very first time. I'll never forget that day as long as I live," Mike said, grinning as I had never seen him.

"I gained new respect that day among all the school students but was challenged frequently after that by tough guys looking for a name.

"Arthur died three years later, just shy of graduation, from an unknown disease. The doctors said it was pneumonia, but I always believed he died of the same disease that he lived with his entire life."

Mike was going to stop there, having already shared more personal information than he could ever remember, but he kept going as he felt something heavy being lifted off of his chest slowly, layer by layer.

"I stalked the head bully who had tormented my brother a few years before," he continued, "hoping to find something to numb the pain of losing my best friend and brother.

Careful and calculating, I was able to make the bully's death appear like an accident, falling out of a three-story window at a drunken high-school party in our senior year.

"I felt a little better after the bully's death, but my pain remained. I would never forget the names and faces of the other three who beat my brother so many times.

"Should I stop?" Mike asked. "I mean, is this too much for you, Lance?"

"No, it's OK, but you know I'm going to pray for you when you're done—right?"

"That's what I was hoping for," he replied seriously.

Mike continued: "I took one on the wharf with only a pocketknife, at a deserted shipyard on a cool October night. A friend of mine and future police partner helped to lure the unsuspecting teen with the promise of a drug sale.

"The final two bullies died that year, with the last one during my academy training. They were sloppy and rushed, with me hoping to feel normal after the final revenge of my brother's torment. My carelessness would cause me many sleepless nights, as I thought the investigation might lead back to me. I wasn't concerned about being caught, but I knew that I couldn't avenge Lily's death from behind bars. A few connections were made during the church trial that could have linked back to me, but nothing stuck."

"Wait a minute," I said, feeling like I was in the middle of a big hoax. "You're serious about this, right?" I had to ask, even though I knew the truth. "And what about your sister?" I added, without waiting for a response. On the one hand, I should have been shocked by his admissions, and on the other, I wasn't surprised and needed to know how the story ended.

"My sister, Lily, was beautiful, smart, and the most popular girl in school. I adored her and would do anything for her. Fighting in Brooklyn's bare-fisted underground fight clubs on the weekends, I would earn as much as $200 for a win. I clothed her and Arthur in the best attire I could find, spending every penny. I gave them everything money could buy, which our mother could not afford, taking nothing for myself. Lily was taken on her senior year prom night. She was ravaged, beaten and killed, left like garbage on the side of a deserted road running deep through the Pine Barrens of north-central New Jersey."

There were tears in Mike's eyes for only the second time I had witnessed.

"I loved her more than anything in this world, after Arthur was gone." He paused for more than a minute, not saying a word and staring straight ahead down the mountain road.

I took the opportunity to look around at the countryside and glance at the map.

"I joined the Academy six months after graduation," Mike continued, "vowing to find her killer. As it turns out, there were three...

"Let's stop for a minute and take a look at the map," he said.

We found the shortcut road David had highlighted with a neon marker, heading from our location straight over to Interstate 25.

"Let's stay sharp and get there in one piece," Mike said.

Pushing my instincts aside to ask him to continue the story, I got focused on the trip forward.

Following the map, one fire road leads into the next, and eventually to the highway.

We turned north on I-25, headed the last few miles down Raton Pass.

The barricade was much the same as the first we had encountered on the opposite end of the pass. Slowing the truck to a stop, we exited. My crutches slowed me considerably, but one of the guards recognized Mike from the other barrier, and our lifetime pass was granted this time.

The lines of people headed to the FEMA camp were decreasing considerably since last time in Amarillo, leading me to believe that more people had either made it by now or headed out on their own.

* * * * * * *

Chapter Fifteen ~ FEMA Camp ~ Trinidad, Colorado

R eaching the front of the camp, we stuck out in the only vehicle not inside the gates. We were ordered out of the truck and questioned as to our intent.

Relaying the story about Vlad, the lead soldier dropped his serious demeanor and asked us to wait while he called the Colonel.

Fifteen minutes later, he came back and shook our hands. "The Colonel is en route to meet with you two."

"That's good luck," I told Mike. "We didn't expect him to be here."

"He's not," replied the soldier. "He's going to helicopter in from a base in Denver to meet you. Hang tight. He will be here in about 90 minutes."

I resisted the urge to make a joke about the Colonel having nothing better to do than fly around to hang out with civilians. It was dawning on me that the sarcastic tone I had carried around since I was a kid could get me in some real trouble now if I wasn't careful.

We hung out at the truck, wondering in earnest why the Colonel would fly in to meet us.

* * * *

"Can I get the rest of the story?" I asked Mike, both interested and wanting to kill time.

"OK," he replied, "but you're hearing things I've never told another person, even Father Corraso. I'm not sure you really want to hear the rest."

"Fair enough, Mike," I told him, surprised at myself for openly engaging what I now believed to be a serial killer with a new girlfriend and next-world adopted son.

"I'm guessing," I continued, "that you have never hurt a woman or a child. Is that correct?"

"I have sworn to protect them both and will never waiver."

"OK, then I'm ready to hear the rest," I replied.

"After my sister's death," he continued, "I worked every tireless lead for months. The break came in a routine lineup, when I questioned a man who was a secondary driver to a bodega robbery apparently gone bad.

"I was able to get an off-the-record confession about the murder of my sister and pulled a few strings to let the man leave the precinct.

"Taking the next four days off, I followed him, observing his daily routine and vowing revenge for my sister. The killer's death was slow, over 18 hours. Drugging him, I brought him back deep into the Pine Barrens of New Jersey, to the same spot my sister was found. The slow torture revealed two more accomplices.

"Two agonizing years later, I had brought all three men to street justice and gained revenge for my beloved sister.

"I met the love of my life, Kelly, during this pivotal time in my life. Of course, I had dated other girls before, but only briefly since they never seemed to get me.

"Kelly was different. I first saw her driving in a bright yellow Dodge Charger while my partner and I were on patrol. Pulling up beside her, I couldn't take my eyes off her. A half-mile down the road, I noticed her left brake light was out and pulled her over for a warning. We hit it off, talking for more than 30 minutes right on the side of the road.

"I courted her slowly and carefully, since she was gun-shy from her last boyfriend, who beat her up on multiple occasions. Even the restraining order she had on him didn't seem to help. It had been more than two months since he beat her last, but she was scared every day and always looking over her shoulder.

"I took care of him one Sunday afternoon on my day off and was still back in time for the Giants game. I had told Kelly that the man was gone and would never be back to hurt her. She thanked me nervously but never asked about it again…

"There were others over the next half-decade that crossed me in one way or another—one trying to flirt openly with Kelly and another cheating in a neighborhood poker game. There were more, and I can't recall the reasoning for a few others, but I'm sure there must have been one.

"You and I, we are even now," he said. "I helped you with Hendrix, and you helped me with Javi."

"That won't last long," I said, "as I'll hopefully owe you in just a minute… I'm asking for a favor now, Mike. That you will talk with me first, should anything go down with you and Jake."

"That's the favor you want?" Mike asked, surprised.

"I have my reasons, but yes, that is what I am asking."

"I will do my best to honor your request, should that situation ever arise," Mike replied.

"Thank you," I said, feeling hopeful about at least one issue.

"Are you going to pray for me now?" asked Mike.

"I already have."

* * * *

The Colonel arrived on a helicopter, landing near the truck.

"Gentlemen," he said, with his hand out. "We were expecting you sooner or later."

"We wanted to check on our friend Vlad and hopefully bring him home. Is he still alive?" I asked.

"Yes, he's alive and recovering well from the surgery. It's complicated, though, this whole thing. I'm sure you can understand that we can't just allow people from the outside to be dropped off here for life-saving medical care, only to turn around and walk right out the door once they're better. It doesn't look good to everyone here, to the residents or even the guards."

I didn't like it, but I understood what he was saying.

"Will you be attending the fights today, Colonel?" asked one of his men. "We've got some good ones on the schedule."

"What fights?" Mike asked him, as we kept walking.

"Look at this," said the Colonel, pulling back the canvas siding of a large circus-style tent. Bleachers on all four sides surrounded a bonafide boxing ring.

"Can I check it out?" asked Mike.

"Sure. See what you think," the Colonel replied.

Mike jumped inside, shadow boxing for about a minute. "This is the real deal," he concluded.

"How is this even here?" I asked.

"There's one in almost every men's facility across the country," replied the Colonel. "It's an essential tool for keeping the peace. All scores are settled right here. Occasionally, even the guards will have a match, but only with each other. It's the only fighting allowed here. We have matches every Monday and Friday. Anyone can fight, and we try to match up the weight classes as close as possible."

"I used to fight," said Mike, hoping for an invitation. "Do the winners get bragging rights or something else?"

"Both," replied the Colonel. "Win a fight, and they get to be one of the first through the mess hall. Win two, and they get to switch jobs with anybody here for a month, minus the guards and other military, of course. Become a running champion with more than three fights won in a row, and they get to be the big man, with eating privileges and no job for the next month."

"Do you get a lot of takers?" I asked.

"More than you would think," replied the Colonel. "Any fighting outside the ring is strictly prohibited, so it's a way to settle differences and a good way for the guys to blow off steam."

"Can I fight your current champion?" asked Mike, feeling anxious for some action.

"That's a question I was not expecting," replied the Colonel, with a chuckle. "I'll think about it."

"Do you know why I flew up here and agreed to meet you guys?" he asked, showing us into a small room with a desk and three chairs.

Mike smiled as he saw the unmistakable setup of a classic interrogation room, complete with one-way glass.

"Who's listening?" asked Mike, pointing towards the mirrored wall.

"When it's just me talking, there's nobody on the other side, I can assure you. I agreed to meet you guys because you remind me of a younger me. My job is to run these camps, and I do it well, but if I didn't hold this position," he said, lowering his voice, "I would be out there on the road, just like you guys and your group.

"And Mike," he added. "I boxed at West Point Military Academy. It's been a while, but I never lost the passion for it."

"Do you miss it?" asked Mike.

"Every day. I miss it every day."

"Do you ever fight here, just to show the men that you can?" Mike continued.

"No. I'd like to, but no matter what happens, it looks bad. If I lose, they will have less respect for me. And if I win, then I'm just a bully, and that doesn't work either."

Mike agreed, smiling.

"Colonel, what if you and I sparred in front of the men, so you can show off your skills, and then you let me fight your champion?" asked Mike.

The Colonel thought this over, not speaking for nearly a minute. "It's not a bad idea," he finally replied. "I can show our guests, as well as my men, that I walk the walk, so to speak."

"What do you want if you beat my champion?" asked the Colonel.

"With all due respect, sir, we would like our man Vlad back and information about the link between your military and the coffee guy, Ronna."

The Colonel grinned, without agreeing to the terms. "And if you lose?"

"If I lose, I'll stay here and work as a guard for you, but Lance leaves here either way."

"Mike," I said, putting a hand on his shoulder. "You don't have to do that. You haven't even seen the champion."

"Is it a deal?" asked Mike, ignoring my statements.

"Eight rounds with gloves and a referee," the Colonel replied. "Three impartial judges that I trust to rule fairly. If you win by KO, TKO or decision, you'll leave with Vlad and some more food, like last time. And I'll tell you what I can about Ronna and how it relates to your group. Understand, though, that even now there is information that is classified regarding him and his team that I will not discuss.

"Should you lose by KO, TKO or decision, then the Russian stays here, and you work as a guard in this camp for 180 days, or longer if you so choose. Now, we have multiple champions. How much do you weigh, Mike?"

"I always fought light heavyweight at just over 175 pounds. I guess I'm still in the category, although I haven't weighed myself lately."

* * * *

"Right this way," said a fit man in his mid-fifties. "I'm Paul, but everybody calls me Pauly," he continued, with an East Coast accent. "I run the Gym here."

"You're a long way from New York!" said Mike immediately upon hearing the accent.

"Jersey City, actually, but we still all talk alike. You sound like me. Where are you from?"

"Excuse me, gentlemen. I'll be back around in a few," said the Colonel, walking away. "Let's get him weighed up, though, while I'm gone, Pauly. He's fighting today."

"Well, this is a first," remarked Pauly, turning back towards us. "So, where did you say you're from, Mike?"

"Brooklyn. I'm from Brooklyn," Mike answered. "But more recently from North Texas."

"What about you?" he asked me, reaching out his hand.

"Born in Louisiana and raised in Northern Colorado, but North Texas for the last couple of decades."

"So, who's going to fight?" Pauly asked.

"I'm just a spectator today," I spoke up. "But Mike here loves this stuff."

"Where did you train, Mike?" he asked.

"Only in Brooklyn, sir."

"Where exactly, I mean?" asked Pauly.

"Gleason's Gym on Front Street. You ever heard of it?" Mike asked.

"Come on, man. I'm from Jersey but it's right across the Hudson River. Yeah, I trained Mayweather Jr., Julio Cesar Chavez, and Larry Holmes, just to name a few at that gym. You don't look familiar, and I trained a lot of guys there for a whole lot of years."

Mike wondered if he was being tested.

"Well, I never had an official trainer, but one of the boxers trained me for a summer before his workout early in the mornings. His name was The Great Bambino."

"You trained with Joey?" asked Pauly.

"Yeah, that's him," said Mike.

"Oh, you're going to love this," said Pauly. "Hang tight, and I'll be right back."

He returned ten minutes later with the Brooklyn legend.

"Hey, Joey!" said Mike, reaching out his hand. "Do you remember me?"

"You look familiar, but I've been in a lot of fights over the years, and my memory is not so good."

"I was 14, and Father Corraso from the Catholic Church asked you to train me.

"Wait a minute. It's coming back now."

"Father Corraso. You remember him, Pauly?"

"Yeah, of course. We went to his church for years," replied Pauly.

"Anyway," continued Joey. "I kind of owed the Father a favor, and he asked me to train Mike here. How's your twin brother, Arthur?"

"He passed a few years later," said Mike.

"I'm truly sorry to hear that, Mike. His brother, Arthur," continued Joey to me, "was slow in the head, but he always had a smile and was great to have around the gym."

"How did I never see you guys?" asked Pauly.

"He trained from 5-6 a.m. that summer. You were lucky to get to the gym by 6:30, Pauly," joked Joey.

"If you decide to stay here for a while, Mike, we'll have to add a 'Y,' like all good Brooklyn names, and change your name to Mikey," added Pauly.

"Just Mike is fine," he said, having a flashback of the name given to him by the news organizations during his trial. More than one of the news anchors jokingly referred to him as Mikey, or Serial Mike, fashioned after a popular cereal commercial where the kids would say, "He likes it! Hey, Mikey!"

"Anyway, Joey here is one of our reigning champions and the only one with any formal training," Pauly said.

Mike felt a pit in his stomach, the same as mine, realizing this was the likely opponent he had bargained everything for.

"The Colonel says Mike is going to fight today," Pauly commented.

"Who?" asked Joey.

"Let's find out," remarked Pauly, motioning for Mike to come over to the scale.

"Boxers or briefs only," he said. "Everyone weighs in the same here."

Mike undressed slowly, as his mind raced. He knew Joey had mostly fought cruiserweight, with a weight range from 176-200 pounds. Last he weighed, a few months ago, Mike was 184 and felt a little chubby. He was certain he had lost a few pounds recently, but how many?

"What's your weight class, Joey?" Mike asked, wanting to have some information at least.

"Cruiserweight baby, just like always. I'm just under the 200-pound limit."

"OK, Mike. Up on the scale," said Pauly.

Mike couldn't look, closing his eyes. His ears were wide open. Ten agonizing seconds fiddling with the scale, and Pauly called out the numbers. Mike and I both heard it in slow motion, "one hundred seventy-four and 1/2 pounds. That's light heavyweight, son."

Mike was relieved, not caring who he had to fight, as long as it wasn't Joey.

"What do you know?" asked the Colonel, walking back inside the tent, but this time from the opposite direction.

"Well, it seems Joey used to train your guy Mike here, when he was a kid," remarked Pauly.

"No shit?" said the Colonel. "What did he weigh in at?"

"He's solid 174 and a half," replied Pauly.

The Colonel chuckled. "Mike, I bet you're a good fighter, but you damn sure got lucky not having to fight this guy," he said, pointing to Joey.

"Who's the light heavyweight titleholder?" asked the Colonel.

"That would be Garcia, sir," replied Pauly.

"OK then. Mike and I are going to spar for the men and moral's sake. Get Garcia ready to fight this afternoon, and don't let him in to see Mike warming up. They both will have the same advantage, not knowing anything about their opponent.

"We'll spar in a few hours, and you'll fight an hour after that. Let's get something to eat, and I'll take you over to see Vlad. He's a funny guy, that Russian," he added. "I like him better now, that's for sure.

"Things are a little different on the men's side," he told us, as we went through the chow line. "Everybody gets the same-sized plate, and you can fill it once—no spillovers on to the tray and no second helpings."

"I don't have to re-weigh after lunch, do I?" asked Mike.

"No, you're good; eat as much as you can fit on your plate."

The food quality was not the same as the women's barracks, but it was still hot and free for today.

As he led the way to the infirmary, towards the back of the camp, the Colonel was still trying to sell us on the charms of the place, although only half-heartedly.

Waiting in the front lobby of sorts in the large medic tent, the staff seemed nervous around the Colonel. Not in a fearful way, but kind of like when the district manager is going to make an appearance in your store.

"Right this way," said a young surgeon, according to the badge on his scrubs. We were led back through a long hallway, flanked on both sides by canvas walls. Nearing the back, we could already hear swearing and joke-telling in a Russian accent.

"You two!" Vlad said, holding his arms out. "You came back for me!" I was happy to see my old friend and instinctively scanned the bed to see if, by some chance, he still had his leg. He was sitting up in the hospital bed with covers pulled up to his chest, so I couldn't be sure.

"It's a good thing you guys got here so quick; I was going to wait until the Colonel left for another property before I assumed leadership of the camp."

"I've made arrangements for the other Vladimir in Moscow to take you in trade for just one pint of cheap vodka," replied the Colonel, touching Vlad on the shoulder.

The staff was laughing nervously at the banter, never before seeing someone joke with the Colonel.

"OK. OK, Colonel, sir. You've bested me once again," said Vlad, still smiling.

"I'll leave you three to talk," said the Colonel. Find your way back to the front of this tent in 30 minutes so we can prepare."

"Yes, sir," we both said.

"Prepare for what, guys?" asked Vlad.

Both of us pausing, I spoke first.

"Mike has agreed to fight the light heavyweight champion this afternoon."

"You mean Garcia, the Southpaw?" asked Vlad.

"I'll pretend I didn't hear that," replied Mike.

"Yes, that's him," I said.

"What do you get if you win?" Vlad asked.

"You!" Mike replied. "We get you and some more food, like last time. Apparently, they like you here so much you're not allowed to leave."

"I see," said Vlad, rubbing his stubbled chin. "What if you lose?"

"Then I stay here and work for the Colonel as a guard. Either way, Lance goes home to his family."

"What happened to your leg?" Vlad asked me.

"Gunshot. What happened to yours?" I asked, still not knowing if they had to take it off, like we were told.

"The leg is no more," he replied, removing the blanket to reveal one good leg and another cut off above the knee. I'm just glad they got the right part," he joked. "You know, this town was well known for transgender surgeries before it all happened, they tell me... How are Jax and the boys?" he asked me.

"They're doing great, and we made it to David's place," I said in a low voice, not wanting to specify a location.

"What about you? How is Sheila?" Vlad asked Mike.

"She's doing good, and we just yesterday adopted a young boy named Javi."

"That is great news!" Vlad said. Waving his hand for us to come in close, he began to whisper.

"Everyone talks around here, and I have developed a system of retrieving information. I knew you guys were here an hour ago. There's been a lot of talk about Ronna and another guy, Bocker, I think."

"Baker," I whispered, "and we don't think he's a Colonel like he claims to be."

"He is certainly not," replied Vlad. "They are headed right past Raton Pass. Did you know this?"

"Yes, Jim and David's son, Mark, have been on the ham radio 24/7, and we are getting information almost hourly now."

"OK, that's good," Vlad replied. "It's about time for you to be going, but one last thing. Ronna knows the Colonel," pointing towards the front of the tent, "and very well, long before this EMP thing ever started. I'm ready to go, and there is no vodka here. So Mike, you had better win today," he said, only half-joking.

"That's the plan, Vlad, for all of us."

The next couple of hours were boring for me but gave me some time to relax. My leg kept me from wandering about, but they were kind enough to change my dressing and give me 60 hydrocodone pills for the pain. I would feel good as long as the truck didn't break down, having me walking home on crutches.

* * * *

I had a front-row seat for the sparring match with Mike and the Colonel. I wasn't surprised at how technical the Colonel's craft was, coming out of West Point Academy, but both the residents and guards were mesmerized by him, proving to me it was a not a waste of his valuable time.

"That was fun," said Mike to both the Colonel and me when they were finished.

"We have a few fights ahead of yours, Mike, so you can rest up a bit," said Pauly.

* * * *

The clock on the wall read 2:30 p.m., and I was getting nervous about the afternoon slipping away. I was sure I did not want to spend the night here, if at all possible.

Joey grabbed Mike, wanting to review some moves from the old days. With nothing else to do, I watched the fights and agreed the matchups were fair, at least by weight class.

Pauly sat next to me, telling me about each opponent, and he placed verbal bets with himself as to each winner.

"I figured you would be announcing the fights," I said.

"Nope. Only the championships."

He had a lot of questions about our group, and I did my best to answer them without giving away any sensitive information about population size, locations or provisions, and especially the firearms.

"How did you and Joey end up all the way over here?" I asked.

"Oh, we're just here for about a week. The Colonel had been to our gym a few times over the years to spar, like he and Mike just did. Anyway, he got hold of us a couple of weeks before it all went to hell and asked us to set up rings like this across the country. The pay was so good, and the contract was for a year, so we couldn't pass it up."

"You mean he got hold of you a couple of weeks *after* it happened?" I asked casually, assuming he switched his words around.

"No, it was before. I'm sure of it because I remember meeting him at a local dive bar and depositing my first-ever government check that same day at the bank. When you deposit an official government check for $250K, it's hard to forget."

I wanted to be very careful about what came out of my mouth next. My mind was racing with the apparent hiring of two civilians by the Colonel a whole two weeks before the EMP attack.

I opted to skip the next series of questions I was wanting to ask, and instead went another route.

"That sounds interesting," I replied. "So, you guys bounce around the country and set up rings in each FEMA camp?"

"That's it," he replied, "and a year from now we get our final payment and a boat ride to any world destination we choose, to retire in style."

I was surprised he hadn't been briefed on the likely confidential nature of his story. I wondered if their final boat ride would just be straight out to sea, where secrets stay forever.

I wanted to tell Mike about this new information but decided against it, not wanting to take his attention off his fight.

My watch read 4:40 p.m., and I was even more concerned about getting home today.

It hit me right then that if Mike lost, I would be driving myself home, bad leg and all. One blowout or engine issue could prove disastrous for me outside of these protected camp walls.

"That's it," I said aloud, getting a few looks from the other men around. All at once, I realized why the camps were so full. It wasn't the showers or electricity, or even free food. They were scared out on their own and quickly became institutionalized.

I had first heard of that watching actor Morgan Freeman talk about it in the 1982 Stephen King novella adapted into the movie *The Shawshank Redemption*. He was talking to his fellow prison inmates, saying, "These walls are funny. First, you hate 'em; then you get used to 'em. Enough time passes, you get so you depend on them. That's institutional-ized."

Most of the pre-fights reminded me of the tough-guy matches I had seen on television over the years, where both men would swing wildly until one was either knocked out or both so tired they couldn't lift their arms anymore.

Pauly had informed us that Mike's fight would be the only championship fight happening today, and something told me it would be cleaner, more technical, and harder to win.

"Do you remember what I always said about your fights, Mike?" asked Joey.

"Yes, I still do. You told me not to leave the results in anyone else's hands."

"That's correct, and especially here. You're the new guy fighting our light heavyweight champion. You can't just win; you have to beat him. Do you understand?"

"Yes, sir, Joey, and thank you."

"For what?"

"For taking the time to teach me how to protect Arthur. The last day he was ever bullied was right before you started training me."

"What happened to him, Mike?"

"Pneumonia was the official cause, according to the doctor," replied Mike.

"Again, I'm so sorry; he was a great kid," said Joey. "Let's get you warmed up. This is the last fight now before yours, and both of these guys are hotheads, so it should be quick, one way or the other."

Mike could hear the men being announced over the loudspeaker.

* * * * * * *

Chapter Sixteen ~ FEMA Camp ~ Trinidad, Colorado

T he wind blew the tent, and the lights inside flickered. Rain out of nowhere pelted the roof of the tent, getting louder by the second.

"Whoooo Whoooo" came the familiar sound. I had heard it dozens of times before, living in North Texas.

"Is that what I think it is?" asked Mike, coming around to help me stand with my bad leg.

"Yep," I replied. "It sounds just like the tornado sirens in Texas. I guess that sound is universal."

It was clear that about half of the men inside understood what was happening, either lying on the ground or running outside the tent. The others just looked around, not having a clue.

We both got down on the floor, under a solid wooden table large enough to shield nearly ten people. It was killing me not to run outside and see what was coming.

* * * *

Before we had the kids, Joy and I had a tornado hit our Plano, Texas, house at 4 a.m. in the morning. We lived on a greenbelt, with large powerlines running straight down it, and were used to strong winds on occasion.

This night we were awakened by a sound like a freight train running through our single-story home. I remember turning on the television to see a map of my area with bright red warning signs flashing TORNADO. The noise was deafening, with cracking, creaking, and crunching sounds coming from the front living room. We got into the bedroom closet, just as it passed over.

There was a pause of absolute silence and then the sound of pouring water coming from the three-foot by two-foot hole in the roof, sending water straight into the living room onto the hardwood floors. Surveying the damage, I found two of our 50-foot trees twisted apart and thrown on top of our roof.

From that day on, I was always the crazy guy out looking around the outside of the house whenever I heard tornado sirens. When asked why I would do something so dumb, I could only respond, "I need to see what's coming."

* * * *

With the three judges, the referee, Pauly and Joey, we were able to squeeze under the table as the roof of the tent was violently torn off.

Sounding like a freight train was crashing through the camp, with the high-pitched sound of sirens wailing and men screaming, it was enough for me to close my eyes in prayer and think of Joy and our boys.

The chaos lasted no more than 30 seconds and stopped just as quick as it had begun, although the sirens ran for another minute or two.

Looking out from underneath the table, the inside of the tent looked like a warzone. The ring was remarkably unscathed, I noticed, with the exception of one of the top ropes on the east side, dangling over the edge of the platform.

Minutes later, the Colonel walked back inside the now-roofless tent. "Well, boys, that was fun," he said, looking up at a nearby clear blue sky.

Pauly was already up and inspecting his ring.

"Is she OK?" asked the Colonel, hollering up at him.

Pauly continued stomping around the platform, replying, "Yes, sir. I think she will be just fine once I get a new rope on."

"All right. I'll be back in about 30. Let's get Mike and Garcia ready to fight, and move the rest to tomorrow. Don't start without me, though!"

"Yes, sir, Colonel," replied Pauly, who was getting to work on the new rope.

* * * *

The Colonel returned in a half hour, sitting down next to me.

"Is everything OK? The camp, I mean?" I asked.

"All is good," he replied. "The mess hall got hit good, but the kitchen and food were spared. The men will have to eat outside for a few days, but everything else looks fine. I could hear Vlad swearing while I was still a good twenty yards from the medical tents," he added, laughing. "I'm going to miss that guy's humor—unless, of course, your guy loses."

"Just a few more minutes, sir," called Pauly. "I've just about got this rope fixed now."

"Take your time," replied the Colonel. "Just make sure it's stable. We don't need anyone getting hurt today."

That sounded funny to me, as Mike was literally about to fight for his freedom.

"We don't need them twisting an ankle falling over a bad rope," I almost said, quickly realizing it might not be so funny to the Colonel.

"I take safety in my camps seriously," the Colonel said, almost as if he heard my thoughts just seconds before. "How's your leg?" he asked, looking at my crutches.

"OK, sir. Your medics got me fixed up pretty good."

"How are you going to drive home?" he asked, "if Mike loses the fight."

"I don't really know, sir. I was thinking about that earlier," I replied.

"Well, let's see what happens, and we'll figure something out," he continued.

"Your guy Mike, he's good," said the Colonel. "I've sparred a lot over the years, and I can tell he's going to be a handful for Garcia. He's a Southpaw—Garcia, that is," he added in a near whisper.

"Interesting," is all I could think to say.

Pauly did the introductions of the fighters, and Mike's borrowed shorts said "Great Bambino" on the waistband.

Mike looked warmed up and ready to fight. He whipped his head side to side, cracking it loudly. Exactly what I used to tell my Chiropractic patients *not* to do.

Garcia was no slouch and looked to be in good shape. I knew he was the champion, but not how many fights he had won in the short amount of time the camp had been open.

Touching gloves, round one started slowly, with each fighter sizing up the other and determining their reach.

The crowd's boos started only one minute into the round.

"These guys booing," said the Colonel, "don't understand the finesse of boxing. The first round is so you can flow with your opponent and understand how they move. It's like dancing with a new girl at a club. You have to follow her moves and slowly introduce your own over a minute, or sometimes more. The more you flow with a guy you've never fought before, the better chance you have of getting them to fight your way.

"These booers here," he said, waving one arm around the crowd "would rather see an all-out bare-knuckle brawl, where someone gets their teeth knocked out."

"I understand," I replied. "Most of the fights before this could fit that category."

"That's why we have strict rules, including weight classes, 8-ounce gloves for everyone, judges, and a referee. We can't tell them how to fight, but Joey is teaching classes for the few who want to learn."

Round one ended with a few light punches connecting for each man.

Round two picked up speed, with Mike getting his rhythm down. Landing a clean right hook to Garcia's nose, he got a smile in return, as blood trickled out of his left nostril.

Garcia returned punches, with one landing squarely on Mike's chin, knocking him back a step.

I held my breath, hoping he wouldn't get knocked out.

Garcia's cornerman yelled for him to finish the fight.

Joey called out to Mike. "We're OK," he said. "Jab and move, jab and move."

The bell rang, with both men red in the face.

Joey, putting down the stool for Mike, gave him clear instructions.

"Garcia is a good fighter, but his cornerman is an idiot. I've seen it in his last two fights, where somewhere in round three or four he gets tired of being yelled at by his corner guy and comes out blazing, with his chin out and wild punches. His opponents couldn't handle the pressure and failed to capitalize on the emotion of Garcia. I think this will happen again very soon and you need to be ready. Pick your shots and you can put him down.

"Is it enough to win the fight, Mike?" yelled Joey, shaking him.

"No, sir!" Mike shouted back.

"What do you have to do?"

"Beat him!" Mike replied, standing for the bell of round three.

Halfway through round three, Garcia's corner guy was screaming at him to finish the fight.

Garcia's shots were wider, heavier, and out of sync. Every 30 seconds, he was yelling back at his corner guy, and Mike could feel Garcia was close to snapping.

"Watch the shots!" called out Joey.

Round three came to a close, with Garcia and his guy arguing in their corner.

Mike watched the commotion for a few seconds.

"Mike, have a seat," said Joey, pushing him down on to his stool.

"This is it round four. He's throwing haymakers, and I've seen him knock out more than one guy with just one punch. He's agitated," he continued, looking over at the man still arguing with Garcia, never sitting on the stool.

"Your opponent is 80% on his way to losing his composure," Joey continued. "You have to get him through the last 20%. Do you understand me?"

"Yes, but how?" asked Mike.

"Jab, jab, jab. You dance around that ring and just keep jabbing until he snaps. His corner guy will help him along, for sure. When he does, you take your shots, or cover if you have to until there is an opening. This isn't live TV boxing of the old days. I can assure you this referee will not stop the fight until one of you is down and can't get back up."

"OK, I can do that," said Mike.

They came out for round four, with Garcia not touching Mike's extended glove. *Jab*, thought Mike. *Just jab.*

In any other fight, Mike wouldn't have worried about his performance, or even getting knocked out, although he never had. This fight was different, with a lot at stake, and he followed his old trainer's instructions completely.

"Nice and easy," Joey called out, as Mike began to jab. Garcia was getting annoyed at the quick pop shots peppering his swelling face. Every few jabs he would throw a wild roundhouse punch.

Mike resisted the urge to try and end it with one blow.

With Garcia frequently looking to his corner and still trading remarks, Mike held back several opportunities to catch him off-guard and distracted.

"This is a good fight," said the Colonel, putting his hand on my shoulder.

Being ringside and near Mike's corner, I heard most of Joey's instructions and agreed with his strategy.

Jab, jab, jab continued Mike, and Garcia lost it. Mike knew it was coming, as his opponent sprang towards him, arms swinging wildly with 1:29 seconds left in the round.

Mike covered, as hard punches connected with his forearms, and occasionally the top of his head.

He was against the ropes when the punch slipped through, catching him square on the chin for a second time. He felt dizzy and stumbled, looking over at the clock, reading 58 seconds.

"Finish him! Finish him!" yelled Garcia's cornerman frantically. Those in the crowd were now all on their feet, chanting the same.

Joey was just behind Mike and speaking calmly. "This is it, Mike. He is coming in hard and fast. Pick your shots and put him down."

Garcia let it all go, swinging wide heavy blows as Mike ducked and weaved.

His head was clearing now, and he got a quick glimpse at the clock—22 seconds—when he saw his opening. A right-hand uppercut knocked Garcia back three steps, followed by a left jab and a right hook, knocking his mouthpiece across the ring.

His opponent stumbled backward, as a drunk man might, running faster to catch his balance. Falling into the ropes, the new one held. Ten seconds was called out as Mike landed the final combination, dropping the champion face-first to the canvas.

The bell rang, with the referee and doctor determining that Garcia could not continue.

"This fight has come to a close at 3 minutes of the fourth round, by way of knockout by our winner and new light heavyweight champion, Mike," said the referee, raising his hand.

Most cheered "Great fight!" with a few boos mixed in.

"Well, we had better tell Vlad the news," said the Colonel.

I agreed, thinking he already knew.

Mike thanked Joey for the coaching today, and we all headed to the medical tent.

"You're going to miss me, Colonel, I know this," said Vlad, pouring on the accent.

"I guess I will," the Colonel replied, shaking his hand.

The medical staff was sad to see him leave, as he kept the typically solemn hospital lively and almost fun.

"I'm already packed, since I knew you would win me back, Mike. Thank you. Was it even close?" he asked, though he already knew the details of every round.

"He's good, the Garcia guy," replied Mike.

"My men have packed some food for you guys to take back to your camp. Let me show you, gentleman, one more thing before you go," said the Colonel, returning to the room. "Good fight, Mike, by the way. You're welcome to stay and defend your title." Mike only smiled, with no response.

Spreading a large map on the table, encompassing both northern New Mexico and southern Colorado, the Colonel circled the cities of Raton and Trinidad.

"Here we are now," he said, writing the words "FEMA Camp," and circling it. "And here is your group," he added, writing out the words "Your Group."

Mike and I looked at the map, showing the exact location of David's property.

"No, fellas. It wasn't Vlad, before you ask. Things have changed, but we're still the United States Military. If I want to find someone, I will."

My mind was numb with the realization that they knew where we were all along.

"Now, about Ronna," continued the Colonel. "I believe you've earned an explanation of sorts," he said, looking at Mike.

"Ronna and I go way back, all the way to Nam. For the past ten years he has led an agency that essentially does not exist and has answered to only a handful of people, including me. He was placed out in the grasslands alone, without weapons of any kind, as a test to see if he could amass a following after that day, posing as the 'coffee guy,' as you say.

"As for the helicopter incident, there are men that need dropping, but he's not one of them."

"So, it was your guys who showed up in his defense at Capulin?" I asked, already knowing.

"Are you working with the Baker guy?" I continued, hoping I wasn't pushing my luck.

"Yes, we helped Ronna out a bit at Capulin. And nope, that guy Baker is an idiot. I'm sure you heard he calls himself a Colonel."

"We did hear that and doubted it from the start," I told him.

"One more question, gentlemen," the Colonel continued.

I had ten more ready to fire but kept my mouth shut.

"Why is Baker still around if he's causing trouble?" asked Mike, "and how did you know where our camp was?"

The Colonel smiled. "That's two questions!

"To the first one, he has friends in high places somehow. But they are getting tired of his actions, so his days may be numbered. For now, he and my guy will work together, I guess.

"Sunset's at 6:45, gentlemen. We've got 5:55 right now," said the Colonel, looking at his watch.

"Do you boys want to stay here tonight?" he asked, waiting for us to come up with three valid excuses. "Let's get some supper, and we will drop you guys off on my way back to base," he added, walking out of the tent toward the mess hall.

Vlad was joking around with the Colonel, creating a distraction as I spoke to Mike.

"What does he mean, drop us off?" I asked. "It's not like he's going to Uber us home."

"And we have the truck," replied Mike, shrugging his shoulders. "I think we need to follow along, since I don't see we have many choices in the matter."

Supper was better than lunch, and it was interesting to see how the men learned to pile the plate high, melding various dishes together without spilling over the edge.

"Now that's an art," Mike said to me, pointing to the tallest plate with mixed dishes of pasta, burgers, French fries, salad and desert.

"Well, it's all going to end up in the same place," I replied, laughing.

Vlad and I were both on crutches, but he was making me look bad. I guessed he had been getting around like this for a bit longer.

It was odd seeing his missing leg, and I had a conscious flashback of the deer coming over the truck, flailing its legs like some kind of cartoon.

I guessed that in the old-world he would have probably kept his leg. Now I wondered if something minor only a few weeks ago, like a simple cut or contusion, could become life-threatening.

I chewed something hard while biting into my lasagna and felt a shooting pain in an upper left tooth.

"Ow," I said out loud, putting my hand up to my mouth. Something pointed was on my tongue and I opened my mouth, dropping my old silver filling onto the table below.

"I'm guessing you would like to get that looked at while you're here," said the Colonel. I nodded my head yes, forgetting all about the food in front of me.

At the Colonel's command, a guard led me back to the Medical tents. The pain was sharp and increased with each breath. Led to an open dental-type chair in the very back of the tent hospital, the guard left me waiting.

"What do we have here?" asked a soft voice. "I'm Dr. Porter, and the Colonel has asked me to take a look at your tooth."

The pain was intense, and I had a flashback to the movie with Tom Hanks stranded alone on a remote island, with that soccer ball he called Wilson. There was a scene when Hank's character has an abscessed tooth, and his only recourse was to knock it out with the blade of an ice skate.

"What kind of doctor are you?" I asked.

"Let me take a look," she said, not answering my question. "Oh, that's bad," she continued, shining a bright light into my face.

"Aren't you supposed to keep that information to yourself?" I asked, only kind of joking.

"Are you paying me for this service?" she asked.

"Point taken," I responded. "Can you fix it?"

"Oh no," she replied. "That tooth has to come out."

"Of course it does," I replied shortly, wondering what else could happen today.

"You're lucky this didn't happen out in the bush," she said.

"I'm sorry," I told her. "You're right. It's just that the timing sucks, and I was hoping to get home tonight."

"You will," she said, with a wink.

"How's that?" I asked, nearly slurring my words.

"The Colonel and I are kind of a thing," she whispered. "And I happen to know that since your friend won the fight and gave my man the chance to spar in front of his men, he will get you all home safe."

"But it's already almost dark," I told her.

"Birds fly in the dark," she replied, smiling.

"Let's get you numbed," she said, giving me several injections around the tooth. I relaxed as the medication kicked in, numbing the entire side of my face and nearly taking away my pain.

"No laughing gas?" I asked.

"No, not this time. Hang tight," she told me, returning a few minutes later with a pliers-type tool. I felt the twisting and heard periodontal ligament around the tooth snap as pressure was slowly increased.

As a teenager, I had my wisdom teeth extracted but I was completely sedated, waking up only after the procedure. I remember them putting an IV in my arm and injecting a cold liquid into my veins, asking me to count down from 100. I remember thinking about starting to count when I went under.

Cracking and crunching, thrusting the tooth side-to-side, she took it with one final pull. "Got it," she said proudly, holding up the bloodied, misshapen tooth. "I'll pack you with some gauze and that should do for now. Do you have someone that can check on this daily for the next week or two?"

"Yes, ma'am," I said, trying not to drool out of the corner of my mouth. Five minutes later, I was headed back to the mess hall with no more appetite.

The clock read 7:12, and it was going to be dark in another hour. *Two guys with crutches headed across the potentially hostile country in the dark*, I thought.

"Maybe we should stay just one night," I told Mike. "It's going to be hell getting back in the dark."

"No worries, boys. I have to get back to Denver, and I already told you we could drop you off on the way," said the Colonel, overhearing me.

"With all due respect, Colonel, even if you could chopper us home, we can't just leave the truck," said Mike.

"You boys ever heard of a Boeing CH-47 Chinook?"

"No, sir," we replied.

"It just so happens to be a twin-engine tandem rotary helicopter that can carry 30-50 troops and a total of 26,000 pounds. I'm pretty sure we can drop you boys and your little truck off at your place on my way back to Denver."

"Can we get just a minute, Colonel?" I asked, sounding funny even to myself with my face still half numb.

"Sure. Let me know when you're ready," replied the Colonel.

Talking quietly with Vlad and Mike, we discussed our options. Mike was fine with driving home in the dark, but Vlad and I considered the free ride.

"They already know where we are at, and it can't hurt to have a US Colonel as a friend," I said. "Plus, I think he likes Vlad more than most of his men here."

"It's going to be crazy landing a military helicopter in our camp," pointed out Mike.

"That's true," I agreed. "But besides you, I can't think of anyone in our camp that would consider taking on a fight with one."

Mike smiled and replied, "I was ready back when we first met the Colonel, but I see your point. It's been a long day anyway, and I want to see my girl and little boy," he continued, yawning.

"Thank you for your invitation, Colonel," said Vlad. "We would be happy to be your guests on such a flight."

"That's good to hear, since they are getting ready to load your truck as we speak," added the Colonel.

"Let's go, let's go," ordered the soldiers, loading us into the gigantic helicopter, already filled with at least 20 soldiers.

"We've got four civilians and the Colonel," called a pilot over the radio.

The helicopter lifted slowly, hovering for nearly five minutes near the ground.

"We're good to go," called one of the pilots over the radio.

"Why all the troops?" I asked the Colonel.

"We have multiple stops," he replied, "but yours is first. I want to talk to your group for just a few minutes," he continued, not asking permission.

"Sure," I replied. "I'm sure they are still awake."

"If not, a big-ass helicopter and a dead man walking, at least on crutches, should do the trick!" added an excited Vlad.

My concerns about the helicopter seeing clearly at night were calmed by the multiple spotlights lighting up the land below.

"Aren't you concerned about being a target up here?" Mike asked the Colonel.

"No, not really. Nobody has the balls to fire first on a machine like this," replied the Colonel.

I wasn't sure of the approach we would take, but as the crow flies it put us right over the group on the opposite side of the river. Slowing, I could see movement below out of the side window.

"That's the..." said Mike, pointing down to their tents. "Wait until they see us landing in this thing on our side of the river!"

Less than a minute later, the movement below was from our group. "Nice and easy, guys," I said quietly, wishing I had thought to try the radio sooner.

It was too late now, with Lonnie out front but recognizing his truck being slowly lowered to the ground.

"Nobody gets off," called the Colonel to the soldiers onboard, "except for you, Doctor," he said, smiling at his girlfriend who had pulled my tooth.

As the ramp was lowered, Mike made sure Vlad and I got off safely. Walking around on crutches was one thing, but exiting a helicopter with a ramp was a whole other ballgame. Everyone was waiting with wide eyes, never expecting this.

The Colonel tasked two of his men with unloading the promised coolers of food.

The crowd quieted, and for the second time our group met one of the top ten most powerful men in this country. The Colonel and his girlfriend exited with us and met most of our group with a handshake.

The kids were mesmerized by the biggest machine, flying or not, they had ever seen, and right then Hudson wanted to be a pilot when he grew up.

A small group of us, including me, Mike, Vlad, David, Lonnie and Jake met privately with the Colonel and his lady friend. Joy, Nancy and Sheila attended as well.

"Officially," the Colonel started, "you all are afforded protection by the United States Military only in our designated FEMA camps. Unofficially, I like you folks. Vlad is still the same smartass we met when you were all out on the road, but I've come to appreciate his humor.

"Mike, you remind me of my younger days, and I think we are a lot alike." *Well, not exactly*, I thought. "And Lance, it takes some stones to take a road trip so soon after being shot.

"As for the rest of you, there are people coming your way, as I'm sure you already know. One leader works for me, and the other does not.

"Once again, I cannot offer you complete protection outside of our official camps, but I will also not stand by idly if you are under attack. I will meet for a few minutes with your radio operators and instruct them on how to reach me, should the need arise...and only under dire circumstances.

"Except you, Vlad. Get in touch with me every now and then so we can shoot the shit." Handing Vlad a brown paper bag, he walked to meet the radio operators.

Vlad laughed, opening the crumpled bag, revealing one unopened 750ml bottle of Beluga Gold Line Vodka. There was a card on it, reading "Happy Birthday, Colonel" and signed "Vladimir Putin / October 25, 2013."

"Mr. Putin has good taste, no?" said Vlad, inspecting the bottle.

Twenty minutes later, the massive helicopter lifted into the air, flying high above the tree line, headed north.

* * * * * * *

Chapter Seventeen ~ Raton Pass, New Mexico

V lad told stories of his time at the camp, having to be occasionally reminded about not cussing in front of the children.

"Where's your leg?" asked Hudson.

"Hudson," I told him. "Let's not..."

"Oh, it's OK," replied Vlad. "The leg is no more," he added, flapping the bottom half of his right pant leg.

"Yes, I see. But where *is* it?" Hudson asked again.

"All right, Hud," as I sometimes called him. "That's enough questions for now."

"Actually," replied Vlad, "it's a valid question, and I don't know what happened to it. Maybe it's in my pocket?" pretending to check his front pockets. "No, it's not there."

"What about in your back pocket?" asked Jax.

"Not there either," joked Vlad.

"I'll need to take a look at your leg in the morning," chimed in Nancy. "And it's time for bed, Danny," she added.

I could tell Vlad was concerned about little Danny's appearance, since he hadn't seen him in a while.

The rest of us had already seen him with his facial bandages off. His wounds from the grass fire were healing well, but it was obvious to all that he would never look the same.

Only recently could Hudson sleep on his back, even for a few minutes, I thought, and Danny's burns were pretty severe, requiring him to sleep that way every night.

David and Jake got Vlad over to Beatrice's house to sleep on Mel's old couch until they could find something more suitable.

"It's good to be back," Vlad told them. "Did you know that Mike won my freedom in a boxing match?"

"I look forward to hearing all about it tomorrow," said David. "Welcome home, Vlad!"

* * * *

My leg was killing me, and I opted for one pill before bed, not believing how long of a day it had been.

"There was a boxing match, a few actually, and a tornado, and I even got my tooth pulled," I told our boys.

"Oh, stop it, Lance," said Joy. "You have only been gone for one day."

"Mike won Vlad's freedom by beating the reigning light heavyweight champion in four rounds by knockout. You had a bad storm here around 3 p.m. today, right?" She nodded her head yes. "And here's where my tooth used to be," I said, holding my mouth open and shining my flashlight on it.

"You are serious!" she said. "That's one heck of a day!"

"Yes, it was. Plus, a free ride on the coolest helicopter I've ever seen—and right over the heads of the group across the river!"

The whole day felt like it had been a week long. "I'm just glad to be home," I added, quickly falling asleep.

* * * *

The morning was bustling, with the children wanting to look into the coolers from the camp. Those in our group remembered fondly the last time Mike and I showed up with stocked FEMA coolers. This time the food was not neatly packed and labeled as last time, but it was cold, on ice, and there was a lot of it.

"How were swim lessons yesterday?" I asked my boys.

"We didn't get to do it since you and Uncle Mike were gone," said Hendrix.

I wasn't sure how I felt about the "Uncle Mike" reference, getting a look from Joy, but left it alone for now.

"Well, it's back on today, buddy," I told him, smiling through the growing pain in my leg and my still-sore jaw.

The first thing the dentist tells you is not to put anything sharp in your mouth. And what's the first thing they do when they have you in the chair?

I smiled, not recalling which comedian I heard this one from, but understanding it better now.

Beatrice was in charge of the cooler lunches today. "Lunch and dinner today are brought to you by the Colonel," she announced. "For lunch, we have your choice of ravioli in meat sauce, roast beef sandwiches, or loaded baked potatoes. Dinner is pork chops (bone-in), potatoes au gratin, garden salad with all the vegetables...and banana pudding, I think. Yep, that's it," she said, dipping her finger into the dessert and tasting it. "Oh, and it's good!" she teased.

"Now, everyone out of my kitchen except for Veronica and Suzie, my little helpers."

Nancy checked my leg before lunch, as well as my mouth. "It's healing, the leg that is, but you have to stay off of it as much as possible, and traveling across the state doesn't help. Your mouth is fine and should be healed up in a few days."

Nancy was impressed with Vlad's healing, thinking they did a good job. "I did everything I could at the time. I hope you know that, Vlad," Nancy said.

"Of course, Nancy. Don't give it another thought. The doctors in Trinidad told me if it were not for the splint you fit my leg with, and the initial antibiotics, I would never have made it to them alive, so thank you for saving my life," replied Vlad.

Nancy smiled and was relieved to hear this news, as she had questioned her own actions in his initial treatment.

* * * *

Jim called a few of us up to get a radio update.

"Our friends from across the river were lively on the ham this morning. The flyover last night caught them off guard, and they nearly fired on it."

"That would have been interesting," I said. "There were 20 combat-ready soldiers on that chopper, ready for a fight."

"There is also a power struggle still escalating between the Baker guy and Ronna," continued Jim. "With the military gone, Baker is trying to establish dominance again. He has three times the men, but as long as Ronna's group has a radio they can get backup if they need it, as we already heard a few days ago."

"Mike and I had a conversation with the Colonel," I interjected, and Ronna is definitely not some crazy nut wanting to build a following. He's military and always has been. The Colonel is his boss."

"Really?" asked Steve, pausing before adding, "but it does make more sense now."

"What about the other guy?" asked Steve.

"He has some connections high up, but I still think he's some crazy fanatic trying to build an army of loyal followers, however he can get them," I said.

"Either way, they are all still passing close to this property, and that can't be good," added Jake.

"Let's keep close radio surveillance of them," I told Jim. "We need to know their every move."

* * * *

I asked a few to help me call a quick meeting with at least most of the adults in both of our groups. I had not had a chance to tell Mike about the information I learned from Pauly regarding the two-week discrepancy between getting the job and the day of the EMP.

As I thought about how I would approach it, I knew it would set Tom and a few others down a deeper path of what-ifs about our government and who would be running the country in the coming months. I was also prepared for more than a few adults to think I was crazy, or simply misinformed.

With everyone gathered, minus a few to watch over the children, I retold the story just as Pauly had relayed it to me. This time, when I got to the part about him cashing the large government check two full weeks before the day, I got the reaction from most I was expecting.

"Why would they do that?" asked Tina.

"Do you mean Pauly and Joey?" I asked.

"No. I mean our government. Why would they let this happen if they already knew?"

"To be honest," I replied, "we should have known something was up when the President declared FEMA camps open in every state, only days after the power went out. Now that I think about it, just the setting up of each camp would likely take weeks, or even months. I'm sure some local news people did small stories on it here and there, but nothing made it mainstream or at least some of us would have heard about it.

"To answer your question, Tina, it was likely something they learned of and could not do anything about in time...or it runs much deeper," I continued.

"You mean like the new world order, where the entire world is said to be run by only a few wealthy and powerful families calling all the shots?" asked Mel.

"Where did you learn about that?" asked Tammy.

"I was the guy right up until the end that you would call if you need the highest quality bunker installation," Mel continued. "I consulted on a few for A-list celebrities and high-ranking government officials. I even did one for Rodman, who was well known for calling Kim Jong-un a personal friend."

"How do you get more interesting every time you open your mouth?" whispered Tammy into his ear.

"Yes, Mel. That's what I mean," I told him. "The only person we know that has the answers is possibly Ronna, and surely Vlad's friend, the Colonel."

I was concerned Joy may be mad that I didn't tell her first, but she never much cared for politics, to begin with.

"That's all I know, and we can discuss any theories as a group over the coming days," I added.

"Joy," called out Mark. "You have someone on the ham asking for you."

"I don't think so," she replied. "Must be another Joy."

"Do you know Kris and Kat?" he asked.

"Oh no, Lance," she said, scrunching her face. "We forgot them," she stated. "What should I say?"

I felt odd, thinking about our friends from back home. We had spent many weekends together, with our kids feeling more like cousins than city neighbors. We had discussed the idea of EMPs and other life-altering ideas over the past year but never had a concrete plan if it all went to hell—only an idea of where my family was headed, including the stop in Raton.

Adan, Shane and I were on the same page with our families, but when it all happened I guess I just forgot to add everyone to the new group. I was hoping they would come by before we left, and maybe they thought the same.

It was enough for me to think about everyone else I knew outside of our immediate neighborhood back home. In a true crisis scenario, where each mile seems like a hundred, how many friends can you get together in a short amount of time, with no cell phones or any other means of communication?

The answer is, you forget some, and likely it's the very ones you started with.

"Let's talk to them," I told Joy. "We have to tell them what happened."

Joy got on the radio, and I stayed quiet in the background.

It seemed that our old friends and neighbors grouped up, following our likely path, as we had discussed more than once the year before.

"Why did you leave without us?" asked Kris, putting Joy in an uncomfortable position.

"It was me," I interjected. "We had a limited amount of time to get things ready, and we all just missed each other."

There was a pause, and I wondered if I was in for a deserved lecture.

"Hey, man. Shane here. We got behind and missed you guys leaving."

"Sorry, buddy," I continued. "We were around for about a week, but we had to leave eventually. We figured you had all found another way to leave."

"We just got behind, getting things squared away," Shane replied. "By the time we got to your house, the whole neighborhood was up in flames. We hope you got out of there OK."

"Yeah, the house was standing when we left, but I knew it was coming," I said. "Where are you and who's with you?"

"We've got Kris and her sister, Anna, and me with Adan, Kat, Doug, Anissa, and the kids of course. We're following the path you told us about a while back."

"Where are you now?" I asked again.

"We're in Des Moines, New Mexico," Shane answered.

"Hold on," I told him. "You're only nine miles from Capulin, and that's the one place you don't want to be right now! How did you get this far?"

"My old company truck," he told me. "It's old and ugly, but it's the only vehicle that started after the electricity went down. I've got that old airstream travel trailer hooked up and it's the only way we could fit everybody.

"It has been a hell of an adventure, with a few scary parts trying to keep the trailer, but we're all here with the exception of two friends who saved our very lives recently. We have been trying to track you down on the radio for a week now," he added.

"OK, Shane, just stay put for a bit. There is a large group of bad guys just ahead of you in Capulin, but they should be moving this way soon. Let them get a day or two out before you move again. I'll talk to my group and see what we can come up with."

"I miss the weekends at Wildwood Ranch," Adan said.

"Yeah. Me too, buddy," I replied.

The three of us couples used to pile the kids into the trucks and drive to Whitesboro, Texas, only about an hour north of McKinney. We rented an Airbnb—the sprawling 160-acre Wildwood Ranch with a large main house, swimming pool, firepit, stocked fishing ponds, and miles of groomed hiking and mountain-bike trails.

"It's kind of like that up here, except it's not near as peaceful and the ladies can't get to a Starbucks in ten minutes," I joked.

Joy and I asked Jim and Mark to wait before talking with anyone about what they just heard.

"Sure," they both replied.

"What's the problem?" Joy asked me, once we were alone.

"The problem is that we have 12 new people headed our way, and I need to convince both our group here and those on Saddle Ranch that they will be assets. Everybody has to agree; those are the rules we set early on."

"But what if they don't agree? These are our good friends, Lance, and we can't just leave them following behind us, like some outcast lot headed somewhere they may not be able to stay."

"I know, honey. We won't likely know anything right away, but I'll start with Vlad and Lonnie."

* * * *

Beatrice called David up to her home. "Sit down, my sweet boy," she said. David used to hate when she did that, but now he understood it made her happy.

"There are three more vacant houses left on our new property lines, is that correct, David?"

"Yes, ma'am. That is right."

"I want you to take your wife-to-be and daughters to each one after lunch and let them choose.

I will not have my granddaughters sleeping one more night in a tent."

"I can do that, Mom, but I'll need to talk to Tina about it first."

"I already have," she replied, smiling. "Vlad can take your room here and stay with Mark and me until we figure out what to do with the other homes."

"Yes, ma'am," he agreed, realizing there was no point in discussing it any further.

"And son," she called out as David was exiting the front door. "Tina is waiting for you to come up with a wedding date. Let me know soon, so I don't have to pick one for you!"

David laughed. "I love you too, Mom—still just as feisty after all these years."

With David closing the front door, Beatrice looked up to the ceiling. "Did you hear that, my love? Our son thinks I'm still feisty!"

* * * *

Mike resumed swim lessons today, with the children excited, having missed a day of instruction.

Beatrice swam again, but this time without assistance.

Taking Tina by the hand, David's new family toured their home choices.

"Do you remember that show 'House Hunters?'" asked Tina. "Where they are shown three houses but have already agreed to make an offer on one of them?"

"Yeah," replied David. "I loved the international ones."

"There were a few off-the-grid episodes," she continued, "and this is exactly what we're doing today... I've never lived in a home before, only apartments," she added. "Us too," chimed in Veronica.

"Well, then, since all three homes are sound and well within our perimeter, I'm not even going to give an opinion. Since this will be the first home for all of you, you all decide which one you like and we will take it," said David.

"Yay!" came the screams of two delighted girls.

Tina let the girls make their final decision and weren't surprised they picked the closest one to "Grammy's" house, as they were now calling Beatrice. It had been a summer home, with David knowing the owners lived in South Carolina during the winter months.

He relayed that information to a concerned Tina, wondering if they would be back soon to occupy the house. "If they make it back, which unfortunately I doubt, we will just move into another," said David.

"Nobody really owns property anymore, but any former house owners who return to this area will be given their home back on the spot," he assured her. "The former owners of this property had a boy and a girl," he added. "With three bedrooms, the girls can decide if they want to share a room or not."

Suzie immediately demanded to room with her big sister, upon hearing the choices.

David laughed, adding, "Then I guess we will have an extra playroom!"

His mother's words about the wedding date ran through his head like a television jingle: *Two all-beef patties, special sauce, lettuce, cheese, pickles, onions on a sesame seed bun*, was the one he remembered word for word but hadn't heard since he was a child.

Lord, if you could find me just one Big Mac™, I would be forever grateful, he thought, smiling at the impossibility.

Pulling Tina aside, he said to her, "It may be some time before things around here are this peaceful again. I would like to marry you while the other group is here, so I can have two best men in Lance and Mel, and I'm guessing you would like Nancy as your maid of honor?"

"If I could have two, yes, Nancy would be my first choice, but I would ask Joy as well, since we have grown close over the past few weeks."

"Of course, you can have two; it's a new-world with new rules."

"Yes, it is," she replied, "but I have to demand that one old rule remain. You boys stay completely out of the preparations and let us qualified women handle all the details."

"Just tell me when to show up and what to wear," he said, kissing her softly.

"Let's go, girls!" she called. "We have a wedding to plan! Out of my way, my handsome logger," she quipped, pretending to shove him aside.

* * * *

It took about an hour for the entire camp to hear about the wedding.

"Did you give him a nudge, Beatrice?" asked Tina.

"Why, I am not sure what you mean!" she replied, with a wink.

"Would you honor me, Tina, and wear my wedding dress? I had it professionally packed over 40 years ago, and I'm sure we can alter it as needed. I hope it's still OK."

"It would be an honor," replied Tina, with tears in her eyes.

It was decided the ceremony would be the next Saturday at noon. David informed me of my co-best man position.

"Thank you, my friend," I told him, adding, "I booked you two into the FEMA camp for your honeymoon!"

"Ha-ha, not a chance!" David replied.

"They have decent food, hot showers, and boxing," I added.

"Maybe my mom would keep our girls for the night. We'll figure it out, one way or another," said David.

* * * * * * *

Chapter Eighteen ~ Saddle Ranch~Loveland, Colorado

"What's going on?" asked Cory.

"I don't know," replied Mac. "It's Sarah. She said I need to come down right away, and now she won't respond to my radio. I'm not sure if it's something personal or not, but I figured I would grab you, just in case it's something I need help with."

"It's probably that Ralph guy, back for more drama," said Cory.

"We'll see," replied Mac, nervous that it could be something between him and Sarah.

* * * *

"I'm guessing she's at the hospital," he said, pulling up and asking Cory to wait outside.

Sarah met him in the empty lobby, and her face said it all.

"What's happened?" asked Mac.

She paused, searching for the right words. She had given bad news to countless families in her residency program, but they were strangers...and somehow, this was different.

"It's Jimmy..." she finally said quietly. Pausing again, she continued: "He's had another stroke, and it's bad."

"How bad? I mean, is he...is he dead?"

"He's in a coma," replied Sarah, "and not breathing on his own."

"Can't you fix him?" Mac asked. The question sounded childish to him as he said it. "What I mean is, does he even have a chance?"

"There's always a chance," she replied, "as long as there is a heartbeat, but it doesn't look good.

We have done all we can do for now, and it's really in God's hands."

"Why is this happening?" asked a distraught Mac. "I mean, what did he do to deserve this? He's a good person and... Oh, no honey," he added, seeing the look on Sarah's face. "I didn't mean to..."

"Excuse me," she said abruptly, walking into the back of the hospital.

"I messed up bad," said Mac to Cory, once outside.

Relating what he knew about Jimmy, he told Cory that he forgot for a second about Sarah's parents and her sister being killed.

"I insinuated that good people don't die," and I just wasn't thinking.

"I'm sorry," replied Cory, putting a hand on Mac's shoulder, "about all of it."

* * * *

Mac took an hour, riding his four-wheeler on Green Mountain, to clear his head.

Running into the Miller boy out for a hunt, he stopped to talk. It seemed odd to both that they could be conversing normally so soon after a major family feud.

When asked what he was up to, Mac replied with just enough information as he was comfortable sharing, keeping it to putting his foot in his mouth with his girlfriend.

"So, where are they?" asked the Miller boy.

"Where is who?" replied Mac.

"I was referring to the apology flowers. You've been riding up on this mountain for nearly an hour, and you don't have even one."

Mac laughed, adding, "I'm sorry, but I was not expecting that out of your mouth."

"No apology needed. I'm complicated, just like you. Now follow me, and we will get you back on her good side."

Mac, exiting his four-wheeler and concealing it in some bushes, cautiously followed the boy into the woods.

"This is a popular deer trail," the Miller boy called to Mac, winding his way through the dense trees and brush. Mac had a flash of being ambushed or caught in a snare as an insult to his guard being down.

"I've got to head back in a few," Mac called out, tightening his grip on his AR rifle, as the boy stopped just ahead.

"Well, then it's a good thing we're here," the boy replied, without turning around.

Mac paused, not taking another step, cautiously scanning his surroundings. He listened, only hearing the wind in the trees and birds chirping.

"Are you coming?" the Miller boy asked, now turning around. "We're OK, you know, you and me," he added. "Come look at these flowers."

Mac made his way to the end of the wooded section, opening into a small field he hadn't seen before.

"Columbine," remarked the boy. "Not the tragic school in the news but the original Colorado State flower," he added, waving his arm around a field full of them.

"The state says you can't uproot them, but the picking fine is variable. I heard the penalty for picking them off private property was a fine ranging from $5 to $50—not that it matters much now. There are more than a few varieties here, with mixed colors that I'm sure your girl will like, Mac."

"I think you're right, son," Mac replied, easing his shoulders just a bit. His rifle, now slung across his back, told of the change in his guard.

He resisted the urge to update the Miller boy on Jimmy's condition, as it was now a past issue.

An eye for an eye, thought Mac, but this time the blame was squarely on him.

Gathering an impressive bouquet, he thanked the boy for his help and headed back to the hospital with a clearer head.

* * * * * * *

Chapter Nineteen ~ Saddle Ranch~ Loveland, Colorado

S arah met him out front, with a neutral tone.

She brightened a bit upon seeing the flowers, and his apology was sincere, reminding her of why she picked him in the first place.

"We're good, my love," she whispered, "and I'm sorry about your friend."

"Is there any change?" Mac asked.

"No. He is the same. Now go and work on other things," she told him.

* * * *

Mac found Bill and they met at John's house. Cory had already filled them in, and Mac was happy not to have to retell the story.

"We're sorry," stated John, "about Jimmy. He's a good man and an asset to our security team.

If he can recover from this, we will care for him as needed; you have my word on that, Mac."

"Thank you, John. "That means a great deal to me. It was all so sudden is all. One minute he is talking and it looks like he will recover with minimal problems, and the next minute he may die."

"I know, Mac," added Bill. "It doesn't make it any easier, but we saw that a lot in Vietnam after a soldier was injured. You just can't be sure how it's going to go until they are up and walking around."

"It's not your fault, you know. Mrs. Miller started this whole mess, and you were the fall guy," added Cory.

"I know," replied Mac, "but it just doesn't seem right is all. It's on me, and I'm still standing while two others are not."

* * * *

Mac took dinner with Bo and spoke with Sarah before bed. He felt better about everything and prayed for his friend.

He remembered his mother telling him to be thankful at the beginning of prayer, before asking for something.

He was thankful for Sarah, Cory and his security team, as well as John, Bill, Sharon, Samuel, and the council for their support.

He then prayed for Jimmy to be healed or taken home quickly. His prayers were answered at 3 a.m. with a radio call from Sarah.

"We did everything we could," she told him. "Jimmy has passed to the other side. It was peaceful, Mac, and I held his hand in those final moments."

Tears ran down his cheeks for the first time he could recall since his dad left him and his mother.

He hadn't known Jimmy long but he was a friend, and Mac never had many of those.

Thanking her for the call, Mac chose to inform Bill and John at a more civilized hour.

* * * *

News traveled fast in both communities about Jimmy, and the funeral service was planned for the following day.

At the service, each person had an opportunity to tell a lighthearted story about Jimmy.

Mac would tell of his first meeting, talking about the fight club he ran in Fort Collins and how he singlehandedly turned a deadly situation into a positive one.

His four-wheeler would be given to Cory, with the gas cap engraved to read "Jimmy."

It was a somber morning, as they lay Jimmy to rest in the Ranch Cemetery.

"He is in good company," Mac told Sarah and Cory, pointing out a few of the headstones of past leaders and prominent community members.

The service was short, as would be the norm from here on. Mac and a few others said nice things about him, with none knowing him for a long time.

* * * *

Mac had dinner with a refreshed Sarah, after a full day off and nearly seven hours of sleep. They talked of his friend and dreamed of the future.

"I feel different, Mac," she said cautiously.

"Me, too," he replied.

"No, I mean different—like my stomach is upset and my breasts are tender."

"I'm sorry you're under the weather," Mac replied.

"Mac, you know I'm a doctor and I've performed births, right?"

"Yes, of course," he replied.

"Then you can imagine I might know what the very early signs of pregnancy may be," she added.

He paused, thinking for a minute before responding. He wanted to be very careful about what came out of his mouth next.

"Just so you know," she added, breaking the tension, "Bradley and I had not been together in a long time before he left for the mountains."

Mac sighed, relieved about his worst fear.

"And we barely spoke when he returned," she added.

"So, I mean...you think you could be...?"

"I don't know anything yet; it's too soon," Sarah replied. "All I know is I feel different somehow, and I have a couple of signs of early pregnancy."

Mac grinned, as a child might when opening a coveted present at Christmas.

"So...you're happy...I mean, if it's true?" she asked.

"Yes!" he exclaimed. "Yes, I would be the happiest man in this world, however many there are of us now."

"Good," she replied simply. "I think you would make an excellent daddy to a little girl or boy.

"We shall wait and see. I'll know for sure in the next few weeks, I hope," Sarah said, with a glow that told him to get ready.

* * * * * * *

Chapter Twenty ~ Saddle Ranch ~ Loveland, Colorado

Cory got Mac back on track with security training, stating it's what Jimmy would want.

The afternoon was back to work, with Cory's old officers returning with their families.

"It's time for the trials," announced Cory, feeling confident his old officers would easily make the cut.

All those trying out for a spot on the team lined up single file and ran through the same drills that Cory and his team had tested on year-in and year-out.

For a number, it was hard and knocked out nearly one-third of the applicants previously on the security team.

The Miller boy, and even Cory's son, Cameron, earned a place on the team, each having outscored many of the applicants.

A few new ones stepped up after hearing they may be able to switch their jobs in housekeeping and gardening to join the security team.

"This is what we've been talking about," said Cory to Mac. "A group of people who really want to be in security and will take it very seriously."

"I see what you mean," replied Mac, impressed with Cory's idea coming to fruition.

John and Bill met with the council, and it was decided that the security hierarchy would remain unchanged after Jimmy's passing, with Mac as the lead and Cory next in line.

* * * *

"Mac," came the call on the radio. "Can you and Cory come down to the southern barricade?"

"Sure. What's going on?" asked Mac.

"It's that Ralph guy. He's back and waiving a gun around."

"This guy is getting to be a problem," Mac told Cory. "The last thing I need is him hearing about Rico and Patty."

Two shots came from the south, followed by three more, seemingly all at once.

"What's happening?" yelled Mac, already headed down with Cory on the four-wheelers.

"I'm sorry, boss," came the reply. "He just opened fire on us, and we had no choice."

"Is he dead?" asked Cory on his radio.

"No. He's down but not dead. What should we do?"

"Just hold tight," said Mac, "and don't fire again unless he does."

A radio call to Sarah had her on the way. With a hospital now empty of patients, she was able to bring one of the new doctors with her. Samuel drove the truck.

"What have we got?" asked Sarah to one of Samuel's border guards.

"Yes, Dr. Melton," he replied. "We have a single male down, hit twice, I think, but that's all I know."

"OK, let's go," Sarah told the other doctor, heading in Ralph's direction.

"Not so fast, Docs," said Mac, blocking them with his arm. "The man is armed, and I can't let you near him until we know it's safe."

"He's already fired on our men," added Cory.

"So, we just let him bleed out?" asked the new doctor, seeming annoyed.

"I'm not saying that," replied Mac. "But he is lowest on my people list to be concerned about right now, so we take it real slow and wait until I'm sure you're safe."

Mac and Cory approached the downed Ralph cautiously, weapons at the ready.

Mac talked calmly as they approached, giving him clear instructions to keep from being shot again.

"Where are you hit, Ralph?" Mac asked.

"In the stomach and the leg, I think," he replied, with labored breath.

"We're going to get you help, but I need to know two things first.

"One: where are your weapons? You will only get one chance at this, so be careful.

"And two: why do we keep doing this? I let you go last time, thinking you would move on down the road and not return.

"Where are your weapons, Ralph?"

"Here," he replied, pointing to a revolver on the ground and a knife he tossed in front of him, taking it from his back pocket.

"OK, that's good. And why are you back here?"

"I came for my wife," he groaned, not able to stand. "Now help me!" he demanded.

"Hang tight, Ralph, and no sudden moves," Mac told him.

Talking quietly with Cory, it was obvious to them both that Ralph had not even mentioned his boy.

"What's the call?" asked Cory.

"It's not ours, but Samuel's," replied Mac, "since Ralph would end up in his hospital."

Mac pulled Sarah and Samuel aside to discuss the next step.

"It's your call, Samuel," said Mac, "as he would likely spend time in your hospital."

"Please give us a minute, Mac," said Samuel, pulling Sarah aside.

"It falls on me to make sure our group is safe and all can sleep well at night. Your job, Sarah, is to do your best to heal the sick with the best tools you have available at the time. We will not have the hospital available for this man," he told her.

"I have spoken to his wife and son, and I recently made the decision to remove him from the property. I will not be bringing him back. You and our new doctor have my approval to treat him here as best you can, and that is all. Do you understand?"

"Yes, father. I understand," said Sarah to Samuel.

Sarah grabbed her medical bag, along with the other doctor, and approached behind Mac and Cory.

"Ralph," said Mac, "our doctors are going to take a look at you now."

"Just get me to your damn hospital," he spat.

"The hospital is not available," replied Sarah, still standing behind Mac.

"What do you mean it's not available, you poor excuse for a doctor?!" he yelled.

"What she means," said Mac, feeling flushed and now completely done with this guy, "is that the hospital is not available to you, and now neither is she," he added, pointing to her walking back towards the security barrier.

"Looks to me, Ralph, like you have one last option," pointing to the new doctor. "And if you insult him, then I'm sure you're on your own."

"Cory, can you stay?" asked Mac.

"Sure, I've got this."

Mac walked back to an upset Sarah talking quietly with Samuel.

"I'm sorry about that," Mac told her.

"It's not your fault, Mac," Sarah replied. "That man is just plain no good. I'm glad to see Patty and her son away from him and moving forward with their lives. What a nightmare it must have been being married to that awful man."

"Rico is ten times the man Ralph is," replied Mac, getting a look from Samuel.

"Is there something I should know here?" he asked, looking at both Sarah and Mac.

"Yes, father. Please take me home, and I'll tell you on the way."

She hung back, as Samuel headed for his truck.

"Nice job," she told Mac, punching him lightly on the shoulder but smiling. "You're going to owe me for this one."

"What did I say?" asked Mac.

"It was hard enough getting one group crossover relationship approved, and now there may be another. Don't worry; I'll take care of it. And Mac," she said, followed by a long pause, "don't let me see that son of a bitch Ralph ever again!"

"Yes, ma'am. That I can surely do," he replied.

* * * * * * *

Chapter Twenty-one ~ Saddle Ranch~ Loveland, Colorado

Mac, heading back up the road, was updated by Cory.

"The doc is taking a look at him as best he can out here. He's insulted the good doctor here twice already, but the doc is still trying to help," said Cory, shaking his head in disbelief.

"Well, I'm done with him is all I know," replied Mac. "Looks like he brought a few friends," he continued, looking down the road, "but at least they are keeping their distance."

"Can you finish up here, Cory, and let me know when it's done? I need to check up on Sarah and should give the generators at the hospital a tune-up while I'm there. Let's get the new security team together for job duties first thing after breakfast tomorrow."

"Sure thing," Cory replied. "I've got this, and I'll let you know when it's done or when the doc here gets tired of helping."

* * * *

Does every day have to be so complicated? Mac thought, riding to The West hospital. *Can't we have just one day to be bored to death?*

He recalled his first few months here on Saddle Ranch, while dating the girl he found hitchhiking from Montana. On their days off, they would explore the Colorado mountains, hiking most weekends with his dog, Bo. He didn't miss her since he met Sarah, but he did miss having an entire day with no violence or drama of any kind—just the wind in the trees and the often-found hidden stream or small lake that most on this earth would never see.

* * * *

Sarah relayed what she knew about Rico and Patty to Samuel on the short drive back.

"It's too quiet in here," said Sarah, entering the hospital with Samuel. "So, I just wait for someone to get sick or hurt?"

"No, it doesn't always have to be that way," said her father. "I believe you have another birth on the way from one of the Ranch mothers-to-be."

"That's right," said Sarah, realizing that she was so caught up in the situation with Bradley, and then Jimmy, that she had put the expectant mother to the back of her mind.

"I didn't abandon her, you know," she told him. "She's had the nurses at the Ranch keeping an eye on her."

"I was not suggesting that," Samuel replied. "I only mentioned it as a positive reason to get the hospital ready."

She smiled, hugging him, whispering, "I love you, father, and always will."

* * * *

The doctor patched up Ralph as best he could, and the small entourage carried him off down the road.

"Is he going to make it?" Cory asked the doctor.

"A few weeks ago, absolutely he would, but now I wouldn't place a bet on it either way."

"We're done down here, Mac" called Cory on the radio. "He's patched up as good as the doc could do, and his friends took him away."

"What are his chances?" asked Mac, not caring much about the answer.

"Fifty percent either way, according to the doc. Can I help with anything else this afternoon?" asked Cory.

"Just let the new security team know we will meet after breakfast. Then spend some time with your boy. And Cory, I was real proud of your son today. He stepped up and earned his spot on the team."

"Thank you, Mac. That means a lot coming from you."

* * * *

Mac left the southern barrier as the guards were being switched out for the week.

He wondered if any of them would be better suited on his team.

Sarah walked the Ranch freely, as all seemed to do. Gone were the days of an invite into either property for the right people.

She checked in on the pregnant woman, who was officially due in 22 days.

"It could be right on time, sooner or later, she told her, and your little girls will be here with us. It will most likely be early, though, with twins."

Sarah was a little nervous about the birth. She had delivered multiple singles over her career, but never twins. She would not relay her concerns to the expectant mother but would get a plan together with the two new doctors, with only one of them having limited experience in births.

"You can stay here until you start having contractions. In the old-world, you could wait until they were maybe three to five minutes apart and lasting 45 to 60 seconds each, but now I want to see you at the hospital after they start. We will transfer you to our hospital when I think you are ready. Sound good?"

"Yes, Doctor. That sounds wonderful," the new mother replied. "I'm just glad I'm not out in the bush or walking down a deserted highway!" she added. "How do I pay you? I mean for your doctoring services."

Sarah paused, as even now it was a legitimate question. "This one is on my father, Samuel," she replied, with a wink.

* * * *

Sarah met up with Mac, this time opting for dinner and a stayover for the first time at his place.

"This cabin is tiny," she joked, having never been in it before.

"It's more of a chalet," he said, with a jokingly fancy tone.

"I just hope there's enough room for Bo and us in here," she joked.

"There is always room, my dear," he replied.

They reminisced about the happenings from the time they first met, tending to a wounded John until now, leaving out the part about Bradley.

He told her of the Miller boy and the flowers. "I knew you didn't think of that all on your own," she teased, punching him lightly on the shoulder. "Who knew the Miller kid was such a lady's man?" she added.

"He's complicated," Mac replied, "but he's still not staying here on the property."

She didn't care to talk about Ralph, now or ever again, but they discussed Rico and Patty's budding relationship at length.

"Now, can we talk about guns and ammo, or hunting and fishing?" Mac asked, only half-joking.

"I'm not sure about hunting, but I will fish you under the table, Mac."

"Is that so?" he replied, playing along.

"It is, and I'll challenge you tomorrow...unless you have something better to do," she added.

"I've got security training until early afternoon, but after that, you're on."

"Three p.m., up at the canal, and I'll even give you first choice of spots," she bantered.

How great is my girl? he thought, drifting off to sleep.

They were awakened by Bo at sunup, pushing his dog bowl around the hardwood floor. "Clang! Clang!" was heard, as he flipped it into the air with his nose.

"A couple more weeks, my friend, and we will be completely out of dog food around here. After that, it's table scraps," Mac told this furry friend.

Bo barked and pushed his bowl toward Mac, getting a laugh out of both the humans.

* * * *

Training this day was different, both Mac and Cory noticed. All took it seriously, and each stood out with their various talents.

"We've got a good group of men and women here," pointed out Mac. "You up for a midnight security check with me, Cory?"

"Absolutely," he replied.

Mac checked his watch, one of the few from the Faraday cage. It read 2:45 as he grabbed his lucky pole.

"Time to show the ladies how men fish!" he told Cory.

"I have got to see this!" Cory replied, dismissing the trainees, pending their upcoming shifts.

* * * * * * *

CHAPTER TWENTY-TWO ~ SADDLE RANCH ~ LOVELAND, COLORADO

M ac and Cory arrived with Bo to see Sarah and Samuel at the ready.

"Good luck, son," said Samuel. "She's been fishing since she was five."

"I'm from Montana, sir, and it's practically a requirement for kids to learn, so I'm ready," replied Mac.

Mac picked his spot, having fished it many times before.

There was a monster (at least for this canal) rainbow trout at nearly five pounds somewhere down below that he had seen pictures of Lance catching and releasing nearly 30 years ago. It had been caught several more times since then, and released, in hopes of another great fish story.

Mac wondered how long a trout could live, since the last sighting was nearly ten years ago. He asked Cory if he knew.

"I know the answer on this one," replied Cory, and unless your fish is supernatural, it's not the same one from before. They live about seven years, and up to eleven occasionally. So, your monster is a great-grandchild of the one Lance caught back in the day. If there's even one in there anymore!"

"There's fish in here for sure!" replied Mac.

"Let's go, tough guy," Sarah taunted. "Pick your spot and the one with the most pounds of fish in one hour wins."

Mac picked his favorite spot at the front of the underground siphon, leaving her to fish the back end.

The canal was full of rushing water 15 feet deep year-round, only slowing to a crawl twice a year during scheduled maintenance and repair, regulated by the Parks and Recreation Department.

Since it last happened, the level remained steady with a strong current, Mac had observed.

Every few hundred yards, the canal ran underground for 500 feet into what was called a siphon, covered by the dirt road and providing the best fishing spots on either end.

Mac put two salmon eggs on his hook, grinning with the thought of his first catch. "You ready, Bo?" he asked, patting his trusted friend on the head. Bo barked once, focusing intently on the line to be slung.

Casting into the opening of the canal where it started to go underground, he let the line sink halfway to the bottom. His pole jerked with the current, pulling the bait under quickly.

"It looks like you've got one on the line!" said Cory.

"Not yet," Mac replied. "It's just a fast current under the surface. The big guys are right down there at the midpoint.

Five long minutes later, Mac got a small bite but couldn't hook it.

"What's she doing over there?" asked Cory, pointing to Sarah in a flowing red summer dress, *probably just to tease Mac about fishing gender roles*, he thought.

Sarah was walking through the tall grass, waving her arms, moving the blades side-to-side. "She hasn't even put her pole in the water," commented Mac. "This will be easier than I thought."

Walking to the edge of the canal, Sarah threw something into the water. Mac couldn't see the juicy green grasshopper, as it was immediately taken by a large fish.

"Just a few more samples and we will be in the fish," said Samuel, excited for the next part.

"I call it the Costco phenomenon," she told him. "Give them just a small taste, and they will fill their carts or, in this case, their fish stomachs."

"I loved those free samples," replied Samuel, "but I always spent more money than I intended to."

"Exactly," Sarah replied.

Mac hooked into a medium-sized fish and made a loud announcement: "Fish on! The first one of the day!" he added, so all could hear.

"I'm sure he's a good fisherman, but this here fishin' hole ain't Montana," said Samuel.

Sarah loved it when her father threw in some good country slang every now and then. "No, it's not, father," she said. "I'll bet he thinks I'm throwing rocks in here."

Fifteen minutes later, Mac pulled up fish number two.

"About a two-pounder!" Cory said. "Nice fish."

Mac was happy to be in the lead, since he felt this was one of his God-given talents.

He was curious why, after almost half the time had slipped away—25 minutes to be exact—Sarah still hadn't put a pole in the water. He was starting to feel bad about the gloating and thought about calling the whole thing off.

"Are you ready to forfeit the competition?" called Sarah loudly. "You're not in Montana anymore," she quipped.

"I'm up to two to none," he said. "You can take the boy out of Montana, but you can't take fishing out of me," he called back, hooking into another good-sized fish.

"Got a big one on the line," he called to Cory, as the monster fish zigzagged back and forth across the narrow canal. He fought to keep the fish towards one side. "That's it, big guy. Stay right there," he said, as the fish seemed to be resting on the side.

Mac kept the line tight and made his way slowly down the metal ladder on the side of the canal wall.

"No, no, no!" he called out, as the fish jerked into the middle of the flowing water, zinging his line in a high-pitched test of his drag tension.

"What's the problem?" asked Cory.

"He's tangled up in the chains!"

The chains he referred to were a series of one-inch link chains spanning the mouth of the canal, just before it went underground. They hung into the rushing water, flowing freely side-to-side. The ten chains across were suspended by a single cable spanning across the top of the cement canal.

Nobody knew exactly why those chains were there, but it was thought that they might be the last line of defense before someone falling into the canal went underground and caught the blades that every kid thought were there to break up ice chunks in the winter months as they headed underground.

There were stories of the canal occasionally drying up entirely, allowing someone to walk all the way through, keeping the scary stories of the ominous blades alive and well.

Rumors of an occasional mountain-bike mishap or a curious child falling into the canal over the years kept a healthy fear in most residents' minds. A small metal ladder, having each rung secured to the cement sides, ran down to the water's edge.

"Gotta let that one go," called out Cory. "He's tangled up good."

"I'm pretty sure I can reach him," called Mac, stretching farther than he was comfortable going.

"Almost got it untangled," he called, as he held on with two fingers to the metal step.

"Fish on!" yelled Samuel, distracting Mac enough to lose his grip. Plunging into the cold water, Mac held on to his pole.

"Grab the chain!" Cory shouted, rushing towards the ladder.

Without losing his pole, Mac swung his left arm wildly to grab a chain moving freely in the water. The current sucked his legs towards the underground blades, and everything slowed down.

Cory yelled, "Drop your pole and grab the other chain!"

No longer panicked, Mac couldn't hear Cory's yelling, but clearly saw his mouth moving.

His grip on the chain was weakening as the current pulled his work boots towards the underground grave. Looking down, he saw his fish caught up in the chain next to him. Mac dropped his favorite pole, letting the current rip it away.

Lunging forward, he grabbed the other slippery chain with his right arm. It seemed to help at first, but his hands slipped slowly towards the end of each chain, link by link.

Memories of his mother, friends from school, old relatives, and new friends flashed through his mind. Sarah and Bo were front and center in the visions.

Cory quickly descended the metal rung ladder, reaching an arm out, but he was two feet short.

Bo ran back and forth across the top of the road, barking and looking at Mac.

Sarah was now at a full run, hearing Cory yelling instructions, followed by a slower Samuel.

Stopping just above the rail, she saw him stretched out, as if he was laying on his stomach feet towards the underground.

He looked at her and said, "I'm in love with you, Sarah," losing his grip on the chains and disappearing underground.

"No!" she screamed, echoing off of the mountain. "No Mac! No." Her love was gone, swept away to the depths of the earth.

Cory doubled over, holding his stomach, wishing he had been only a little closer. Bo ran this way and that, barking frantically, with Samuel saying a prayer for both Mac and Sarah.

Seconds turned into a minute, then two, as the three were frozen. Sarah collapsed on to the ground, praying for some sort of miracle.

All was silent, with the exception of the tangled fish slapping its tail on top of the water and Bo's barks getting further away.

"He's tracking him," Cory pointed to the dog, nose to the ground and headed towards the other end of the siphon.

"I hear something," said Samuel, looking to where his daughter had been fishing at the end of the underground lair.

"It sounds like coughing!" replied Cory, with all three running towards the sound, following Bo's lead.

"It's him! It's him!" cried Sarah, seeing a figure balled up and clinging to the ladder at her fishing spot.

Mac's coughing was hoarse and deep.

Cory called a few of the security team to "bring a truck on the double!" It took all three witnesses to bring a half-conscious Mac up the ladder and back on to the road.

Sarah turned his head to the right side. He was conscious and breathing but did not speak. He was only staring straight ahead without expression.

"Let's get him to the hospital *now*," commanded Sarah to the men who brought the waiting truck.

Samuel drove, with Sarah and Mac in the bed. "Hold on, my strong man. I love you, too."

Cory had a slew of questions about the happenings from the security team dropping off the truck.

"He's in good hands now, and we will discuss this later," is all he said.

Hanging back, Cory worked on a surprise for Mac, hoping he was going to recover.

Sarah radioed the other doctors at the hospital to be ready for an incoming.

"This one is a VIP to me," she called over the radio, realizing immediately how that may sound. She thought about toning it down and continued, following a self-pep talk. "F-it," she told herself. "This man is mine!"

"All hands on deck in five," she called out with confidence, getting a smile out of a still concerned Samuel.

Just over five minutes later, they sped into the hospital parking lot. Sarah, with the other two physicians, unloaded a groggy patient.

"Let's get him in quickly, and everyone else out," she commanded, with an apologetic look towards her father.

Samuel nodded his head, signifying a respectful agreement of her terms.

* * * * * * *

CHAPTER TWENTY-THREE ~ SADDLE RANCH ~ LOVELAND, COLORADO

Cory, feeling helpless and completely out of his element as the man who always has the answer, vowed to catch Mac's fish.

Using Sarah's pole that she had left at the canal, he hooked the fish in the mouth after several tries. Rigging his open pocketknife to a long skinny tree branch, he carefully maneuvered it to cut the old line, freeing the fish from the initial snag but remaining captive on the new pole.

Mac was right. This fish was a monster, once raised over the top ledge and on to the hard ground.

"It's Lance's fish's children's, children's, children!" he said aloud.

He radioed Sarah for an update, but none came.

* * * *

"I need your help, Rico," said Cory, relaying the story of Mac and the fish. "Mac trusts you to keep things confidential—correct?"

"Absolutely," replied the chef, floating on a budding-relationship high.

"Can we keep him on ice for a day or two, and then serve him up to Mac? Assuming he is all better, of course."

"We can do just that, and I know he will be back soon. He's as tough as well-done steak."

* * * *

Sarah stabilized her patient and vowed not to leave his side for the night. Confirming his vitals were OK, she let him sleep, switching off with the other doctors for 24-hour surveillance. She slept for short intervals but would not leave his side.

The morning offered renewed hope, with Mac talking and asking what happened yesterday. Sarah told him small pieces at first.

"I remember putting my pole in the water and catching a fish," Mac said, "while you threw rocks in on your side."

"Is that so?" she asked, relieved to have him talking. "Have you seen those fishing shows where they chum for shark?"

"Yes, I have," Mac replied.

"Well, then you know the way to catch a shark is to give them a small taste of what they want—right?" Sarah continued.

"Yes, that sounds right," he responded.

"I basically chum the water in the summer months with their natural food source—grasshoppers. After a few of those, these fish will immediately hit anything that touches the surface of the water."

"So, you were about to smoke me in the last half of the competition?" Mac questioned her.

"I don't know," she replied. "But from now on, I will only fish with you."

Samuel stopped by early and was relieved to see Mac talking and alive. Pulling Sarah aside, he told her he needed an update for John and Bill on the recovery.

"He has some temporary memory loss about what happened, but it's probably PTSD."

"Is it serious?" Samuel asked.

"It can be," she replied. "Think of it like a soldier returning from active duty in a war zone or hostile environment. They may end up with several, or even dozens, of situations such as Mac has gone through, and their PTSD can last months or years, and can also be permanent. Mac's should be temporary as his mind deals with what happened; he will likely recall everything in the next few days."

"That's good to hear. Are you going to ask for a rematch? You do love to fish, Sarah."

"No, father. I *like* to fish. Mac *loves* to fish, and that's what matters to me, so I'll only be fishing with him from now on. Plus, I already told him my secret," she added.

Samuel relayed the good news to Bill and Cory, standing just outside the hospital. John was there as well, surprising Samuel. Still in his wheelchair, John was walking more unassisted each day.

"You didn't have to come down here," Samuel told John.

"I know, but I wanted to check on Mac and get out of the house for some fresh air."

"Would you like to join me for breakfast, old friend?" asked Samuel. "Patty makes a mean omelet. Plus, I have some things to discuss."

"Sounds great," replied John, asking Bill and Cory if they could return later to pick him up.

* * * *

The West's kitchen and eating facilities were much smaller than the Ranch's.

John was introduced to Patty, who was working the morning shift, and Samuel asked if she could please make them each The Special. "Please 86 the shrooms on John's, though."

"Yes, sir, two Specials coming up," she replied, with a smile, disappearing back into the kitchen.

"What's 'The Special'?" asked John, "and is the number 86 something I should know about?"

"I'll let Patty tell you what's in The Special, but 86 just means to cut something out. In your case, it's the mushrooms, since I know you don't like them," replied Samuel.

"Back in the 1930s, it's said that bars would use 86 as a code to get rid of a drunk or someone getting rowdy. It spilled over into restaurant lingo and is still used today, only now it's to cut an item or signify when the restaurant is out of something."

"Patty is the one with the boy and that Ralph guy as the ex, right?" asked John.

"Yes, she is, and she is thriving now. I had no idea she was a highly rated chef when I asked her if she wanted to stay, but I'm not complaining about it either. That leads me to the first topic I wanted to discuss with you," Samuel added. "It seems our two chefs have started somewhat of a crossover relationship, like we saw with our Sarah and your Mac. I suppose it won't be the last, now that our groups are intermingling more."

"Do you mean Rico?" asked John. "I thought he was gay!"

"I don't think so," Samuel replied. "I mean, they seem to like each other is what I hear from Sarah."

"I'll talk with Rico," said John, "and see what his intentions are."

"I'm glad we have known each other for so long," said Samuel. "If it were anyone else leading your group, I might be concerned about them trying to lure key members away from our side. We will just need to take each one as they come and make sure it's not distracting from our work. Few things are worse than a hard breakup in these tight quarters, except maybe for infidelity that may require our direct intervention, should it come up."

"Two Specials, gentlemen," said Patty, smiling.

"Wow!" stated John. "That omelet looks incredible! What's in it?"

"I call it my City Slicker Cowboy Smothered Omelet. Inside three extra-large, free-range, no-antibiotics eggs sits six ounces of grass-fed (also free-range) porterhouse steak, cooked medium and diced. Hand-churned butter and homemade cheese sits on the innermost layer, surrounded by sautéed onions and bell peppers—organically grown, of course.

The entire gutbuster comes obnoxiously smothered with a killer chunky ranchero sauce recipe, passed around Northern California gypsy camps in the early to mid-1970s."

"I'm not sure if you're joking," said John, "or just poking some fun at the fancy Starbucks crowd of days gone by. But I, for one, think it sounds great!"

Looking at the huge omelet in front of him, covered in thick sauce, he thought it must all be true.

"You've had one of these before?" he asked Samuel.

"Yes, this will be my third. But I'm going to limit myself to one per week, just so I have a better chance of staving off a massive coronary."

"I would say that's a good idea," John replied, thanking Patty.

John took a sip of his water and started to tell Samuel he had something to discuss, as he caught a smiling Patty standing right where she had been.

"Thank you again," he said. "I'm sure it's delicious."

Samuel laughed. "I did the same thing the first time, but Patty is not like our other chefs here. She will wait until you try it and give her your honest feedback."

"OK," said John, cutting into his first bite. "No mushrooms, right?"

"No, sir, not on yours."

John paused after taking a bite, carefully considering each flavor.

"Hmm," he finally said. "You say you have had this before, right?" looking at Samuel.

"Yes, a couple of times, to be exact," Samuel replied. "Do you not like it?"

"No, it's not that. I'm only wondering how I have never had something this good for breakfast before!"

Patty smiled as John thanked her for the best breakfast he had ever had, pre- or post-Apocalypse.

"I'm telling you, her cooking is going to send me to an early grave," Samuel replied, chuckling.

They spent the next hour discussing what John had learned from Lance about the Topeka group and how close they may come to the Valley.

"Either way, they will be permanently residing less than 15 miles from this very spot soon, and eventually it could be a problem," John added.

Mac was talking more each hour and remembering his ordeal much more clearly now. Sarah made a hospital exception and allowed Bo inside for just a few minutes to check on his dad.

Mac petted Bo, thanking him for sticking close all these years.

"Where's my pole?" he asked abruptly. "I let it go when I grabbed the other chain."

"I'm not sure," she replied. "I'll have Cory take a look downstream and see if it popped out."

"They're right," said Mac. "They're right."

"Who's right and about what?" asked Sarah.

"The kids always said there were huge blades at the very bottom of the siphon to cut large chunks of ice. The blades are real. I saw them, or maybe I felt them. I don't know for sure, but I remember wedging between two of them, hoping to pop out on the other side, and that's just what happened. There are other things underground I was caught up in, like fishing line, sheets of plastic, and wet clothes or something like it. I'm guessing I know what it's like to be buried alive. Do you think I'll have nightmares about it, Sarah?"

"You may at first, but if so, they will be fewer with each passing day."

"It was pretty scary under there," he continued. "I thought about getting back to you some way, any way. I fought hard and held my breath until near the end. My throat burned like fire, and I swallowed some water right before my head popped up on the other side. Then you were there waiting for me, like some kind of Angel in a red dress. Who wears a sexy red dress fishing, anyway?"

"I do, and apparently it distracted you more than it should have. It was Bo who told us where to look. He followed you all the way through the siphon."

* * * * * * *

CHAPTER TWENTY-FOUR ~ SADDLE RANCH ~ LOVELAND, COLORADO

"How are you feeling, honey?" he asked. "I mean with your...well, uh, your..."

"Morning sickness? It continues," Sarah said, answering her own question.

"Samuel is going to be upset at me if it's true, since we have only known each other for a short amount of time," Mac said.

"Don't worry about that. I'm a grown woman, and he's had a few girlfriends over the years as well, but that's between us... Now get some rest, and I'll check back on you in just a bit. With any luck, you will be out of here by tonight," she said, kissing him on the forehead.

"I bet you do that to all your patients," he quipped.

"Only the real cowboys!" she stated, walking out the door.

* * * *

Mac got hold of Cory on the radio to check on things.

"You find my lucky pole yet, Cory?"

"Not yet, but we're looking. Are you sure it's lucky?"

"Well, I'm not dead," replied Mac. "So, I would say yes!"

"I'm surprised the doc let you get on the radio so soon," Cory said.

"Oh, she doesn't know, but in my defense, she never said I couldn't! Anyway, it looks like I'll get out of here by tonight. We still need to do a midnight recon of our new team, but it will probably be a few days out, at least for me."

"Sure, Mac, whenever you're ready. Just let me know."

"What happened to that monster fish I had, caught up in the chains? It probably died there eventually."

"Let me check on that, Mac," said Cory, already of course knowing the answer but not actually lying.

"That's a lie by omission," his deceased wife used to say. He smiled at the memory and spoke to the sky.

"I miss you, honey, every day, and so does Cameron. We're in a different place, but I'm taking great care of our boy, just like I promised you I would. Don't worry about us down here; we'll be up to see you in good time."

* * * *

Cory grabbed a few security members and had them check up to 500 yards downstream for any sign of Mac's pole.

After nearly two hours, the search was called off without a find.

Cory went to tell his new friend the bad news in person, meeting Samuel outside the front of the hospital.

"Any word?" asked Samuel.

"Yes, sir. I talked to him on the radio a couple of hours ago, and he wanted us to find his lucky pole. Anyway, it's gone for good, and I wanted to deliver the news to him in person."

"I'm sorry to hear that, son," replied Samuel. "A lucky pole means a lot to a fisherman, and I know that firsthand. Please tell him hello from me, and I'll talk to him later."

"Yes, sir. I'll do that."

Cory was eager to get inside, since taking to Samuel was like talking to a President or high-level politician. Basically, anyone who made you think about every word you uttered or where your hands were placed, or even if your socks matched.

Cory broke the bad news to Mac but vowed a surprise when he was better.

* * * *

Samuel headed back to his house, pushing a couple of meetings back by 30 minutes.

He had always been in the teach-a-man-to-fish camp, having studied the art for many years, including the finest equipment for the sport. He instructed a fishing class as an elective at a local community college in Loveland a few years back and enjoyed the comradery amongst his students.

Digging through his back closet, he was looking for the one. Not the new one, or even the oldest one, but the special one.

There it was! The Fenwick Yellow Jacket in an unopened custom-made wooden box. A bright yellow spin rod that was a match for any freshwater fish in the country.

* * * *

Mac was given early release by Sarah at lunchtime, so he could meet Cory and Rico for the special surprise.

Samuel met them all up at the Ranch for lunch. He handed Mac a long case. Every fisherman could guess the basic contents.

"This was given to me by my old friend, Ronald Reagan, back in 1985. Back then, he was getting ready to serve his second term in office. We had become close over the years, as I guided him in the ways of the spirit. He had once told me to call on him if I ever needed anything.

"I never dreamed I would...until that day. It was February 5, 1985. It was a Tuesday, I remember, and the city had given all of us in this Valley official notice that they would be taking our land by eminent domain, to be used as the new City dump. It was even signed by the Governor himself.

"I couldn't just stand by and watch our pristine Valley be turned into a refuge pile, so I used my get-out-of-jail-free card. I called the sitting President and asked for a huge favor.

"When he got back to me the next day, he asked if I knew it had been signed by the Governor of Colorado. I told him I had seen that in the document.

"OK, old friend," he told me. "Let me work on this."

"One week later, the City informed us that they had found a more suitable spot for the dump on the other side of town. Two days later, a package arrived from Washington, DC, with this Fenwick Yellow Jacket fishing rod, signed by the 40th President of the United States, with a note saying: 'May you have happy fishing days in your valley for years to come.'

"Those are the stories you never hear on the 6 o'clock news.

"Now, I want you to have this special rod, Mac."

Mac didn't know what to say, looking to Sarah for help, but she only shrugged.

"Samuel," he started slowly, wanting to pick the right words. "This gift means a lot to me, and I will take great care of this keepsake, as you have all these years."

"I know you will, son," Samuel replied. "Just promise me you will catch some fish with it. The darn thing has been collecting dust in my closet for too long."

Rico appeared with a large silver platter, with steam pouring out the sides of the cover. "Something smells good, and I'm starving!" said Mac, as Rico set the plate in front of him.

"Please do the honors," said Rico. Mac slowly lifted the cover, revealing a whole monster rainbow trout, complete with its head.

"I remember you, big guy!" said Mac, looking around the table. "How did this happen, Rico?"

"It wasn't me; I was only helping Cory with the surprise."

"Are you kidding me? The fish that nearly cost me my life is in front of me and smells delicious! It's like that movie *The Jewel of the Nile*, where the crocodile swallows the jewel and Michael Douglas's character dives in the water after it, with just a knife. Then, in later scenes, he is wearing crocodile boots."

"Yeah," said Cory. "It's kind of like that, but this one you get to eat."

"I still don't know how you pulled this off, Cory, but thank you. And I can't wait to try out my new rod!"

"In good time," Sarah told him. "You still need to rest up a bit before jumping full-throttle back into everything, including work and play."

"Yes, ma'am," he reluctantly agreed, "but only for a day or two."

* * * *

"Cory!" came the call from the Miller boy, running into the dining room at full speed and startling a few of the residents.

Stopping at the table, catching his breath, he asked, "How are you feeling, Mac?"

"Better, thank you. Now what's going on?"

"It's the MacDonalds. They're, well, what I mean is...they are...I don't know, but their property is being overrun right as we're talking."

"By who?" asked Cory.

"I'm not sure," replied the Miller boy, "but there's a lot of people up there, and they never have folks over to their place. Unless a bunch of cousins done showed up without a call, I think they're in trouble."

"I thought you two didn't get along," questioned Mac.

"He and my pops never saw eye to eye, but that don't mean we stop looking out for each other up there on the mountain. When something bad happens like this, it has a way of bulldozing everything in its path, including this here Ranch."

"Thanks, son," said Cory. "Do you know anything about how many are up there and if they are armed?"

"I was huntin' and did some spyin', and I figure there must be 50 or more up at the MacDonald place right now. Some have rifles, but most carried shovels or pitchforks, looked like."

"Did you see old man MacDonald or his wife?" asked Mac.

"Nope, but they always stayed close to the main house, or inside."

"All right, that's a good job. Can you wait outside for just a few?" asked Cory.

"Sure," the Miller boy replied, heading out the front door of the Pavilion.

Mac stood quickly and swayed enough for Sarah to demand he sit back down.

"I have to see what's happening," Mac said, standing again, but this time holding on to the table with one hand.

"Let me take a couple of my former officers up and see what's going on," said Cory. "They may even know some of the people, and if we're lucky, maybe we can get things under control before they get out of hand.

"You're not well enough to go up there yet, Mac," he whispered. "We both know that, and Sarah is going to kick your ass if you try."

"You're right on both accounts," Mac conceded, feeling helpless to lead his team. "I want radio contact with me at all times, though," he added. "And yes, I'll keep an eye out for your boy, just as always."

"Yes, sir," replied Cory. "And I'll take the Miller boy also, if that's OK."

"That's a good idea, since he knows the MacDonalds and the terrain up there better than anyone else here. This is a recon only, unless you're fired upon," added Mac.

Cory was excited to get back to work with some of his old team, but the rules were different now, and he wished he had Jimmy with him.

* * * *

Parking their four-wheelers at Moon Rock, one of the new security team was left to watch over the machines.

"Nobody takes these machines," Cory told him. "Nobody. Radio me if you see any trouble."

The Miller boy led them by foot around the east side of the MacDonald property line.

"There's a spot up on the cliff," he told Cory, speaking low, "that offers a view of their entire spread. It's how I always knew what they were up to. If we're quiet, we will have the advantage, but if one of us slips up, we'll have to fight our way back down to survive."

Cory had chosen two of his former officers, one male and one female, plus three other men from the security team, bringing the total to 7, not counting the ATV guard.

"I'm sorry, but I don't remember your first name," said Cory to the Miller boy.

"It's Drake, sir, just like the little town up the canyon a ways," he said, pointing up the mountain.

"That's it. I remember now," replied Cory. "Drake is going to lead us quietly up to a vantage point above the property, where we hopefully will learn what we are dealing with. Stay low and don't fire unless I give the go-ahead. Are we all clear?"

"Yes, sir," replied everyone, even Drake.

* * * *

Sounds of laughter and rowdiness came from the direction of the main house, giving Cory a reason to be concerned. The short one-mile hike was harder than it looked, quickly increasing in elevation. Each team member carried a small daypack with enough provisions for an overnight stay in the bush, if absolutely necessary.

The first vantage point gave them a clear picture of the outside of the east and part of the south side of the house, surrounded by men, women, and some children.

Cory pulled his binoculars, scanning the crowd, looking for anyone he may recognize from days earlier or from his former position in Loveland. It dawned on him that most formerly clean-cut men would now be sporting beards, and the women would not be made up.

Still, he scanned the crowd, wondering how long it took them to get all the way up here. A few days, he heard in his mind, just a few days to get from the southern border of the Ranch, following my boy and me here, right after Mac's duel with Ralph.

"It's them," Cory said out loud, only now realizing his team hadn't been there for the action.

"Them who?" asked Drake.

"The townspeople that gave us some trouble before. They promised not to return to the Ranch, but they didn't exactly leave either."

Cory, with others, watched with their binoculars as the side door of the main house was thrown open and Mr. MacDonald, along with his wife, was shoved out and onto the ground. They were pushed to the side, further and faster still, until they tripped over their own feet and went on to their knees.

Cory held his breath, not ready to engage but also not willing to sit by and watch an execution.

A man had his pistol out and leveled at the back of old man Macdonald's head.

"Fire on three," said Cory quietly... One...two...wait, wait, hold fire," he said, as the man with the pistol became distracted and walked down the road towards a small incoming group.

Cory flashed a pocket mirror, sending a beam down in front of the old man, getting his attention.

Waving his arm in a sweeping motion, Cory gestured for them to run. They ran up and around, climbing slowly up the back of the steep cliff. Near the top, Drake lent each of them a hand, getting a nod out of Cory as Mr. MacDonald took it, with a "Thank you, son" added on.

"Do we call for backup or hold tight?" asked one of Cory's former officers.

"We are the backup plan," replied Cory, speaking quietly.

"I doubt they are going to put out much of a search for Mr. MacDonald and his wife here, so we will stay put for now and see if we can find out some more information about our new neighbors."

Minutes ticked by, with most mulling around the property aimlessly. The small incoming group was receiving lots of attention from others as they gathered around, blocking Cory's line of sight.

The small crowd whooped and clapped as the procession came into view.

"Oh, hell," said Cory, still looking through his binoculars, as the group made way for the man being carried on a stretcher. "How can we not get rid of that guy?" he said aloud.

"Do you know them?" asked Mr. MacDonald.

"I know one for sure," replied Cory, "and he appears to be their leader."

"When do we get our house back?" asked the old man's wife.

"I honestly don't know," replied Cory.

* * * * * * *

CHAPTER TWENTY-FIVE ~ WESTON, COLORADO

Sheriff Johnson felt a bit better, having a new rival locked up in his jail, but it was still too quiet.

He thought about how to get the loud-mouth obese man, who had disrespected him more than once already, inside as well.

Talking it over with his girlfriend at lunch, he told her he was thinking about asking the Judge's permission to arrest the man on a civil unrest charge.

"Are you frickin' kidding me?" she responded immediately. "You are the Sheriff of this town and the most powerful man here. Why would you ask his permission to do anything? Are you going soft on me?"

"Give me a minute," he told her, walking outside, with his head spinning. Never before had anyone suggested he was soft about anything, and now he had recently heard it from the two people closest to him.

Could it be true? he thought, questioning his sanity for a split second, before the fear and anxiety turned to anger. "I am the sitting Sheriff of Weston, voted in by the citizens in a landslide victory, and nobody tells me how to do my job," he mumbled.

"Say it again," she told him, overhearing the first attempt, "and this time with conviction!"

He stood, his voice booming across the small house. "I am the sitting Sheriff of Weston, voted in by the citizens in a landslide victory, and nobody tells me how to do my job!"

"There's my man," she said, smiling flirtatiously and pulling him into the back bedroom.

An hour later, he emerged, confident and resolute, calling to his deputies to arrest the man on-site for civil disobedience.

"He's a big boy," he added, "so it may take a few of you. Throw him into the same cell as the former councilman, just for fun."

He thought about telling the Judge what he had done. *He'll find out soon enough*, he thought.

His deputies found the fugitive in the midst of a multiplayer bastardized version of craps, right on the sidewalk downtown.

"What's your name?" they asked the man, easily tipping the scales at 350 pounds.

"My name?" he responded, looking around at his fellow players. "Why, my name is you rent-a-cops better move on down the road."

With that, he turned his back on them and continued his game.

"Sir," called out the lead deputy, "you are under arrest for civil disobedience."

"You mean because I said a few things in front of your boss and hurt his feelings?" He got a laugh out of only a couple guys with this last statement.

The other players were getting nervous. "His...his name is Richard," called out one of the players.

"That's right," added another.

"Thank you, gentlemen," the officer responded.

The hulk of a man, overweight and at least 6'5", had a path opening to him, man by man, as the other gamers backed away from him.

"Now, Richard," said the lead deputy calmly, "we can do this one of two ways. I would prefer option number one, where you slowly and quietly walk over here, turn around and put your hands behind your back. However, it's completely up to you, and my boss has given me carte blanche permission to do whatever is necessary."

"I don't know what the hell you're talking about with that cartey blankly Spanish crap, but I haven't heard option two."

"Fair enough, Richard. Option two is a hostile and assuredly unpleasant removal of yourself from this area, and one way or the other ending up in our jail cell."

The rest of the men around him scattered with this final statement.

Richard paused, silently mulling over his options. The air was still, with nobody speaking.

"I choose," he finally spoke slowly, "option number 3!" he announced, grabbing one of the male spectators around the neck and putting a small pocketknife to the man's throat.

The hostage let out a stifled scream, his eyes wide with fear of what could happen next.

The deputies didn't react, but each had a hand on the butt of their holstered pistols.

Richard slowly backed away from the crowd, with the deputies following five yards behind.

"Where are you going, big guy?" asked one of the officers.

"Wherever I want! And if you try anything, you're going to have a dead man on your hands."

Judge Lowry was promptly notified by one of the spectators, who had been making a small amount of side money each week to keep him informed of out-of-the-ordinary town happenings.

"That's enough, deputies," called out Judge Lowry, rounding the street corner. "Who authorized this?"

"Sheriff's orders not to let anyone interfere, even you," replied the lead deputy.

Judge Lowry was taken aback by this brazen attempt not to follow the chain of command. He turned without another word, walking the short 3/4 block back to the courthouse.

* * * *

Richards's resolve was failing as he walked slowly backward, his heavy arm tiring of holding the shaking shield before him.

Looking behind him, he caught the two old-time ranchers on horses, blocking his exit. His gaze moved wildly from right to left.

"Just let me know, deputy, when you've had enough of this," called out one of the ranchers in a casual, conversational tone. He quickly pointed to his lasso before Richard could turn around.

The old-time rancher was known to most for his numerous rodeo trophies, spanning several decades. The deputy nodded, understanding where this was headed.

"Richard," called out the deputy. "As you may know, I was a sharpshooter in my former military days and while on the force in New York City, before moving out here to God's country."

"What's that got to do with shit?" Richard spat.

"Well, sir, it's like this. We have orders to bring you in, and the Sheriff will typically specify clearly if a person is only to be taken alive. I received no such clarification with you."

Slowly walking back to his truck, he pulled the impressive Sniper rifle from behind the backseat.

He made a point of showing it off to a few of the spectators, pretending to ignore the situation at hand.

Richard was getting nervous, and his captor even more. "What are you going to do with that?" asked Richard, his smug confidence now waning.

"It's really a distance rifle," the deputy replied, as he walked backward 25 yards.

Richard held his man closer now, peering just around the whimpering man's head. "You'll have to shoot through him first!" called out Richard, now intentionally hiding behind his shield.

"Way I see it is you have a, what is it, about a 350-pound man hiding behind a 170-pound shield? There is just no way to cover all of your parts. It could be an elbow or shoulder hanging out, or maybe even a knee. I would stay completely still for hours on end in my former jobs, waiting for the kill shot. With you, I don't need just one shot. I can just hit multiple body parts until you let him go."

He instructed his deputies to clear the path in front of and behind the soon-to-be-captured man.

The deputy made an obvious gesture to inspect his rifle, slowly loading one round. He pretended to check the wind direction, as he had done many times before when the shot was a much longer distance. Nodding to the readied cowboy on horseback, he aimed his weapon.

On cue, Richard dropped the shaking man from his clutches and turned to run. "Watch this," the deputy said to his fellow officers, as the cowboy's rope began to swing. "That man there has been the steer-roping champion in both Trinidad and Pueblo six straight years, with the last one only a few years back."

The big man ran wildly, heading somewhere, anywhere away from where he was.

The cowboy let him run nearly 50 yards down the main road before giving chase. Closing in and whipping the lasso over his head, he let it fly over the accused man's head and around his midsection. He was careful not to get him around the neck and possibly kill him as the horse stopped abruptly, tightening the rope.

Richard was thrown violently backward, landing on the ground with a loud thud, knocking the wind out of him. The cowboy was off his steed in seconds, binding Richard's arms and feet as he would a steer's legs.

The crowd from the earlier games gathered around the spectacle, with a few laughing and pointing, but most staying silent.

The deputies handcuffed him, escorting him on foot to the jailhouse, only a quarter of a mile up the road, to see the Sheriff.

"Why didn't you just shoot him?" asked one of the deputies to the man with the gun.

"That's a good question, since I used to be ordered to shoot bad guys from quite a distance. These were very bad men that, left alive, would cause major problems to innocent people. This guy here," he said, squeezing Richard's shoulder lightly, "is just an a-hole with a big mouth. He deserves a rundown by a rider cowboy, but he's not bad enough for me to consider shooting—unless, of course, he gives me no choice. Now he's soon to be someone else's problem."

* * * * * * *

Chapter Twenty-six ~ Weston, Colorado

"Howdy, big boy," announced Sheriff Johnson, with his feet propped up on his desk. "I wondered if you would make it in here alive, and I see that you have. You must have just surrendered peacefully," he added, having already been briefed over the radio by another of his men.

"No, sir," he replied. "They ran me down like a damn animal and tied me up. I was minding my own business, playing games with other townsfolk, when they started harassing me for no reason. Now let me go! I'm getting tired of this crap!"

"Is that so?" replied the Sheriff calmly. He was determined not to get upset or out of hand, at least in front of his men.

"What do you like to eat, Richy boy? I mean, besides the ravioli sauce you had all over your T-shirt the first time you disrespected me at the hangings."

Richard stammered, playing the moment over in his head. Fear filled his eyes, as he realized this was a coordinated effort all along, and he had only seen people leave this jailhouse by hanging on the end of a rope.

"I'm sorry, sir...I mean, Sheriff, about that," he stated, with his voice cracking.

"I can't quite recall what you were eating when we met again in front of the new greenhouse land, where you disrespected me a second time," continued the Sheriff.

Richard had no response to this, and his knees weakened, causing him to stumble forward, only caught by the deputies.

"So, I'll ask again. What do you like to eat? I like to make sure all of our guests are well fed while in our company."

"Anything, sir," was all he could muster for a response.

"Well then, you just may be one of our easier guests, after all."

"How long will I be here, if I could ask?" said Richard.

"Oh, probably not too long. I don't like taking good food out of the mouths of our lawful citizens, only to redistribute it inside these walls. Let's introduce him to the former councilman, gentlemen," he said to his deputies, pointing down the hall.

* * * *

Judge Lowry headed back to the courthouse, keeping his anger off his face. Once inside, he dismissed his longtime clerk for the remainder of the day, calmly telling her she deserved an afternoon off and locking the door behind her.

He paced the smooth tile floor back and forth, growing angrier by the second. While he wasn't exactly surprised that this scenario could happen, he just wasn't fully prepared yet.

He always knew the Sheriff would eventually make a power move against him, and his plans were in motion but this was too soon, and the story of his orders being questioned would spread through the town quickly over the coming days.

Think! he thought, pacing faster now.

Finding himself in his study, a small room void of windows and secured by a padlocked door in the basement of the 100-year-old courthouse, he reviewed his plans.

Nobody else had ever set foot in this room, or even knew it was there, since he took over as town Judge years ago.

Lighting the oil lantern, he locked himself in with two deadbolts, one just above the door center and the second a foot above the first.

A glass of James' finest was poured into his favorite glass he had received years ago from an old college buddy when he first became a judge. It was a whiskey glass with the scales of justice on one side and a custom saying on the other. He laughed every time he read the words: *I shall only rule when my glass is empty.* Only he knew the truth that he only ever drank alone...well, almost always.

Walls were covered with pictures of various people, including Sheriff Johnson, his deputies, the former town council, and other prominent citizens. James' photo covered the former Mayor's, as the newest art hung.

The Judge was fully aware that, to anyone else, his study would look like a scene from a television drama, where the serial killer had pictures of his victims he has obsessed about strewn around the dimly lit room.

This was not the obsessed dungeon of a crazed man with no filters but a carefully calculated working space of a sitting Judge, and arguably the smartest man in town, he thought.

Opening his black spiral notebook, he reviewed his simple five-step plan typed one day after "the day" on his old manual Smith Corona typewriter. Each step, separated by ten spaces, had ample room for handwritten notes.

Step 1: *Gain the trust of the sitting Sheriff and establish a hierarchy.* "Check," he said out loud.

Step 2: *Find a man who can win an election in a landslide.* This had the name "James VanFleet" handwritten under it.

Step 3. *Give an impression of weakness.* Written underneath was "Be intoxicated in front of those listed above one time, and then purchase alcohol by the case."

He smiled, as he looked to the corner of the dimly lit room, with the cases of moonshine he had purchased from James VanFleet stacked neatly and nearly undisturbed.

He found it difficult to let himself drink in front of the Sheriff and James, as he didn't like the taste and disdained not being in complete control over himself or any situation. He made exceptions only when alone and mixed it with any type of soda he could find.

After first learning of James' still, he spent several hours practicing the drinking parts in his mind, careful to say only enough to make him appear compromised but not spill any of his future plans. James and Jason assumed the Judge had ruled on the hangings of the vegetable thieves after a night of drinking, but in truth he had already made the decision.

Step 4: *Strip the sitting Sheriff of power, shifting it all to the court.* This one seemed to be working to plan, until today's happenings. Judge Lowry was agitated but remained calm. He would not allow his anger to beat him or be shown as a weakness, like the Sheriff had done.

Step 5 was blank.

* * * *

Saturday was trade day, and the Second Chances Ranch bunch were all excited to attend. Chance would tag along this day, giving James some anxiety about leaving the ranch unattended.

The girls filled in Billy on every possible thing he might see or eat there.

Working all week, gathering items to sell, the trailer was extra heavy this morning. As they pulled the trailer behind the bright yellow truck once again, James and Jason got waves, thumbs-up signs, and even a few hoots as they made their way into town for the official traders' morning kickoff with the Sheriff.

The vendor list had nearly doubled this week, but James kept the same stand number.

After a short introduction of the rules for the new vendors, Sheriff Johnson once again pulled James onto the back of a semitrailer for a short speech about the greenhouses starting construction next week.

"We just keep reminding them why they voted for us, so come election time again, we can run unopposed," he whispered to James.

"Plus, the occasional hanging to scare the hell out of them," James said sarcastically, almost holding his tongue.

"Exactly. And speaking of that, I've got another one coming up soon," the Sheriff replied.

"Really?" asked James. "I hadn't heard that. Judge Lowry has already ruled?"

"Not exactly, but we will see what happens," he replied with a grin.

* * * *

Heading back to the jailhouse, the Sheriff hadn't checked on his guests since earlier last night.

"How are my boys?" he asked, walking in the front door, as his deputy came up from the back.

"Well, there seems to have been an altercation with those two, and the former councilman didn't fare so well. I'm not sure what happened," the deputy said.

"Maybe I should have given them two dinners last night, instead of just one. Big guys love to eat. Is he alive?"

"Yes, sir, but he will need some medical attention."

"OK," said the Sheriff. "Get Doc Walters up here to take a look at him and get your boys to help put him in a different cell before the doctor arrives."

The good doctor arrived nearly 45 minutes later, medical bag in hand.

"How can I help you, Sheriff?" he asked, with a handshake.

"I've just got a man I need you to take a look at is all. It seems he likes to fight but didn't fare so well."

"Sure thing," the doctor replied. "Anything for the town."

It took Dr. Walters a full hour to return from the cell with an update.

"He's got three fractured ribs, near as I can tell without an X-ray. He also has a mild concussion and several lacerations on his face. Two fingers are broken on his right hand, with no X-ray needed to confirm. Other than that, I think he will survive. I patched him up as best I could. Oh, and Sheriff, will you please feed those two separately from now on?"

"Thank you, Dr.," the Sheriff replied, without answering the question.

* * * *

Trading today was robust, honest, and fair all the way around. Jenna, Carla and Candice kept both Chance and Billy close, carefully examining each booth for candy and other items kids like.

Each girl and Billy were given a small amount of walkaround junk change that Jason was able to trade a few silver coins for.

The girls scouted every booth, finding plenty to consider purchasing. Billy only wanted a yo-yo, like the one he used to have a few short weeks ago. He accidentally left it behind at a road stop while traveling with his father. When they finally found one he liked, he was short on money, so Carla made up the difference with most of her change. "Thank you, sister!" coming from Billy made it all worth it.

James' stand was inundated with well-wishers and average folks hoping to gain his ear for new ideas.

"You're going to have to take over the stand," he told Janice and Lauren. "We're not going to sell anything like this."

He and Jason slowly made the rounds to each vendor, talking about the future of the town and the upcoming greenhouse project.

Judge Lowry made an appearance, leaving the courthouse for the first time since yesterday afternoon.

Knowing he would have to face the Sheriff sooner than later, he maintained a casual demeanor.

His chance would come quickly, running into the Sheriff only 30 minutes later at James' booth.

"Are you back for more moonshine?" asked the Sheriff jokingly.

Judge Lowry smiled, clenching his teeth. "No, not today," he replied. "I hear you have a couple of men in the jail now," he continued, coming out as a statement. "A former councilman, as we already discussed, and the big guy."

"Yes, that's right," replied the Sheriff, waiting for the part about him not asking permission.

The air was thick, and even though Janice didn't know what was happening, she could tell it was some sort of passive-aggressive standoff between the two most powerful men in town.

"Well, I'll need to gather all of the facts before making my ruling in the coming days," continued the Judge.

Sheriff Johnson pretended to get a call on his radio, as he did more frequently now. He was getting better at the ruse, and this time he had both Janice and the Judge believing it was real.

"Excuse me" is all he said, talking to the radio as he walked away.

The Judge stayed a few more minutes, making small talk with Janice and Lauren. He spent the next two hours visiting each and every booth for more of the same. Although he didn't particularly like talking to people who were not standing below him in his court, he made an effort today, just in case he needed their support, sooner or later. Thankfully, no one asked about the large man, Richard, or anything about the happenings yesterday.

In all the booths he visited, be bought only one thing. It cost him a pretty penny—four silver dollars, to be exact—but the item fit seamlessly into his future plans for the town.

James and Jason met praise at every booth, and their popularity did not go unnoticed by the Judge. As the trading came to a close, James and Jason returned to their stand to good news.

"We nearly sold out today!" announced Lauren, pointing to the picked-over tables in front of them.

"Chance was really good also," added Janice. James noticed the new collar straightaway. It was bright red, contrasting with his dark fur, and could be seen from quite a distance.

The tag looked like a miniature green Colorado license plate but contained the name "James VanFleet" and "Second Chances Ranch," along with their address.

"Phone numbers don't matter anymore," interjected Jason, noticing it was missing.

The girls returned soon after, with little Billy in tow. Proudly holding up his yo-yo, he declared that Carla had bought it for him. She beamed with pride, hugging her new brother. "I really only helped 'cause it cost more than he had."

Each child had a small amount of candy and gum for the coming week. They quickly packed their few remaining items so they could head home before dark.

Following a great day of trade, Janice announced they would all be eating out after church tomorrow.

The Weston Grill and Tavern owners passed around a reservation sheet among the vendors, citing 20 confirmations would be needed for a special secret Sunday lunch menu to be prepared.

Janice signed in the number 24 slot, as rumors ran regarding what would be on the menu.

* * * *

James was happy to see the increased parade of traders, causing a country-style traffic jam going beyond his property.

"The lock is still on," called Jason, pointing to the front gate.

With the kids waiving to the now occasionally passing trader, the adults observed the property with binoculars for a few minutes, with nothing appearing out of sorts.

Chance made the final house sweep, declaring "All clear!" with a single bark.

* * * *

Sunday morning had the VanFleet and Davis clans decked out in their finest. With Chance in tow, they headed back to town.

Sunday church would be a regular happening from here on out, and the ladies didn't mind pressing two suits for such an occasion.

The families were treated like royalty by their fellow parishioners, giving James a good feeling that they were doing something good for the town.

James' offering of 10% of his recent sales, including the steer, to the church surprised the pastor, and he made a special after-service visit to meet with the expanding family.

"Thank you, James," the pastor said quietly. Most of my worshipers used to tithe regularly, but now they are not able to do so. They still need God and the church, now more than ever, and your contribution today will ensure that they may return here, regardless of financial ability to donate."

"We are always happy to help the church," James replied, adding, "Janice's and my faith are the only reason I am still alive today."

"Would you please say something at our next service, James, about where this God-fearing town is headed?" the pastor asked.

In a lower voice, almost a whisper, the pastor added, "My parishioners sometimes have trouble speaking out when they witness injustice. I know the Good Lord will right the wrong, and those on the wrong side of good will pay the price when it is time. They don't realize it's that simple and so they try to overthink it, I believe. To them, the Judge and sitting Sheriff are men to be feared, but you are a man of hope and generosity, someone they can trust. You, James, are a true leader of people, as I am. Does that make sense to you, James?"

"Yes, pastor," James replied, so nobody else could hear. "I never asked to be put in this position, but since I am now, I will do everything I can to help our fellow citizens have a better life."

* * * *

Heading to the restaurant, the girls were excited about the secret lunch menu.

The banner out front said it all in only two words. "Daddy, what does 'Old School' mean?" asked Carla.

"Well," replied Jason, "it usually means something authentic from days gone by. As for the menu today, I'm guessing it won't be anything fancy, but you are likely to find various foods we all love and have had many times before."

Under the same heading on the chalkboard hanging off the wall, in smaller letters, read the menu, separated into categories.

Mains: char-grilled hamburgers, foot-long hot dogs, Fair corn dogs, turkey legs, and grilled cheese sandwiches.

Sides: tater tots, onion rings, French fries, collard greens, smashed potatoes, and corn off the cob.

Desserts: chocolate or vanilla ice cream, apple pie, and pecan pie

* * * * * * *

CHAPTER TWENTY-SEVEN ~ WESTON, COLORADO

The lunch seemed to be a hit with the growing crowd, and indeed was to the VanFleet and Davis clans. This lunch was taken outside and consumed on a picnic bench, with James ordering an extra double hamburger, plain, and pretending to accidentally knock it on to the ground near Chance's head, where it promptly disappeared.

"You did that on purpose!" Janice announced, calling him out in front of the others. "That's a waste of good food."

"Tell him that," James replied, reaching down to pet a grateful companion. "You girls sure did make a good find with Chance here. I wasn't convinced at first, but now I'm sure of it." Chance barked, wagging his tail.

* * * *

Judge Lowry considered himself an outdoorsman, fishing and hiking growing up back East. and even more the past years in and around Weston. In all these years and adventures, he never owned a gun or weapon of any kind, unless one counted a Swiss Army knife.

Truth be told, he had never shot a pistol before and only knew the very basics of the Smith and Wesson model 10 .38 special. The six-shot revolver was recommended by the booth trader over a semiautomatic pistol for less experienced shooters, and it came with 50 rounds of ammunition.

"Can we keep this purchase between us?" the Judge asked the only man running the booth.

"Yes, sir. All sales at my booth are final and confidential, and this here pistol shoots straight every time. You will want to clean it, though, periodically."

The Judge thanked him, without concern about the last advice. *Who needs to clean a gun that will only be fired once, or maybe twice?* he thought.

Thankfully, the weapon came with basic instructions on proper loading and firing, and he studied in earnest this quiet Sunday afternoon.

* * * *

Sheriff Johnson spent some time today messing around with his captives. They would remain in separate cells from now on, following the previous altercation.

He started with the councilman, asking him to please not fight in this building. "It's just something we have zero tolerance for in my town," the Sheriff added.

"I can't have you and Richard over there," pointing down the hall towards the other cell, "putting our good citizens at risk of being harmed because you guys think it's fun to brawl."

The former councilman listened intently, with an idea of where this was headed. In a plea attempt, he explained what happened, as if the Sheriff didn't already know.

"Sir," he started quietly and respectfully, not the same cocky man from before. "Sir, he attacked me after I tried to get some food off the only plate you gave us."

"That's a lie!" came the response from down the hall. "He attacked me first!"

This got a slight smile from the Sheriff, who didn't care either way, as long as his two captives were under his roof.

* * * * * * *

Chapter Twenty-eight ~ Raton Pass, New Mexico

W e could hear the dogs barking loudly.

"Some raccoon is in for the race of his life," said Tom, joking.

"Mr. Lance! Mr. Lance! Come quick!" said Lonnie's daughter, running up, out of breath.

"What is it?" I asked, now getting the attention of Joy, Lonnie, Jake and Nancy.

"It's Hudson and Jax! Something has happened to them, I think!"

"Where are they?" I asked, now feeling panicked and jumping up.

"Ow!" I yelled, as my leg buckled. I fell, reaching out as Jake tried grabbing my arm. Hitting the ground hard, a shooting pain went down my leg.

"I'm sorry, buddy. I tried to catch you," said Jake, helping me to sit again.

"Honey," said Lonnie to his little girl, "where are they?"

"I don't know, Daddy. I think somebody took them."

"This is important, honey," Lonnie added. "Tell me everything, exactly as it happened."

"We were playing and Hudson had to go potty, so he went behind a tree. We heard some screaming and Jax went to see. The rest of us went to check, and they were gone. I could hear them screaming, but it kept getting farther away. Ringo and Mini are barking like crazy, but we can't find them."

"Show me right where they were," he told her. "And you're not going anywhere!" he added, pointing squarely at me.

"I'll find out everything," Joy told me, hobbling with Tina and Lucy's help towards the edge of the property, trailing a running Jake and Lonnie.

"I'm staying with you, Lance," Nancy told me.

"I need to be there!" I shouted, attempting to stand on my own. My leg buckled for a second time, with Nancy catching me.

"Ahhh!" I yelled in frustration, feeling helpless to do anything for my children.

"They are going to be OK, Lance," Nancy told me. "We have all the right people here to make that happen."

"You mean Jake and Mike, right?" I snapped. "Now there's a pair!"

Nancy's face was calm, and she was unfazed by my last comment.

"I'm sorry I snapped at you, Nancy. I feel useless, and there couldn't be a worse time to be laid up, but it's not your fault or anyone else's."

"It OK," she replied. "I've been doing this for a long time, and I never take anything said in a time of crisis personally. And to answer your question—yes, I believe my husband and Mike are going to have to work together on this. I'll grab a four-wheeler, and we will get you down there, but no walking. Understand?"

"Yes, ma'am. Thank you."

* * * *

Joy and her helpers, with Lonnie and Jake, headed to the group of children huddled at the far end of the property.

"Show us right where you saw them last," Lonnie said to his daughter.

"Here, Daddy," she told him, taking them all behind a large group of pine trees. "This is where Hudson went potty, and then Jax went to see if he was all right."

Calling out their names...with a few seconds pause between each attempt...there was no response, only the rustling of trees.

Joy looked to the ground for shoe prints, and the necklace caught her eye, balled up and barely sticking out of the pine needles strewn across the ground.

Picking it up carefully, she recognized the smashed penny on the end of the chain Hudson always wore as a good luck charm. He, Jax and Hendrix would get a smashed penny each year from a restaurant vending machine near the camp their Louisiana family had owned for years.

Hudson had not taken the necklace off for more than a year, even to shower or swim.

"This is Hudson's necklace!" she announced, "and he never takes it off, not ever!"

Lonnie called Mike and David on the radio. "We need you two down here on the west perimeter right now!" is all he said. Both came running and were quickly briefed on the situation.

Joy walked briskly into the woods, calling their names. It took both Mike and Lonnie to turn her back.

Mike asked everyone to stay behind a line he carved into the dirt with his boot.

Joy kept me informed over the radio.

"I'm headed down there, with Nancy's help," I told her. "Where's Hendrix?"

"He's right here with me and said he didn't see anything."

"What about the other children?" I asked.

"Most are down here now, is all I know. I found Hudson's penny necklace," she told me, starting to cry.

"Honey, we will find them. I know it."

"Mike is looking for tracks and clues as to what happened," she added.

"Don't let anyone else over there except for Lonnie. We don't need anyone contaminating the area," I said.

With Nancy and me arriving on a four-wheeler, we all waited anxiously for Mike and Lonnie's report.

"Why are they taking so long?" asked a frustrated Joy, holding a whimpering Hendrix in her arms.

"This is a crime scene," I told her. "They didn't just wander off, and I'm pretty sure they will tell us the boys have been abducted." My mind raced, and I couldn't believe I was actually speaking those words about my own children.

I remembered the first time hearing the heart-wrenching story of a popular television personality who literally hunts bad guys following the abduction and killing of his young son. Since then, I always kept that possibility in the very back of my mind, wondering what I would do as a father myself.

Mike and Lonnie huddled, as a group of NFL referees on a controversial call might, before announcing their findings to the group of adults and children.

"Joy and Lance," Lonnie said, "your sons have been taken, from the looks of the scene behind us."

The news, while not surprising to me, still stung with the finality of it.

"It's them…those bastards!" shouted Katie. "We should never have left, and now they are mad. I'm so sorry this happened," she tearfully told Joy and me.

"This is not your fault," Joy told her, "or anyone else's here."

"Nancy?" asked Lonnie. "Will you please take the bike and bring Vlad down here?"

Joy helped me off and on to a sitting position on the ground, and Nancy rode back to the camp.

David called Mel and Steve to come down, and told Mel to bring his drone. He told Mark and Jim to monitor the radio for any news relating to the boys.

"Don't leave the radio unattended for even a minute," he ordered, "and let me know if you hear *anything*."

"Will do, Dad," Mark responded.

Mel and Vlad made it down at the same time, quickly being filled in on the situation.

"How can I help?" asked Vlad.

"We may need your influence with the Colonel to bring these boys back safe, but we don't know anything yet," Lonnie told him.

"Of course," Vlad replied. "Whatever you need, we will get it done together."

Mike pointed out the tracks to Lonnie, with Jake, Mel, and an insistent Joy observing.

"It looks like three men ambushed the boys. Two waiting here," he said, walking behind a large clump of bushes, "and the other one over here," he added, pointing to a large pine tree. "Judging by the footprints and cigarette butts, they had been waiting a while, maybe even a day or two."

"We would have smelled the smoke," pointed out Joy.

"Not today," Mike replied. "The wind is blowing away from us."

"So, they hunted our kids?" asked Vlad.

"Yes, basically, that's what happened," replied Mike. "We were monitoring the bridge border, but not the other sides. They took advantage of our weaknesses and capitalized on their position."

"We have something on the ham," came the word from Mark over the radio.

"What do you know?" asked his father.

"They have the boys across the river and want an exchange."

"They are asking for three to trade for two?" David said, as more of a question.

"No, Dad. It's something different."

* * * * * * *

CHAPTER TWENTY-NINE ~ RATON PASS, NEW MEXICO

Hudson, playing with his friends before it happened, had kicked the soccer ball back and forth across the flat field at the edge of the forest. He was trying to impress Lonnie's daughter with his footwork, making sure she saw every play.

Ducking behind a tree to pee, he smelled the cigarette odor, turning around to see a man dressed in camouflage from head to toe. He let out a scream as the man covered his mouth with a cloth and dragged him, kicking, into the bushes.

Jax, hearing Hudson's cries, ran into the bushes, hoping to help.

"This is even better," a man called out as he grabbed Jax, folding his arms against his side and lifting him off the ground.

"Do you see her?" he asked the third man, without a captive.

"No, that's it," declared the third man. "Let's head back to base."

Jax and Hudson resisted, from the beginning of the river crossing in the slow section and back up the hill to the captors' camp. Their captors took no care to keep them from banging into trees and bushes, scraping their arms and legs while being carried back to the camp.

They were given a quick potty break before being locked inside one of the main tents. Both scared, they were glad not to be completely alone.

"We've made contact," announced Jim over the radio.

"What do you know?" asked Lonnie.

"I have some information," said Jim, "but I'm not sure everyone should hear it."

"Jim," said Joy, grabbing Lonnie's radio. "Those are my boys out there. Tell me everything now!"

"Yes, ma'am. They have your boys at their camp across the river."

"What do they want?" she added immediately.

"They want a trade—one for two," he said soberly.

"We have three," added in Jake.

There was a long pause on Jim's end...

"Are you there, Jim?" asked Joy.

"Yes, ma'am."

"So, what's the problem?"

"They only want the girl," he replied.

This time the pause was on our end.

Katie froze for a moment, old enough to understand what she and everyone else had heard. She turned and led her brother back towards Mel and Tammie's house without a word.

"Katie! Katie! Come back," Tammy called out, wanting to chase her.

"Just give her a little time," said Mel, putting one hand on her shoulder, "and then I'll check on things."

"That's why I didn't want to tell you in front of everyone," Jim said.

It didn't much matter now, but I could see his point.

"OK, what's the rest?" asked Lonnie.

"That's it," replied Mark. "They said they would be in touch and jumped offline just as quick."

"What do you think?" Lonnie asked Joy and me.

"We're not trading kids with those animals," Joy told him.

"And trading guns or food will just bring a guaranteed fight when they think we have more to take," I added. "Let's get back on the line and have them believe we are negotiating for a trade with all of the specifics. We need to spread this out over a few days, giving us time to make a plan."

"I'm sorry, honey," I told Joy. "I want them back as soon as possible, but it has to be a calculated play on our end. We can't just bulldoze our way over there without a solid plan."

"I know," she replied. "You're not going anywhere with your bad leg," she told me, "and neither am I with my foot. You're too close to the two guys we need the most for my plan to work, so I've got this," she told me.

"Mike, Lonnie and Jake!" she called out. "Let's talk over here."

They all gathered out of earshot of the rest of us.

I couldn't hear what she was saying, but I saw Mike and Jake keeping their distance.

"Okay, gentlemen. My boys are out there, and with both Lance and me down, I'm taking the lead on this, at least for the planning stage. You two," she said, pointing squarely at Mike and Jake, "are my best chance at getting my children back. You may as well move in closer because you will be shaking hands in a minute."

Neither man moved.

"I have respect for both of you, and I know Lance does as well," Joy continued. "With that being said, I need you both working together for a rescue mission. That means cutting this macho bullshit I've seen since we started this journey. I'm not saying you have to like each other, but you *will* work together to make our group whole again. Agreed?"

Both men nodded their heads slightly.

"That's *not* good enough!" she said, raising her voice.

Lonnie stayed put, in case things got out of hand, and tried hard to keep in a smile.

"I said, are we *agreed*, gentlemen?" This last statement, loud and stern, was heard by all, with both men answering "Yes, ma'am."

"Now, shake hands, signifying you will work together to save our boys!" Joy commanded.

Mike and Jake shook hands for the first time since initially meeting back in McKinney, in what seemed a lifetime ago to both men. It was quick and awkward, but it was done.

Sending everyone back to Beatrice's house, the four, along with David, Mel, Vlad, Nancy and me, made plans for a rescue mission.

"Don't forget about me," said Tom, slowly running up, with rifle in hand.

"I'm not as fast as I used to be, but I'm still one hell of a shot at a distance."

"OK, everyone," called out Joy. "We know where they are likely being held, since Mike has been there before. I want us to make a detailed map of how to get there, using Mike's information and at least two alternate routes that I'm sure David, Mel and Tom can help with, as they have been up here and all through these woods for years.

"And Mel, if you're holding out anything that could help us, now is the time."

"I may have a few things up my sleeve," he replied.

"That's not going to do this time," she told him. "I know you love to surprise everybody with your gadgets, but I need to know what you have that can help us, and right now works for me."

I thought about chiming in, but she was plowing ahead, forcing unlikely alliances and not allowing anyone to remain vague or anonymous. It was clear she didn't need my help at the moment.

"OK," replied Mel. "I have a small arsenal of distractions, including flares, smoke bombs and fireworks, not only the small ones like firecrackers and bottle rockets but Roman candles, Screaming Serpents, and the big ones you would see at a finale of a city-sponsored fireworks show. Bottom line: we can create mass confusion for at least 10 minutes, but we had better know exactly where Hudson and Jax are, because we will only get one chance."

"That's good! That's just perfect," I said, feeling hopeful and silently praying for their safe return.

Mike drew a map with key points, including our location, their camp, the river crossing, and the former bridge for reference.

David, Mel and Tom worked on alternative routes to and from the other side, with David wishing his dad were here to help.

* * * *

Katie took her brother into their room, reaching Mel and Tammy's house. She told him what happened to Jax and Hudson, even though he was there.

"I always want you to be safe," she told him, "and that is why I have to leave. You will be taken care of here and will grow up to be a person I can be proud of. It's my fault that Hudson and Jax were kidnapped, and I am the only one who can fix it."

He pleaded with her, saying, "Sissy, please don't go!"

"Stay quiet, Jonah," she told him, "and we can be together again." Slipping out the door, she confessed her lie to her parents in heaven and walked back into the woods.

* * * * * * *

Chapter Thirty ~ Raton Pass, New Mexico

"They want to meet tomorrow afternoon on their side of the bridge for the exchange," called Jim over the radio. "We tried to push it back a day or two, but they were resolute about it being tomorrow. We have 30 minutes to respond," he added.

"OK," said Lonnie. "We will agree to their terms—3 p.m. tomorrow afternoon on their side. The exchange is one for two, and nothing more."

"You've got just over 24 hours, guys," he said to Mike and Jake. "We are counting on you two to work as a team and make this happen. Can you do that for us?"

"Yes, I can," said Jake first, followed by a "Me, too" from Mike.

To Lonnie's amazement, and my own, Mike and Jake calmly discussed recon plans for this afternoon, with an extraction plan well before the scheduled meet tomorrow.

Joy and Nancy worked with Sheila and Tammy to camouflage the two men, where they could not be spotted within five yards if completely still.

This afternoon would be the first of at least two missions dubbed "Project Intercept."

Mel headed home to gather his contribution for the finale, whether tonight or tomorrow. He entered his home to see little Jonah crying.

"What's the matter?" asked Mel.

"Sissy's gone!" is all he could say. "Sissy's gone..." he cried over and over.

Mel was able to get the story out of him, with his own stomach churning with worry. He called down on the radio with the news, asking if anyone had seen Katie.

"No!" came the response from all with radios.

"She's gone back over to help the twins," Mel called.

"This makes things more complicated," said Jake.

"Agreed," added Mike.

Twenty minutes passed, with Mike with Jake now both ready for a recon mission.

"As careless as they were, sneaking up on our side without being detected, we should have the upper hand now," called out Jake.

"This first one is recon only, guys," said Joy. "I want my boys and Katie back all at the same time."

Tom stepped up, talking with both Jake and Mike. "Upriver, maybe a mile and a half, there's a large tree that fell across the river some time back. I've never crossed it, since we had the bridge, but I used to hunt over in that area. From there, it's about a mile back to their camp. It's one hell of a drop down the river, though, if it doesn't hold."

"That may work," replied Jake. "They won't be expecting us from that side."

Heading upriver in full camo, each carrying a small day pack, Mike and Jake worked as a team, using hand gestures mostly and talking only when absolutely necessary.

Covering for each other, they advanced to the crossing.

Mike gestured to the fallen trees, two actually intertwined, with branches sticking out in all directions.

"Let's cross one at a time, and watch close from each end," suggested Mike. "If we both get caught halfway out, it's not going to end well for either of us."

"Agreed," said Jake getting low and covering for Mike.

Edging out, Mike did a little jump to test the natural bridge of sorts and it seemed solid enough to him, for a few crossings at least.

Even with something to grab hold of, crossing the old logs, was harder than just walking across a smooth one.

I've already been swimming once, Mike thought, looking down in case it should come down to it.

Jake scanned to the opposite side of the bank with his scope, as Mike made it across, occasionally snagging his daypack on a branch, and did quick scouting of the other side.

He gave a thumbs-up, and it was Jakes's turn to navigate the difficult crossing.

Once clear to the other side, they huddled up.

"This is good for scouting, but there's no way we're getting three kids across here, being chased by bad guys," said Jake.

"It has to be across the river where they took the trailers," replied Mike. "I nearly lost little Javi trying to cross too soon."

* * * *

It was obvious to Jake that the camp was not far. It sounded like a drunken high school party, with music playing, and not like a ruthless outfit who would execute anyone with their own opinions and kidnap two small boys.

Observing with binoculars, they saw both captives and pseudo soldiers mulling about. Viewing from a safe distance for nearly fifteen minutes, they hadn't spotted Hudson, Jax or Katie.

"Do you think they are there?" asked Jake.

"Yes, I do. I'm not sure about Katie, though. She might be hiding out, observing, just like us," replied Mike.

Forty more minutes went by, with no signs. The men in charge would take turns taking the adult women into a tent separate from the others, as their husbands looked on helplessly.

This parade of disrespect for the women, in particular, made Mike's blood boil.

He carefully studied the face of each captor, now counting four participating, and vowed to send them all to an early grave. This promise he would keep to himself.

Minutes passed in silence.

"There," said Jake quietly. "I see Jax." He came out of a back tent, asking a guard if he could use the potty."

"That's the same tent they had Javi in," whispered Mike.

The guard let him go, waiving his rifle towards the nearest bushes.

"Where's Hudson?" Jake asked aloud, not expecting an answer.

Jax returned slowly to his tent, pausing for a moment, looking towards Mike's and Jake's direction. This caught the attention of one of the guards, who started walking towards them as Jax returned inside the tent.

"Stay completely still," Mike whispered, "and only fire if we have no choice."

The guard walked straight towards them without alerting the others.

Mike and Jake lay perfectly still, with camouflage blending into the surrounding bushes and trees.

The smell of alcohol wafted before the man, now five feet from Mike. The man took two more steps and paused, staring Mike straight in the eyes.

It's the moment, Mike thought, as the guard's casual drunken demeanor turned to terror when he saw the whites of Mike's cold eyes. Springing up fast and spinning the guard around, he wrapped his arm around the man's throat.

Laying down, stretching out his victim, he tightened his grip, holding the man in submission.

Jake didn't like it but didn't interfere. They had taken the children, and it just as easily could have been his Danny.

"One man down," Mike said casually, letting the deceased man out of his grip.

"You're up," called out another guard, searching for him. They could hear a discussion amongst the remaining guards about where he might be, eventually giving up the half-hearted search around the camp.

"I only count four guards left," whispered Mike. "If we could lure them up, one at a time, we would have the boys home for supper."

"I get it," whispered Jake, "but I don't think it's going to go down that easy. I'm willing to give it another hour, though, just to find out."

Jake was uneasy about Mike and the operation, but he felt good doing something that would make a big difference for Lance and Joy if they could pull it off.

Another hour revealed no new information about the guards, Hudson, Jax or Katie.

"We should head back and make a solid plan," suggested Jake. "Should we grab his rifle?"

"Not yet," replied Mike. "But it will be recovered soon," he added, without elaborating.

Heading back the way they came, both men wished they could give visual updates on Hudson and Katie.

"I'm going to take them out," said Mike coldly, once they were both back across the log bridge.

"Them who?" asked Jake, believing he already knew.

"The rest of the guards hurting those women. I'm going to take them all out while you rescue the kids," Mike replied.

"OK," replied Jake, figuring he didn't have much choice in the matter.

* * * *

Hannah and I had been working closely with Mel on his fireworks stash and other distractions for a potentially hostile rescue, prisoner-of-war style—minus the helicopters, of course.

Several possible plans were discussed but would only be decided upon with everyone's approval and using the information gathered by Jake and Mike.

Emerging from the trees, Mike and Jake wished they could have presented three young children to their parents.

Neither man spoke of Mike's altercation with the guard, and Jake for the second time saw him kill up close, with no remorse or emotion of any kind.

"We have two choices," Mike started, "and both leave us crossing the river where the trailers did. The tree crossing is too dangerous for kids and adults alike.

"First, we can put off a rescue attempt until tomorrow at the trade site, hoping to recover Katie before then. We did see Jax, and he appeared unharmed from our vantage point but we did not see Hudson or Katie."

Joy and I were only partially relieved at this news.

"Second," continued Mike, "we can launch an all-out assault tonight, taking out the four guards and freeing the entire group."

"I thought there were five guards left," said Mel, confused.

"There were," added Jake, without elaborating. "But now there are four."

"What do you think?" Mike asked Joy and me.

"I want all three kids back together," said Joy, "and before they all decide to move on down the road."

Mike then looked at me. "My concern is…"

"Hold on a second, Lance," said Lonnie.

* * * * * * *

CHAPTER THIRTY-ONE ~ RATON PASS, NEW MEXICO

M ark pulled up fast on the four-wheeler. "Jim is on the ham with them now, and they are confirming the trade tomorrow."

"Wait a minute. They don't have Katie?" asked Mel.

"No, they are still asking to trade for her."

"We go with Plan B," Joy and I decided. "If Katie is there, she will be rescued; and if she's not, then she will surely show up after seeing our victory," I announced.

"I want to strike at 4 a.m.," said Lonnie, "while they are still half hungover. The kids will be well rested and ready to run, and the guards will be sober enough not to do anything too stupid, but still groggy enough to let us get our job done."

"You will need to bring the kids across the slow river crossing, as you already mentioned," I added, talking to Jake and Mike. "I will be on our side of the river with Tom and Mel. Sorry, David, Joy and Nancy. We can't have everybody down there, in case it gets bad. Mike and Jake will bring over some of the fireworks and, with Mel's help, will get within 50 yards of their camp before creating the diversion."

"Jake's on rescue," Mike added.

"And you?" I asked.

Mike grinned. "Me? I'm on cleanup."

Most looked puzzled at this statement, minus the few of us who knew him best.

"Kids out first, right?" I asked Mike.

"Sure thing, buddy. You will get your boys back, and your girl too, Mel. After that, I can't promise you anything you're going to want to hear." He turned without another word and headed to his tent.

"You're not going into the woods with your bad leg," said Nancy to me, with Joy nodding in agreement.

"Yes, he is," said Vlad, "and so am I. We are both compromised, but we can still shoot. Help us down to the river and we will give them hell," he added.

I hobbled over to Vlad and said, "I'm glad you're back, my friend," patting his shoulder, "and thank you for this."

"And when they are safe, then we open the Beluga!" Vlad added.

"It's a deal," I told him.

I was suddenly overwhelmed by the sacrifice each member of our groups was willing to make for someone else's kids—for my boys and Mel's daughter.

In the old-world, I thought, *most wouldn't knock on a neighbor's door to ask for an extra egg or coffee creamer, and these fine people with us would risk their very lives for another family's children.* I felt truly blessed and vowed to return the favor. I would get my chance in the coming weeks, more than once.

David was not exactly happy about staying behind, but we convinced him that he had an entire group to lead, and one more body in the line of fire would not help the cause. Tina agreed and helped convince him of his duties and promises to her and his mother.

Mel left the drone for another time but unpacked the impressive arsenal of fireworks.

They would be divided, 2/3 among Jake and Mike on the other side, and 1/3 with me, Vlad and Tom, on our side of the river—all of us with night-vision goggles.

We ate an early supper, vowing to turn in early.

Joy and I, both holding a still-scared Hendrix, prayed aloud for the safe return of our boys and Katie.

Mike, with Sheila, told Javi what he had to do, leaving out the adult-only parts. Sheila was worried but didn't ask any questions or ask Mike to stay back. *Maybe this is one way I can start to give back,* she thought, *to make amends, one step at a time.*

Tammy held Jonah close, vowing that her Mel would do everything possible to bring his sister back to him.

* * * * * * *

Chapter Thirty-two ~ Raton Pass, New Mexico

Katie had slipped out of the house, leaving her crying brother behind. She was doing the one thing she swore she would never consider. She left him, her only family, now alone but safe.

Ringo and Mini greeted her on the edge of the property, giving her a startle. "I'm sorry, doggies, but you have to stay here," she said, petting each before entering the woods closest to her house and making a large arc around the property, disguised by trees and hills.

Keeping the daypack she had from before, it was now stuffed with borrowed food from Mel and Tammy's house, including a small life-straw water filter from one of Mel's bug-out bags he kept scattered around the house, a working flashlight, a Swiss Army knife with a can opener, and several days' worth of food.

She vowed to remain hidden in the woods until she could confirm the twins were unharmed. Only then would she sacrifice herself in trade to the same men she fought so hard to leave.

Finding her way to the makeshift camp by the river that she had used with her brother only days before, she found it undisturbed. Leaving her supplies concealed, she made her way to the camp to spy on the group mid-afternoon.

She missed spotting Mike and Jake by a full hour, hearing nothing but music, as well as birds in the trees, singing as always now since they were quite used to the loud distractions.

Weighing her options for more than 30 minutes, she climbed a large pine tree about 100 yards from the camp. The vantage point was crucial, as she had not thought to bring binoculars with her, now remembering seeing more than a few pair in Mel's house.

They can only spot me if they really try, she thought, and it seemed unlikely given the drunken stupor of the guards.

For a split second, she thought about a rescue plan, with her taking both boys to safety, as she had done with her brother, then quickly dismissed the thought.

Sitting high up in the tree, with the breeze gently swaying the branches, Katie daydreamed of her former life... Family and friends, even teachers and dozens of random people, went through her mind, as the innocent girl she used to be treasured the thoughts. Christmases, birthdays, and an overall happy childhood, where she always felt safe, flooded through her as if she hadn't a care in the world...

A disturbance in the camp jolted her back to reality. One of the women was refusing to enter the "special" guards' tent, with her husband attempting to pull her away by the arm. She couldn't make out the faces clearly but it sounded like her mother's very best friend, Martha, now screaming to be released.

She could clearly make out the guard's hat, signifying he was directly responsible for her mom and dad's deaths, as well as the others. She knew it was him because she had never seen him with his hat off.

The guard kicked Martha's husband in the stomach, doubling him over before he was beaten down by another, and she was forced inside the tent. Music was slowly turned up, drowning out her screams for help.

Katie decided right then that she would not voluntarily go back; and if captured, she would end her life before they could.

Thirty minutes later, the guard emerged alone, turning the music down. Katie felt her stomach turn and vowed to make sure he would pay for his crimes.

Still vowing to help the boys, she stayed still for another hour before getting her proof of life. The music was once again turned down, and each child was ordered out of the tents by name, including Jax and Hudson, for a bathroom break. *They are both in the same tent Javi occupied before!* she thought.

Heading back the way she came, she unexpectedly met Mike on her side, and Jake at the other end of the river crossing.

"You're back!" called out Mike casually, continuing his work.

"Maybe and maybe not," she responded confidently. "What are you two doing down here anyway?"

"We're putting a catch rope across the river," Mike replied.

"What's that?" Katie asked.

"When we rescue the kids, minus you now, of course, we..."

"I'm no kid!" she spoke up immediately.

"OK, sorry... When we rescue Hudson and Jax, we will cross the river above the rope, and if we stumble, any of us can catch the rope and follow it to the other side. I should have had one when I got Javi."

"Those men over there," she said coldly. "Those animals..." she continued. "I want them all dead!

"*Why is that?* Mike thought, but didn't ask.

"The one with the Indiana Jones hat, he's the one who killed my parents. That evil excuse for a man had me stuck in a tree, watching as he hurt my mother's best friend in the whole world, and had her husband beaten up. He's the same man that wanted to trade for me, and he's the first one I want gone off this earth."

"I'll take care of it," Mike whispered.

Mel dropped his full-sized backpack at the river's edge, near Jake, and began setting up, without spotting Katie.

"Your girl," said Jake quietly, pointing across the river.

"Oh, thank God!" Mel said aloud, dropping his pack to the hard ground.

Jake put a hand on his shoulder. "Take it slow," he told Mel. "It's just my intuition but we don't want her scared back into the woods."

"I get it," Mel responded, slowly crossing the knee-deep river to Katie.

"Your brother misses you, Katie. Tammy and I miss you too. Are you ready to come home?"

"Not until that evil man is dead," she said loudly, getting a look from each man.

"I'll bring you his head," Mike whispered. "Now, go back home with Mel and take care of your brother before I change my mind."

* * * *

Katie crossed back over the river with Mel, believing Mike would keep his promise.

She was distracted, as Mel asked her to help set up the fireworks, talking to her like his own daughter. "The Screaming Serpents," he told her as he held one up, "sound like a thousand feral cats in heat," getting a smile out of her.

"They are going to have no idea what hit them," he continued, "and we will get the twins back."

"What about Martha and her husband?" she asked.

"I don't know yet, Katie. We will have to see."

Twenty minutes later, they all walked back to Beatrice's house together.

Jonah was there, playing with Javi, when he saw his sister. "Sissy! Sissy! You came back for me!" he cried, running into her arms.

"I'm sorry, Jonah. I'm so sorry... I'll never leave you again!"

Tammy welcomed her back with a big hug and genuine tears. Mel hugged Tammy, telling her it's going to be OK and reassuring her they would be a happy family soon enough.

Mike lifted little Javi and swung him in the air, surprising Sheila and most adults in the room. "More!" he yelled out. "More! More!"

Beatrice made her way over to Mike as he put Javi gently on the floor. Putting her right hand over his heart, she whispered, "I know who you are..." followed by a pause, with neither speaking. "You are a slayer of bad men and a protector of the innocent. Thank you for bringing Katie back to our side. Now bring those sweet boys back safe."

"Yes, ma'am," he replied honestly. "I'll do just that."

"What was that about?" David quietly asked his mother minutes later.

"It's my job to make sure everyone is welcome here, and that's what I am doing."

"Mark and I have a surprise for you if you're up to it," David told his mother.

"Of course I am, son. I'm not getting any younger, so let's have it!"

David let an excited Mark take the lead, showing his grandmother to the underground gallery. Beatrice was taken aback by all of the paintings featuring her, year after year, and started with the one on the left side.

"What are these?" she asked David.

"Dad painted one every year that you were married, and they have been here the whole time."

"Why didn't Dean show them to me before?"

"I'm not sure, Mom, but I think he would have if he'd had more time," David said, whispering so Mark would not hear.

"Well, they are just lovely," Beatrice replied, not acknowledging his last statement. "I especially like the early ones, with zero wrinkles!" she quipped.

She noticed they were in order by years since they were married. With the exception of the fifth year, which was missing, the rest were all in order. She hoped the boys would not notice the discrepancy.

"Should we take them down and move them into the house, Mom?"

"No, David. I like them just where they are, in your father's hideaway studio. Now I can come down here as often as I wish and view each one at my leisure. Besides, cooking, swimming, and being a new grandmother to your girls—oh, and planning a wedding!—I now have a few extra minutes a day for this precious gallery."

"Can you please excuse us, Mark?" asked David.

"Sure, Dad. I'll just head back to the house."

"You noticed, right?" she asked about the missing portrait.

"I've known about it for a long time, Mom," he replied. "Dad told me when I went off to college, after I asked him about the missing painting."

"He told you everything?" she asked.

"Yes. He said he made a mistake that nearly cost him his marriage. I didn't have to ask questions to understand why he didn't paint that year."

"What do you think the mistake was?" she asked, puzzled.

"I assumed he had an affair and you two were able to move on past the mistake and stay happy for all those years."

"You're partially right, my son, but it was me who cheated on your father all those years ago."

"I don't understand," David said, confused.

"Your father was traveling a lot back then. I got lonely and made the biggest mistake of my life. We had a tough year after that, which I assume is why he did not paint. But he forgave me completely and we remained the closest of couples the rest of our days."

David paused, processing the information he always thought to be different. "I love you, Mom, and I forgive you too."

* * * *

Dinner this night was solemn, with a hint of hopefulness as well as prayers for our boys' safe return.

Although it wasn't spoken out loud, David had a sense that since there were only four guards left across the river, they would be liberating an entire camp that would assuredly affect his group in either a positive or negative way.

Jake seemed confident in a stoic military-type way. "This is going to work," he told me. "We have superior firepower, planning, the element of surprise, and eventually good always triumphs over evil."

"If you can get the boys to the river, Vlad and I will make sure you're covered from there," I said.

"I can do that," he replied.

"Mike's going to take all the guards out, isn't he?" I asked.

Jake nodded his head without saying a word.

"OK. Let's make sure our plan is solid and everyone knows their roles," I added.

Mike, Jake and Mel would leave camp at 2 a.m., crossing the log once again and eventually making their way to the other side to set up the fireworks close to the camp.

At exactly 4 a.m., the first of them would be set off. Mel was solely in charge of detonation, planning a five-minute initial launch, keeping low in the trees in case of random gunfire.

Jake would head to the tent they hoped the boys would be in, after spotting Jax and hearing Katie's confirmation on both the boys.

Mike opted not to give any details about his part, beyond a few instructions to Jake, Mel, Vlad and me.

"Jake," he said, "you bring the boys back to Mel, and both of you get them right down to the river crossing. Lance, you and Vlad will cover them from our side. I'll be back when I'm done."

"You're going to have some work tomorrow," Lonnie said aloud, looking at David.

"I know we will have to set a meeting with Nate, if he's still alive," added Joy. "I'm betting he won't be cocky at all this time around."

* * * *

Forcing myself to go to bed early, Ringo barked just outside the tent. I awoke in a panic, thinking I had slept in and missed the window.

My watch read 2:17 a.m. *No going back to sleep now,* I thought.

"It's just me, Ringo," I heard Vlad saying outside the tent. "Let's get you up on the four-wheeler, Lance," he called out, "and I'm driving. Tom will be around in a few minutes on his machine, and we will head down to the river together." We disengaged the headlights, opting for small flashlights to show the way.

Our camp was bustling, with all being sure to keep the noise level to a minimum.

"Where are Jake and Mike?" I asked.

"They took off with Mel about a half hour ago. They should be in position soon.

"My leg was hurting again, and the bumpy road did not help. I opted not to take a pill until it was over. If there was going to be anyone shooting towards my boys, I wanted to have a clear head. I was happy to have Vlad and Tom along and knew I would have to trust their shooting as well.

Joy, Nancy, David, Lonnie, Steve, Sheila and Tammy waited at the edge of the property, where we would all be headed back to soon.

Jim and Mark monitored the radio for any outgoing messages from the other side of the river.

As we bounced down the bumpy, washed-out road, my leg was on fire. I wondered how Vlad felt, remembering my experience as a Chiropractor with a group of amputees, both legs and arms, who nearly all described phantom pain where the limb used to be. He wasn't making any noise, though gritting his teeth, as I was, so I thought it best not to ask.

By the time we reached the river, my leg was feeling better. Oddly, it was so numb that the pain level came down from an 8-10 just an hour ago to a steady 4. I was thankful, knowing it would be bad again soon enough.

Vlad and I positioned ourselves, with Tom's help and wearing our night-vision goggles, behind two large pine trees, where we had an expansive view of the river, 100 yards in each direction.

Easily finding the fireworks Mel had not even tried to hide, Tom was instructed by Mel not to move or reposition them in any way.

"Just start on the left and move to the right, lighting each, with ten seconds in between each block," he told him, "and only when it is time."

"It's a solid five minutes of craziness," he added, "but that's it, so wait until you see the kids ready to cross the river before you start."

"Thirty minutes, boys," I told them, looking at my watch that read 3:32 a.m.

Mike and Jake were in position, having navigated around the entire camp, with Mel 20 yards behind, setting up the new fireworks.

The body of the soldier from the day before lay undisturbed.

"They didn't try too hard to find their comrade," whispered Jake, with no response from Mike.

"You OK?" Jake asked him.

Mike's eyes were fixed ahead, in a trance-like state, as he slowly nodded his head up and down.

Jake was a planner by nature, and his military background only added to the trait. He looked at his watch, already 3:39, and was getting anxious, not totally knowing what they would do in exactly 21 minutes.

He waited another ten minutes, watching Mike help Mel check each firework bundle, thinking he surely would want to get on the same page with the plan.

"OK, Mike," Jake whispered. "Can we make a plan here?"

"Sure," Mike replied, looking through the trees at the kid's tent.

"Give me five minutes to get up to the camp, and then light the fireworks, Mel, one after the other. Jake, if you can get positioned close to the kids' tent before Mel lights them off, then just grab the twins as they come out to see what's going on. Then both of you head straight for the river crossing, and don't forget to go in just above the catch rope."

"What about you?" asked Mel.

"I'll see you boys back at camp later," replied Mike. "And tell Katie I have her hat."

* * * * * * *

Chapter Thirty-three ~ Raton Pass, New Mexico

J ake and Mike slowly crept towards the camp, careful not to break twigs as they quietly moved closer.

Jake crouched down near the same bush Mike had used for cover when he rescued Javi.

Mike disappeared in between the tents, as Jake checked his watch.

He made sure they had all synced watches on both sides of the river, mostly thanks to Mel's stash.

Jake read "3:58," mouthing the words…"3:59," followed by a long pause before hearing the first "Whoosh!" of a high-altitude firework arcing above the trees, with a single "Boom!" at the end. Two more in succession got the tents in camp stirring.

Jake had eyes on his tent, drowning out the increasing noise and smoke around him. He heard the first sound of the tent zipper cautiously opening when the first wave of Screaming Serpents was flown into the air, with a high-pitched whistling scream that could be heard for miles.

As Mel predicted, chaos ensued throughout the camp. Flashlights inside tents, and now outside, shone in all directions.

Mike, with his night-vision goggles, had the advantage against the guards, knowing that, even if they had the same equipment, they would likely not have a clue as to where they were located. He also left his rifle across the river, in trade for a pistol and six-inch skinning knife, better suited for close-quarter combat.

He had eyes on three of the four men, all running around and yelling at the others. "Get back in the tents!" they hollered at the terrified men and women running around.

Mike had his eye on one coming right towards him. *Just a little closer,* he thought. *Only two more steps.* He smiled, with his face not more than three feet from the guards. The anger turned to terror on the man's face, as Mike took him swiftly with his blade across the throat, and the single scream was blocked out by the continuing barrage of explosions above.

Three more to go, Mike thought to himself, compromising his position to stalk each one.

The second guard was easier, with a short rope pulled tightly around his neck as he fumbled into the trees, trying to flee, in a drunken stupor.

Mike had eyes on the third man and wondered if one of them was the man with the hat Katie had talked about. He was still missing the last one, sure he had not miscounted.

Jake watched the kids pile out of the tent and counted seven in all. He had no choice but to call out Hudson's and Jax's names. They seemed scared at first in the midst of all the noise, and with Jake's face painted and covered in camouflage from head to toe.

They recognized his voice, and he told them he could only take the two of them for now.

Hudson and Jax wanted to help the others in their tent, turning around as the others asked where they were going, but reluctantly followed Jake into the trees.

The third soldier ran fast past Mike, shooting into the trees after Jake and the boys.

Mel returned fire with two shots, once the boys and Jake were behind him.

Running full out, the four ran to the river's edge, only stopping along the way to catch their breath. After the nearly three miles, the boys were exhausted as the adrenaline dumped out of their small bodies.

The soldier followed, and I saw him across the bank as our guys, and my boys, started to cross the river.

"Light them up!" I told Tom, not realizing he was way ahead of me.

The flurry of fireworks lit up the sky, illuminating the river as I saw my boys edging across, holding the catch rope. I wasn't sure how many others were coming, but I couldn't let the one in my sites fire on my boys and new friends.

My leg ached badly, and I wondered if I was getting an infection. I trained my rifle on the man across the river. My thermal rifle scope showed a figure but I could not tell for sure if it was Mike or not.

"Lord?" I asked. "What should I do?"

My answer came immediately and without question. The man shot twice towards the river, towards my little boys and my friends risking their lives for them.

I aimed for center chest and squeezed the trigger. "Boom! Boom!" I heard, watching the man drop.

"I am still a threat," yelled Vlad, as I realized he had fired the other round.

I was impressed with the care Mel and Jake took in getting my boys back across the river in the dark of night while being fired upon.

I asked myself if I would do the same for their children, realizing immediately that I would without question. They both now had children, even if only for a few days, and somehow I knew I would have the chance to return the favor sooner than later.

"It's Families First!" I yelled into the darkness, like some kind of crazed man. "It's Families First!" I repeated, now drowned out by the remaining Screaming Serpents.

Moments later, my two little guys were hugging me, and their only concern was for my leg.

"Let's go! Let's go!" called out Tom and Vlad. Tom drove a machine with Hudson and me while Mel drove Vlad with Jax back to camp and a crowd of people cheering at 5 in the morning.

Only Jake held back, waiting for Mike.

* * * *

Smoke filled the camp, and Mike wondered it there would be a fire started by the debris falling from the sky in every direction. He was still missing one guard and it made him anxious. The picture in his mind he had carried since yesterday was the removal of all four soldiers, with an immediate regime change, and that meant taking out all of these guards.

Did the last guard leave camp earlier? he thought, still wondering who the man in the hat was.

Pausing, frozen in place, he took stock of the camp and remained still amongst the chaos. The shrieking sounds, paired with thick black smoke, surrounded him, filling his ears and nostrils. It was his element, a place he could feel comfortable, like your average person would feel watching a light-hearted holiday movie at home, wrapped in a blanket in front of a toasty fire.

A woman's scream came from a tent 20 yards away, as a woman scrambled out, screaming "That's it! No more, you filthy bastard!

"Mike, at a run, met her just as she was scrambling out of the tent. She was taken aback by his appearance, with camouflage on his face and body.

"Does the bastard wear a hat?" asked Mike. "Like a Paul Hogan one?"

"Yes!" she cried. "That's him!"

Mike smiled, knowing he had found his last man. *This should be fun,* he thought.

Without a thought for retaliation, Mike quickly zipped the tent back up. Grabbing the tent from the bottom, he began to walk, ripping the stakes out of the ground and bouncing the man inside over rocks and branches.

The man inside swore and hollered for him to stop.

Mike headed down the steep embankment towards the river, easing his struggle dragging the 180-pound man through the woods and picking up speed. At the river's edge, he pulled the tent into a calm, waist-deep pool, not wanting to lose him in the rushing river.

He had made a promise to Katie about the man who killed her parents and he intended to keep it.

* * * * * * *

Chapter Thirty-four ~ Raton Pass, New Mexico

N ate, no longer hearing the guards barking orders, took inventory of the camp and its residents. "I think we are safe now," he said, gathering as many as possible near the center.

"I believe our captives are now dead or prisoners of war. Today we will take stock of our injured and supplies and try to move forward once again, like we used to. I am truly sorry for what happened here, and especially for the women. We will do everything in our power to make sure it never happens again."

* * * *

Mike smiled broadly in the darkness lit only by the moon and stars, as he spun the man with the hat inside the tent—first left three rolls, then right. *What if he finds his gun inside and shoots you?* Mike could almost hear Sheila saying.

"Then it becomes more interesting," he said aloud, now increasing the rollercoaster of twists and turns, getting screams and now choking sounds, as water rushed through small rips and tears in the tent after being dragged across the woods.

"So, I hear you like to hurt women and bargain for little girls..." said Mike, pausing just long enough for the man to hear.

"Let me go, or you're a dead man!" he screamed back.

"Wrong answer," replied Mike coldly, resuming the shaking and now dunking the entire tent under the water for ten seconds at a time.

Nate's group could hear the commotion but not anything that was being said. "Every adult, look for weapons in all the tents!" he called out. "If they come back, we have to make a stand."

Most adults fanned out, scouring the camp for anything that could help their cause.

The excitement of the last man was wearing off for Mike, and his arms were getting tired. "OK, this is it!" called out Mike, holding the tent on top of the water. "But I have to know, why do you always wear the hat?"

He received no response.

Mike pulled the remaining material out of the water and onto the bank. Locating an end zipper, he carefully worked it open, as a child might wind a jack-in-the-box after seeing what happens several times over.

He searched with his flashlight inside to find the man slumped in the corner, along with two sleeping bags with only one out of its case, a rifle with shoulder strap, and a small cooler with its contents strewn about the tent floor.

"Where's the hat?" he asked loudly. "Hey, buddy! Where's your hat?"

The man was silent.

Barely able to reach the rifle, Mike used it to poke the drowned man hard enough to spot a fake. Three pokes in, and the man fell to the side, with the hat clutched loosely in his hands.

"Yep, that's the one I need," called out Mike, using the rifle to hook the leather hatband, with six realistic-looking crocodile teeth sewn in, and pull it toward him.

"Drop your weapon!" came the call from behind him.

Mike smiled, recognizing Nate's voice with the same tremble he had when he was driving the trailers across the barricade.

"Put down the gun, Nate. It's Mike and I don't want to have to kill you, too. I'm going to turn around slowly, and I will not be dropping any weapons. If you fire on me, it had better be a perfect shot."

There was a pause...and only the sound of the river could be heard.

"Lower your weapons, everyone!" came the call from Nate, as his people all made their way towards him. "It's Mike, and I don't think he's going to hurt us."

"That's true," Mike agreed, turning slowly. "I don't hurt men I like, and you're a hell of a lot more likeable than the Keeper guy."

"Thank you, I think, Mike...I mean, sir," replied a nervous Nate. "I'm sorry about your kids," he added. "They just took them and didn't give us a choice."

Mike stared into the blank eyes of ghostlike women and their husbands who would never be the same, along with the children who witnessed the injustices firsthand.

"I know, Nate, and they're done—your captors, I mean... Take this," Mike continued, handing the AK-47 to Nate. "You'll find three more around camp if you all fan out at daylight. There should be one more down by the river, as I'm sure my guys took care of that last guard. You will need these in the coming days, assuming there is still ammo lying around for them.

"Do you know where the road crosses the river, Nate?"

"Yes, sir. I do."

"OK," Mike said, "that's where the last rifle should be, and I want to meet with you and any of your top people there this afternoon at 3 to discuss future plans. Do you have a watch that works?... Never mind, grab one off of one of the soldiers. I'm sure they work."

"What about the hat?" asked Nate, pointing down towards it and annoying Mike just a bit. "Can we have it back?"

"Absolutely," replied Mike, making an obvious gesture to hold it out in front of him. "I was going to give it to someone, but I'll trade it straight up for five AKs..."

"We will see your group at 3 down by the river," Nate replied, turning back towards his camp.

"And Mike!" Nate called over his shoulder. "Thank you for saving us and for the weapons."

Mike headed down to the river, crossing to find Jake waiting. Stepping around the soldier's body, he spoke. "It looks like you got the boys back safe."

"We did just that," replied Jake. "And you?"

"I got my job done, as well," replied Mike. "We have a meeting here at 3 this afternoon with Nate. I'm sure David will want to see what they know."

"You got about 30 minutes?" asked Jake, with a grin.

"I just might," said Mike.

Jake reached down under a log and pulled a string, end over end, until six shiny cans floated to the surface of the river.

"Lance's idea," he said, tossing the first beer to Mike without asking.

"So, he thought you and I should have a beer together at 5:30 a.m.?"

"Or six!" Jake replied, getting a laugh out of both of them.

The conversation over the next half hour started out awkward and slow but morphed into something positive and mutually respectful that would run through the camp like wildfire over the next few days.

It would be a while before it happened again, but an unlikely alliance of sorts was forged this day, which would set the groundwork for more talks between the two toughest men in camp.

Walking back to camp, most of the greeters had dispersed, with the exception of Joy and me, Mel and Tammy, Sheila with Javi, Nancy, as well as Katie, who hung back from the crowd.

I stood, with Joy's help, and called them both over.

"It's not even 6 a.m. and I can smell cheap beer on both of you!" I said, keeping a straight face.

"He did it!" they both replied simultaneously, pointing at each other.

Joy looked at me like I had parted the Red Sea, watching the two men shake hands and give a guy hug without prompting. The rest of the group was just as shocked.

Mike then embraced Sheila and Javi, who were elated that the operation had gone well, with the safe return of Hudson and Jax.

Mike made his way to Katie. Dropping his small pack on the ground, he unzipped it, whispering, "I couldn't bring you his head, but I do have his hat," pulling it out and handing it to her.

"Is he...? I mean...is he dead?" she asked hesitantly.

"He just drank too much river water," said Mike, with a wink... "He's gone and never coming back."

Katie cried. Not the angry cry of a hardened young woman who lost almost everything she cared about but the soft cry of an innocent young girl who had her demons slain, never again to haunt her dreams.

"Thank you, Uncle Mike," she whispered. "I'll never forget you, as long as I live," she added, embracing him tightly for the second time in only a week.

This time he held her close, stroking her head and saying that everything would be OK now.

Beatrice went all out for lunch at noon, with many adults sleeping until 10 a.m.

Joy and I had a chance to talk with Jax and Hudson about their ordeal, believing that the only real mental trauma was the initial abduction. Once they were in camp, they were kept together and in the company of other kids, with one older woman watching out for them all.

Hendrix was so happy to have his brothers back and presented them each with a hand-made card that Beatrice had helped him create.

* * * *

Nate used the morning to talk with his people and plan the next step.

He was aware that more than a few families were wanting to move out of the area and deep into the mountains on their own, believing more soldiers were headed this way.

He understood their pain, having watched the abuse go on for far too long.

* * * * * * *

To be continued...

ABOUT THE AUTHOR

Lance K. Ewing lives with his wife, three boys (Hudson, Jax and Hendrix), Ringo, Mini and Bobo (dogs and a cat) in McKinney, Texas. When he is not at work, he can always be found with his family, preferably outdoors. Lance grew up in the foothills of the Colorado Rocky Mountains, with the Rockies quite literally in his backyard.

Families First is his debut series. The final volume of the series (The Change) can be found at

https://www.amazon.com/dp/B09S3SLF4P

His new series Long Road Home can be found below.

https://www.amazon.com/dp/B09S3SB3GH

Lance is a Chiropractor in Dallas, Texas.

From the author: "As a young man, I was fascinated by the writing of Stephen King. I can still remember getting a used, or sometimes brand-new, copy of classics, such as *The Shining*, *Firestarter*, *Christine*, *Cujo*, and *The Dark Tower* series. One book, however, topped them all: *The Stand*. To this day, that is the book I measure all other Post-Apocalyptic work against, including my own. As I grew older, I never left for a vacation or camping trip without a book by James Patterson stowed away in my backpack."

If you enjoyed this series, please leave an honest review. In this new age of publishing, reviews are heavily tied to the success of Indie authors who don't have the backing of a large publishing house. I read every review and they fuel my writing.

Honest reviews can be left on Amazon for the volumes 1-3 box set here.

https://www.amazon.com/dp/B09Q2VN7ZF

For those interested in this series, please consider keeping in touch by visiting my website at *lancekewingauthor.com* for upcoming books and projects, as well as updates on what I am up to. Join our e-mail list for news about upcoming volumes and sneak peeks. I will not distribute your e-mail anywhere. Contact Lance at *Lancekewingauthor@gmail.com*.

Visit the Facebook page: *Families First*. https://www.facebook.com/groups/44730539 2509202

OTHER TITLES BY LANCE K EWING

Families First A Post-Apocalyptic Next-World Series ~ **Volumes 1-7 (EMP) (PG-13)**

Volume 1: Families First

Volume 2: The Road

Volume 3: Second Wind.

Volume 4: Hard Roads

Volume 5: Homecoming

Volume 6: Battle Grounds

Volume 7: The Change

Long Road Home ~ a Post-Apocalyptic Next-World Series (EMP) (PG-13)

Book 1: Long Road Home

Book 2: The Plan

Book 3: Turning Point – In Production

2030 ~ An Apocalyptic Series

Book1: In Production

Book 2:

Book 3:

Coming of Age stand alone titles under my pen name Kendall Ewing

Bonze (Bo-nes) – On Pre-sale **(Live May 2023) (PG-13)**

Fragile – In Production

Children's Picture books (ages 3-8)

The Super Great Adventures of Rico, the Monkey-Tailed Skink

The Great Toy Revolt (Lost Toys Series)

Nonfiction Health and Medical

The 30 Days to a Better Back Challenge

Printed in Great Britain
by Amazon

48677861R00173